I0537326

Call It What You Want

Written By

Qiana N. Moss

Three Mindz Publishing

P.O. Box 1583 Columbus Ohio, 43216

ThreeMindzPublishing@gmail.com

Call It What You Want

This is a work of fiction. Names, characters, businesses, places, events,

locales, and incidents are either the products of the author's

imagination or used in a fictitious manner. Any resemblance to actual

persons, living or dead, or actual events is purely coincidental.

Library of Congress Control Number: 2018909011

ISBN# 978-0-692-72223-7

Cover design by J R Jackson, Wicked by Design Inc.

Editing by Paper True Editing & Proofreading Services

Copyright © 2018 by Qiana Moss

First Paperback Edition Printed August 2018

Manufactured in the United States of America

Call It What You Want

For Tish

There comes a time in life when you have to let go of all the pointless

drama & the people who create it & surround yourself around people

who make you laugh so hard that you forget the bad and focus solely on

the good. After all, life is too short to be anything but happy.

-Author Unknown

Call It What You Want

Chapter 1

May 20, 2011

I woke up on Friday morning, grinning like a Cheshire cat. It was the
eve of my husband's40th birthday—a huge milestone that deserved
some extra special attention, considering how he had managed to go all
out to honor my birthdays even when we were in the middle
of a tiff.

Thanks to my best friend Symone's assistance, Isaiah was in for a
remarkably sexy weekend—deep tissue massage, front-row tickets to
Maxwell's concert, a candle-light dinner, along with a thick slice of
"kinky" pie!

Back in December, Symone had tried to con me into joining a pole
fitness class with her and a few of her married peeps from church. From
the very moment that she had asked me about joining the class, I had
been apprehensive about it. I thought she was trying to be funny and

wanted to indirectly hint that I needed to lose some weight, without

using those exact words and taking the risk of getting cussed out.

Symone was tall, slim, and curvy; she could easily pull off that pole

dancing stuff naturally— unlike me, who was super cute in the face but

thick around the waist.

At 5'5", I weighed over 230 pounds at that time. I thought to myself:

What in the hell am I gonna do in a pole dancing class besides turn my

nose up at all the skinny, flexible, half-dressed chicks who can manage

to effortlessly swing and sway around those metal bars?

I had told her then, "*Nah*! I'm straight, Symone. I'll leave that pole

dancing business to you thin chicks, and stick with my Zumba classes."

But as expected, Symone refused to accept my "No" as the final answer.

"Awe c'mon, Kayla! Don't knock it till you try it! Live a little, dang!"

was Symone's exasperated response to my self-pitying rant.

"Gurl, this class is super fun. Oh, and let's not forget it's super, super

sexy! Trust me boo, there are women that are twice your size in the

class, working the HECK out of those poles! It's not like you can't dance, punk! You've always been the better dancer ANYWAY! I've got

very little rhythm when it comes to regular dancing, but I can *shake it*

fast when I need to! So If I can do this so can you, *scaredy-cat*!"

Symone and I shared a laugh as I thought back on the house parties we

used to attend back in the day. While she spent most her time flirting

and slow grinding on some of the neighborhood cuties, I would be right

in the middle of the dancefloor, with a crowd cheering me on as I

emulated some of the dance moves I had snagged from the Janet

Jackson videos I was once obsessed with. "Umm . . . yeah, you can stop

trying to pump me up Symone. It's a 'no' for me, friend. Uhn-uhn!

Nope. Nata! I ain't doin' it!" Symone chuckled. "Oh stop it. Ain't

nobody tryna gas up your ole big head; it's big enough as it is! I'm just

tryna pull you outta that mundane hut you've been living in for years.

Listen Kayla, if you agree to take *one* class with me, I promise I won't

ask you for anything else until sometime next year... In fact, I'll even

pay for your first few sessions! All you have to do is show up! What do

ya say?"

"Symone, what if I don't like the class, hmm? Hell, what if I fall and bust my ass?" I whined. "And doesn't those women practice in heels and leotards? I am *not* goin' to be spinning around in anyone's freakin' leotard Symone! I don't even own a swimsuit. So, what in the world am I gonna do in a skin-tight leotard besides look like a hot-ass mess! No, Symone . . . just no!" Symone was cracking up laughing by this time. "Kayla . . . gurl, you are something else, you know that? Ain't nobody gon' be dancin' around in no coochie-cuttin', tittie-smashin' leotards! This is a pole dancing class, silly—not ballet! We wear shorts, T-shirts, and sometimes heels—nothing more, nothing less. Have I ever misled you, punk? NOOOOPE! So, I ain't gon' start with that crap now. I promise you're gonna love this class—you and the mister! C'mon now, don't make me report you to the *boss*, Kayla!" Symone threatened teasingly.

"*Mm–hmm*, I'll tell Isaiah that you punked out on the sexy upgrade like a sucka and have your butt on 'Ram-Rod' suspension for weeks! We all know how cranky you get when that kitty needs some scratching. Sooo .

Call It What You Want

. . what's it gonna be, eh?" I laughed my ass off, as if Symone was sitting in front of me instead of speaking through the cellphone. My best friend appreciated my marriage to Isaiah as much as I treasured our 20 plus years of friendship. In her own little way, she made sure Isaiah and I stayed connected. She kept the twins for the weekend once a month, so that Isaiah and I could spend quality time together. And to make sure that I my bedroom skills were sharp, Symone always included me in on the kinky sex-toy parties that she often attended.

Over the next few days, Symone badgered me too damn much over that stupid pole dancing class. She texted me pictures of the studio, the pink sparkly stilettos she danced in, along with a pair of plus-size homemade booty shorts that she had designed for me. The last picture I received from this unrelenting friend of mine was of a thick metal pole with my name inscribed on it—in bright red lipstick!

My best friend was beyond determined to make me agree to attend that damn class, and she knew if she plucked my nerves enough, I would eventually give in to her pleas—as I always did.

Call It What You Want

So, the Thursday following Symone's last text message regarding the pole dancing class, I pumped myself up to visit the studio, if only for the sake of saying, "*I tried*." After watching a few plus-size pole dancing videos on YouTube, I had become intrigued by it; plus, I wanted to see for myself how all of it looked in real life.

The studio had not been hard to find. I had typed the address into the navigation system of my car, and within 10 minutes of leaving my office, I pulled into the parking lot of the studio. With my knees knocking, as though I was about to meet a great Zulu king in the flesh, I held my breath and sauntered through the door like a boss!

Symone was the first face I noticed— standing at the reception desk, flapping her lips at a heavy-set blonde woman who was dressed in a pair of "daisy dukes," a cute pink crop top, and a pair of royal blue stilettos.

"*Yaaaaasssss!*" Symone bellowed the moment she noticed me. "I knew you'd come, Bestie-Boo! Did you bring something to change into? If not, I've a few things in my trunk for ya . . ."

Call It What You Want

As I sat on one of the studio's chairs, my legs crossed and my handbag sitting on my lap, I witnessed a group of 13 beautiful curvy women gliding up and down, all around the metal poles with grace and pure sensuality to an old school jam by Usher- *Nice & Slow*.

Symone was absolutely right—I was NOT the chunkiest chick in room, as I had feared from her initial invite.

I counted a minimum of three women who were at least 40–60 pounds heavier than the 230-pounds of fun laden on my 5'5" frame.

Yet, they were more flexible than I had ever imagined being possible for a 'thick chick'. I was thoroughly impressed and ended up joining the class that very day! And, after almost six months of pole dancing, I lost well over 30 pounds, improved my flexibility, and even mastered a few of the gravity-defying holds and inversions that used to intimidate me once upon a time.

To claim that the sensuous pole dancing class had hand delivered my ultra-sexy card would be an understatement. I had been introduced to my lascivious alter ego— *"Desire."* And now, I was ready for her to

meet my husband . . .

Chapter 2

I reached over to the nightstand to turn off the alarm clock that was set

to 5 am on the dot. I didn't want to risk its annoying sound killing the

frisky mood I was in, nor did I want it to startle Isaiah who was sound

asleep next to me.

After tossing my short, lace nightgown on the floor and popping a

cherry jolly rancher into my mouth to veil my morning breath, I rolled

over and mounted my husband, planting cheery-flavored kisses on his

neck and chest.

Isaiah was quick to "rise" to the occasion, and within a matter of

minutes, my body was erupting with back-to-back orgasms! My

husband was a G-O-D when it came to the bedroom. That man had me

so "dick-whooped," a knock-down, drag-out fight couldn't keep me

from dropping my panties for him! All he had to do was whisper my name, flash his breath-taking dimpled smile, and I was sure to melt like a fist full of M&Ms!

 At the end of our astounding amorous session, we collapsed on our bed—satisfied, sex funky, and completely out of breath. Drawing me into his arms and kissing my nape, Isaiah whispered into my ear, "Kayla, I want you to always remember that I love you with all my heart and soul. I'd marry your fine ass over and over again if you wanted me too. . ."

Blushing like I did the day he proposed to me in front of my family, I kissed his strong chocolate arms and muttered, "I love you more . . . Isaiah."

Once his bear-like snores ensued, I quietly slid out of our bed and jumped into the shower. When I returned to the room, less than 20 minutes later, wrapped in my favorite purple, plush towel and adorning a matching head wrap, I was surprised to find Isaiah sitting on the edge of the bed, scrolling through his cellphone with a painful expression etched onto his face.

Call It What You Want

"*Oh boy*...what, or should I say who in the heck has pissed you off this morning? You look like you wanna take a bite out of that phone and toss its remains into the garbage, Isaiah!" I joked as I sauntered past him and grabbed my jar of shea body butter from the bureau and pulled out a lace, black lingerie set from the drawer.

"*Ugh*!" he groaned, with his eyes still glued to the cellphone's screen. "It's just fuckin work as usual . . . nothing for you to worry about babe."

"*Mmm,* but I thought things had been going well at work, especially with the recent promotion and those generous bonuses we've been receiving..."

"Yeah . . ." He nodded. "It can be a lot worst, I guess. But, you and I both know that the more money you make, the more problems you'll have. Regardless of how transparent you try to be with folks, some just ain't never fuckin satisfied— you're damned if you do and even if you don't! Anyway, my beautiful lady . . ." Isaiah chuckled, tossing his phone on the nightstand and bopping his naked body towards me.

Call It What You Want

With a sly grin on his face, he continued, "I've been thinking . . . since the boys are gonna be in Florida for the summer, we should book a little getaway or something—just the two of us. I ain't talking about taking a drive down to Cincinnati or Cleveland, like we normally do. I'm talking about taking a trip that includes using our passports and shit. I dunno about you babe, but I am muhfuckin' tired of Ohio!"

I spun around so fast to face my husband that I almost tripped over my feet. "Oh my God, are you serious?" I exclaimed, gawking at him with excitement dancing in my eyes.

"Hell, yeah! I'm serious, babe! I'll be 40 years old in less than 24 hours; I wanna start traveling the world, like we had planned to do back in our younger days. On top of that, I have been so tied up with work and other *stupid shit*, I haven't been able to spend as much time with my sexy wife as I would like to. I miss you, Kayla, and I wanna take things back to the way they used to be. . ."

Cupping my face in his palms, Isaiah kissed my lips and looked into my eyes. "All I need you to do is make the arrangements, text me the dates so I can notify the office . . . then we're outta here babe . . . just you and

I!" I jumped up and down and squealed like a piglet. "Oh, I love me

some you, Isaiah! I love you so, very much!"

Excited as a child in a candy store, I leaped into my husband's arms,

kissed his lips several times, and began harmonizing the chorus of John

Legends' song *Take me away*— "I don't care where we go, as long as

I'm there with you, baaaybeee!"

In that moment, I felt like the luckiest woman in the world and could not

have ever envisioned a life without the man whom I loved with every

fiber of my being.

Chapter 3

I had become smitten by Isaiah during my senior year of high school.

Not only was he as fine as aged wine—the way he moved, laughed, and

interacted with people intrigued my curiosity more than any other fella

around my way. I met Isaiah through his cousin/best friend Chase Floyd,

a mighty hilarious cat who lived in the red brick house at the end of our

street.

Call It What You Want

Chase and I attended the same high school, shared a few classes, and even teamed up for a couple of class projects. Regardless of the many times he had asked me out on dates including our senior prom, I always turned the fella down. Chase was a cutie, no doubt, and had a reputation for being compassionate and very attentive to his lady friends.

Yet and still, it was his cousin that I wanted—Isaiah Maurice Ward. From the first day I had laid eyes on Isaiah, I wanted to learn everything about him. He stood nearly six feet tall, had an athletic physique, smooth brown skin, and dark curly hair tapered in a boxlike style, like Bobby Brown used to flaunt back in the 80s.

Besides the fact that he was a few years older than me, with a management position at the local Footlocker athletic shoe store in Eastland mall. He possessed his own ride—a burnt orange Chevy Cutlass with a booming music system *and* had a set of deep darling dimples that winked each and every time he opened his mouth!

The warmer months of the year were the times when I would see Isaiah the most. I'd spot him picking Chase up from school from time to time and I often noticed the two of them strolling back and forth from the corner store for rainbow slushies, chips, and other junk foods.

Isaiah and Chase were such respectful young men, that whenever they strolled by the house and noticed my parents or my brother Maxwell sitting behind our enclosed porch, they'd stop by just to say hello, or to see if my parents needed anything from the store. I think it was those type of small and thoughtful gestures that made me adore Isaiah even more...

On a rainy April afternoon, I arrived home from school to find Isaiah's Cutlass parked in front of our house. At first, I figured he might have simply parked at our house and rode away somewhere with Maxwell-since my brother was always looking to recruit people to work out with him at the local YMCA. But, as I got closer to the car, I realized that Isaiah was sitting in the driver's seat with his head down, as though he was reading or was even asleep.

"*Boy*, what in the world are you doing here?" I asked, stretching my neck to look through his window from a distance. He flashed a wide grin, as if he had just won the Ohio lottery, and then quickly stepped out

of the car. Jogging over to where I was standing near our fence with an

apprehensive look on his face, he had said, "*Uh. . .* I thought I'd swing

by to holla atcha' really quick. If that's cool…"

"Um . . . yeah. . . but, about what? My parents aren't home, and I am not

allowed to have anyone in the house. Sooo?" I had asked, reflecting the

same concerned expression he had on.

He chuckled, "Damn girl, I don't think your parents would mind if I sat

on the porch with you. They all know that Imma good guy. I ain't gon'

take up much of your time. I just wanna pick your brain for a sec about

this chicken-head you go to school with."

"Chicken- head? Who are you talking about?"

"Lisa Mendoza . . ."

For a hot second, the crush that I had on Isaiah had flown straight out

the window, like a loose piece of paper! I had only dreamed of sharing a

private conversation with this guy, but never had I imagined that our first real exchange would include a love interest, especially not Lisa's loose-bootie tail!

Lisa Mendoza was what some refer to as a *blaxican*. The hue of her skin was a warm light brown; it reminded me of the color of tea with milk. She was short, cute, with a well-developed figure, and funny colored eyes, but a *terrible* human being! In addition to her trashy, whorish reputation, Lisa had only been a student at Central High for about a year and a half, yet she had allegedly *hunched* and *slobbered* on the knobs of at least 11 seniors and a sophomore student who looked like the comedian Ricky Smiley!

During our junior year, a video was circulating from school to school in which Lisa was recorded performing fellatio on some guy who seemed old enough to be her father. Symone was the first to bring the video to my attention, which was crazy considering she was attending a school on the total opposite side of town. We watched that mess in horror; as a matter of fact, I didn't even have the courage to finish the 5-minute video, because I had become sick on my stomach, watching a teenage girl deep throat a massive penis without gagging or even batting an eyelash!

To further exacerbate the situation, Lisa had the audacity to be a darn bully! She and her "high heeled" crew would carelessly strut through the school halls, cracking cruel jokes, and picking fights with those they assumed to be easily daunted. Lisa only had one chance to bark up my tree, because that was going be the day that I would've had a legitimate reason to lay her ass out-FLAT!

Before Isaiah could dive into his story about Lisa, I asked him to hang on, so that I could run into the house and do the things I normally did when I arrived home from school—letting our two German Pinschers out of the basement and into the backyard and ensuring they had fresh food and clean water. Once I had completed my tasks, I returned to the front porch holding two bottles of ice-cold water.

"Here ya go, Isaiah. I wasn't sure if you were thirsty or not, but I thought I'd offer you a cold drink anyway . . ." I explained, handing him a bottle. "Good thinkin', Kayla!" he declared, accepting the drink an appreciative chortle. "You're a little sweetheart. It's easy to see that

you've been raised by good people. I *like* that about you. You know

what I mean, right?"

"Gee, thanks Isaiah!" I blushed. "So, what was it that you wanted to talk

to me about? Lisa, right?" He nodded and sighed. "Yo, I dunno if you

know Lisa all like that, but that girl is on some crazy-ass shit! This broad

called my momma's house at like five in the morning, bawling and

yapping about how she missed her period and thinks she that she may be

pregnant!" I gasped, nearly choking on the water I was drinking.

"Oh my God! Please tell me you used protection with that girl!"

"*Hell yeah*! We always use protection, that's why I was trippin' like—if

you're pregnant, that baby ain't mine! I'll admit, there was a few times

when the condom broke or whatever, but as soon as I realized what had

happened, the party was over!" He confessed, thumping his chest

proudly.

"Actually, before I even hit it, she told me that she was on some kind of

birth control pill that would keep her from gettin' pregnant for like five years. I figured with birth control that damn potent, a slip up would be

harmless, ya' know what I'm saying, eh?"

I listened intently, as Isaiah reflected on his *nonromantic* relationship

with Lisa, and couldn't help but think back about the last time I had seen

"Ms. Hot-to-trot" in action—a mere two days prior. It was right before

8th period ended, when a girl named Lacy Mae and I had decided to

slide out of class for a quick trip to the bathroom before the bell rang.

Just as we had turned the corner leading to our planned destination, Lacy

Mae and I were sidetracked by none other than Lisa Mendoza and her

whorish shenanigans!

Lisa was so consumed with pressing her tities into the dude's face, and

squeezing his crotch like a stress ball, she never realized that she had a

live audience. We watched in pure disbelief, as Lisa grinded her coochie

against the dude's legs and flicked her tongue against his chin like a

serpent.

In a seductive tone, she purred into the dude's ear in Spanish, "¡ Sé que

quieres a este MARICA, papá, pero ni siquiera tendrás la oportunidad de olerlo! Eres débil, papá. Eres feo, papá. No vales nada, papá, y tu aliento huele a culo de un maldito vagabundo... Suicidarte, papá. ¡ Estoy seguro de que no te echarán de más!

"Oh my god, I wonder what she's saying to him?" Lacy Mae whispered, turning to me. Without a second thought, I recited Lisa's vile words to Lacy Mae, verbatim, "*I know you want this pussy, papa, but you'll never even get the chance to smell it! You're weak, papa. You're ugly, papa. You're worthless, papa, and your breath smells like a freaking bum's asshole . . . Kill yourself, papa. I'm sure you will not be missed!*"

Bearing a slack-jawed expression, Lacy Mae replied, "Oh my God, Kayla, Lisa is a total bitch! I dunno which part is more jacked up—the fact that the dude doesn't have the slightest clue that he's being disrespected in Spanish, or the fact that he's more than likely to continue pursuing her drawls, after this! I freakin hate *mean* people like her, ugh!"

Silence fell between Isaiah and I for a few seconds, as I tried to verbalize a balanced response to his situation, without inserting my negative views about Lisa. I glanced at him from the corner my eye a

couple of times, hoping that he wouldn't break down in tears. Because,

if he had, I would have been bawling my eyes out along with him.

"Look, I just ain't tryna' have no kids right now." He said. "I just turned

21, and there are a lot of things that I want to do with my life, before

claiming the title of someone's daddy and shit. I ain't tryna' be like any

of my brothers or uncles— walking around at the age of 30 with like ten

kids, living in my momma's basement, with a minimum wage job and

shit! Lisa might not wanna' do shit with her life, but I've got plans for

mine, you feel me?"

"Yeah, I understand where you're coming from. Have you discussed this

with your parents? I'm sure they can give you better advice than I can."

"*Oh, hell no!*" he shrieked with a grave look on his face. "My pops died

a few years ago, and if my momma heard a word about the pregnancy

stunt Lisa is tryna pull on me, she'd lose her freakin mind, and toss my

black ass out of the house, like she did with my brother, Ace, when he

came home with a baby.

Call It What You Want

I dunno how things go down in your household, but uh, there ain't no 'Leave It to Beaver' type of shit where I come from. My momma can be cool when she wanna be, but she's raw and don't play any games when it comes to these '*scalawags*,' as she calls the chicks my brothers and I have brought by the house."

"Well. . ." I sighed. "Try to look on the bright side of things. Lisa's missed period can be linked to other things besides pregnancy, including the birth control pills she's on. I've missed countless periods over the years because of my birth control pills, and I'm still a *virgin*! If I were you, I'd just tell Lisa to *chill* and wait it out. If her period doesn't start within a week or so, she can take a home pregnancy test, see a doctor, or do both. . ."

Isaiah tried hard to suppress his guffaws but ended up bursting out in loud laughter. I already knew what he was laughing about, so I simply covered my face and started giggling with him.

"Maaan, I know I ain't trippin' . . . but did you just say you're still a virgin, Kayla?" he asked, thoroughly amused.

Call It What You Want

"Yeeeesss, boy, I'm still a virgin! What is it to you? Just because you've been *bumpin* and *grindin* since you were two years old, doesn't mean we all get down like that! Call it what you want, but I am saving my goodies for that special someone— preferably the man who'll be my husband . . ."

"So, wait . . . are you saying you've never had a boyfriend? Are you gay?"

"Gay?" I chuckled. "Boy NO!"

"I ain't tryna be funny, but as fine as you are, I find it odd that you've never let anyone hit that. Imma have to do a little "hood" research to check the validity of your claims. Cause right now, I ain't buying it!"

"Aye, I've no reason to lie to you or anyone else for that matter. And, as far as boyfriends are concerned, I'm dating someone now and have dated a few other dudes in the past. But sex?" I scrunched my nose and moved my head from side to side. "No suh! I ain't ready for all the drama that comes with meaningless sex.

Call It What You Want

I'd much rather focus on my education so I can live a good life, take care of my family and travel the world. All of this may sound a little corny to you...but oh well- *this is who I am!*"

Isaiah's posture stiffened, as he pondered on my words. Rubbing his chin slowly, he turned his gaze towards me and smiled. "Wow, Kayla, that is the *dopest* shit I've ever heard! How old are you again?"

"I'm 17," I muttered. Isaiah nodded his head approvingly. "Only 17, eh? And already you're some grown and classy shit . . . I like that about you, lil' mama! I *really* do."

Early the following Saturday morning, Maxwell busted into my bedroom with his eyes red and swollen, as if he had been crying. "Sis, hurry up and turn to the news, you ain't gon' believe what happened last night..."

"What happened, Max?" I asked nervously, shifting from my Indian-style position in the middle of the bed, rising to my feet and fumbling around with the bowl of frosted flakes that I had cupped in my hands.

Call It What You Want

"The little homie down the street, Chase, got killed last night in a high-speed chase with the cops... "he replied, nodding in sorrowful affirmation.

Tears streamed down my face like rain, as I listened to the newscast describe Chase and his friends as thieving thugs. The unenthused reporter elucidated that the stolen vehicle was spotted by police officers a little after midnight, leading to a five-mile-long, high-speed chase, before the 16year-old driver lost control and crashed head-on into a light pole on Livingston Avenue. *All of them died instantly.*

My entire family and I attended Chase's home-going services, and I do not think there was a single dry eye in the church that day. Especially when his eulogy was read explaining how a high school senior was snatched entirely too soon from the world.

Not only was Chase an honors student and couple of months from graduating from high school, he was also the primary caregiver for his mother who had been battling breast cancer for the past five years.

Call It What You Want

The next time I heard from Isaiah was the day of my graduation, which was sort of bittersweet. Chase was supposed to be amongst the graduating class of 1995.

Our landline started ringing just as I was making my way out the front door to join my family in the car, and head to my graduation ceremony. I was literally standing right next to ringing phone, so I decided to answer it. "Hello?" I asked, in a rushed tone. "Aye! Wasup, graduate? I wish I could be there to see you walk across the stage, but I've gotta work and shit. . ."

"Huh? Who is this?" I questioned, not recognizing his voice immediately. "It's Isaiah, girl. I know you haven't forgotten about a brotha already." I blushed. "Oh, hey you. I was wondering how you've been doing. I haven't seen or heard from you since Chase's . . . you know—"

"Yeah, yeah, I know," he quickly interjected, "I've been doing aight'. Just had to lay low for a while and process things…you know what I mean? But look, I ain't tryna hold you up, lil' mama. I know you've got a lot going on today, with the graduation and shit. But uh, I've got a quick question for ya . . ." I released a quick breath, hoping that his "quick question" was not going to turn into another Lisa Mendoza saga. "*Hmm*... okay, what's the question, Isaiah?" I asked, trying hard not to sound pushy or disinterested. "Aight . . . when you gon' be 18, lil mama?"

"August . . . August 11th. Why?"

"August 11th. August 11th. *Cool*! Only a couple of months from now." He mumbled to himself. "So, dig this... If you've already made plans for your 18th birthday, you mine as well go on and cancel that shit. Matter fact, you can cancel the dude you're kicking it with too! I really, *really* like you Kayla, and I wanna be your man. I'm taking you out to celebrate your 18th birthday, girl, and I will not take no for an answer...." Before I had a chance to process his words, or even formulate a suitable response to the demands tossed on my lap, Isaiah had hung up . . .

Chapter 4

I felt like I was floating on a bed of clouds, when I pulled my Honda

Element out of our two car garage and waved at the retired couple across

the street, out for their morning walk. Everything in my life seemed

perfect at that moment . . . and with Isaiah's proposal for a trip out of the

country, I just knew life was only going to get better!

I stopped by a gas station on my way into the office for a quick refill and

bought a few instant lottery tickets. My goal was to make sure all of my

minor responsibilities were taken care of, so that when the next day

arrived, I could dedicate all of my attention to celebrating Isaiah's 40

years of life.

I arrived at the C&O Counseling Center soon after leaving the gas

station—the place where I had been employed as a licensed therapist

and life coach for the past 7 years. I completely adored the work I did

for the community, even on the terribly exhausting days.

 I still distinctly remember how one of my favorite professors, Barb

LoFrisco, had described the counselling profession in one of her classes,

Call It What You Want

"On the best days, counselling is like sipping tea with your best friend, only you cannot talk about yourself. On the worst days, counselling is like facing a bully in the school yard, only you cannot speak up for yourself." Mrs. LoFrisco couldn't have been more on point with her theory, as those words definitely defined my life; at least the professional side of it. "TGIF, Mrs. Ward!" the receptionist, Maybelle Lynch, bellowed as soon as I walked through the sliding double doors. I grinned at her and then had to clear my throat, as her tawdry perfume, smelling like a concoction of potpourri and church incense, tickled the back of my throat.

"Yes, TGIF, Mrs. Maybelle," I replied, my voice slightly hoarse from the irritation. "*Mmm* . . . well, I guess there is no need to ask how you're doing this morning darling, because that radiant glow on your face says it all! Mm-hmm . . . that's the look of a woman in love with a man who can still make her '*feel good,*' if ya' know what I mean," she chimed playfully, flashing me a toothy smile.

Call It What You Want

Mrs. Maybelle was my absolute favorite at the counselling center. She reminded me of one those bold, old school, no-nonsense relatives, always speaking her mind openly and freely, without a care in the world. Mrs. Maybelle was wise, protective, loving, and had all those genuine traits, which sometimes made one forget that she was as unattractive as a gargoyle! She was as tall as a beanstalk, stout, olive-skinned, with pencil thin eyebrows, angular cheekbones, and a pointed chin that I assume was inherited from her father or some other male ancestor.

She reared 8 children on a receptionist's salary and was currently raising four of her twelve grandchildren. Believe it or not, this superwoman had also managed to keep up a 40-year marriage with a presumptuous EL DeBarge look alike, who at his grey age, STILL roamed the streets like a horny adolescent!

A couple of years back, Mrs. Maybelle had confided in me that she had decided to separate from her husband after a frightening altercation with one of his lovers. She explained that she had come home from work one evening to find her husband *surprisingly* missing in action. As a replacement for his absence, she stumbled upon with one of his drunken

paramours, who was fast asleep on the hammock in their front yard.

Mrs. Maybelle said that she hadn't wasted time waking the woman up

and bombarding her with a bunch of questions—as I probably would

have done. She said she took a good look at the sleeping woman,

sauntered into the house, and called the cops to report an intruder.

Then, returned to the yard seconds later with "Junjun"— her steel

slugger— and whacked the woman across her knees and legs, until she

jumped out of the hammock, and took off down the street whimpering

like a gimp legged dog!

I had laughed so hard when she animatedly reenacted the events, that I

almost peed my pants! However, it was only a matter of days before she

was right back with her two-timing husband, on blissful honeymoon

mode, as if nothing had ever happened. . .

"So, do ya' have any big plans for the weekend, darling? I hear the

weather's gonna be really nice— upper 80's according to the news . . ."

Mrs. Maybelle inquired, with an anxious grin. I smile and nodded my head. "Ooooh yes, ma'am. I have an awesome weekend planned . . . it's

my husband's birthday tomorrow, and I am going to spoil him rotten.

I'm taking him to a concert of one of his favorite R&B artists—front row

seats. And I've scheduled a swanky dinner for two. . .along with a few

other things. . . " I winked at her, before we both busted out laughing.

"Ooh, Kayla you're such a romantic. I hope that handsome fella realizes

what a good woman he's got in his life. Because, there are a BUNCH of

women—young and old—strutting around town with smart mouths and

nonexistent morals and principles! HECK, I don't even know if these

girls pray anymore, and if they do, you've gotta wonder who or what

they are praying too! I don't wanna too sound cynical, but it seems like a

LOT of these women are selling their souls by the pound, and are too

dang on stupid to recognize it . . . *umph, umph, umph*!"

While nodding in agreement, I quickly changed the subject, to avoid the

extended 'Essay' she was preparing to deliver. "Enough about me, Mrs.

Maybelle. What do YOU have planned for weekend? Bingo with the

sisters from the church?" My question made her eyes sparkle with enthusiasm. Excitedly, she exclaimed, "Bingo? ABSOLUTELY, sweetie

pie! I'm tryna hit the jackpot soon, so Emerald and I can take a few

cruises after I retire in September. "But uhh, our baby girl, Gina Lynn, is

coming to town for this weekend and will be staying with us for about a

week or so.

You know Gina the one doing all of that modeling stuff for the bigshots

in California. I am quite sure that I've told you about my little beauty

queen . . . right?" I nodded, as I clearly remembered the daughter she

was speaking of.

Gina and I had never met, but I knew she was Mrs. Maybelle's daughter

who had been battling with a drug/alcohol addiction, for as long as I'd

been working at the counselling center. From what Mrs. Maybelle told

in me, Gina, although she was living a lavish life, occasionally suffered

physical abuse by the hands of her wealthy Caucasian husband. I had

seen multiple pictures of how that man had beaten Gina black and blue.

Yet, regardless of how much Mrs. Maybelle *prayed*, she refused to leave

him. "Praise the Lord, Gina has been clean for almost a year now. And guess what? My baby and her husband completed marriage counselling and are expecting their first child in a few months. God is sooo good, I tell ya! Hallelujah! Their first few years of marriage were difficult, but it seems like they are finally gettin' back on track . . ."

As Mrs. Maybelle continued to excitedly talk about Gina's visit, she turned her back to me slightly, clutched her mouse tight, and with several tiny clicks and a few little thumps on the keyboard, my daily calendar popped up on one of her two monitors. She shot me a glance and said, "Okay darling, for the most part, you have a pretty light schedule today. With three cancellations from earlier this week, you only have one session scheduled for this afternoon, which, uh . . . I have a few concerns about."

"Concerns?" I asked, as I slid into the empty office chair beside her. With genuine concern hardening her eyes, the receptionist took off her red plastic framed reading glasses and tossed them on her desk. She leaned closer to where I was sitting in an attempt to shield our conversation from potential eavesdroppers.

Call It What You Want

"Listen . . . As God is my witness, speaking with this new client of yours was probably one of the most horrifying exchanges I've experienced with any client. From the very moment I answered the phone, this woman began mouthing off, as if I had stolen and worn her favorite underwear and flaunted them in her darn face! I dunno if this woman is mentally challenged or simply ornery. Whatever the case, she was as mean as an ole constipated wolf! By the time the call ended, I was so fired up, I had to pop a few Advil to calm my frazzled nerves! That woman was just mean and rude, for no good reason!"

"Oh my goodness! What on earth was she so agitated about?"

"*Hmph*! For starters, she was ticked off because she had allegedly requested an appointment through the company's website and didn't get a response from our end as early as she'd expected. After I apologized and tried to explain that our online scheduling is handled by a separate team. She became irate, suggesting I was being '*unprofessional*' and 'talking down' to her, which you know is a lie. Then hear this . . . she demanded to be seen by you and only you, TODAY! I thank the good

Call It What You Want

Lord you had openings, because had you not, she probably would have

cussed me out about that!"

"Yikes, that's weird. Has she been counseled at C&O prior to today?

What's her name?"

"Her name is Odessa Starr, and she is a new patient. I don't mean no

disrespect towards this woman and whatever it is she's going through,

but Kayla, that woman is a fry short of a doggone happy meal, for sure!

I can tell by the things she allowed to fall out of her mouth, she's not

well . . .*mentally*." I covered my mouth, trying not to laugh at the little

"fry short of a happy meal" jokey-joke Mrs. Maybelle had managed to

slip into the conversation, but both she and I ended up laughing

anyway—not at the strange behaviors of my new client, but the phrase

used to describe her. "Mrs. Maybelle, you are hilarious! For a minute

there, you had me feeling like I was gonna be interviewing Charles

Manson, without protection, or security! I'm hoping that the session

works out in perfect peace, because I'm entirely too high on life right

now to allow someone else's issues to stress me out. We have to think positively, Mrs. Maybelle! Positive! Positive! Positive!" I

enthusiastically said to her.

Mrs. Maybelle shot me a quick glance, then said, "Yeah, I hear whatcha

saying baby doll but, uh . . . I suggest you take a little extra caution with

this one. As a matter of fact, do you still have the anointing oil I gave

you a few months ago, when you were having trouble with your mother-

in-law?" I pondered over her question for a moment, then nodded, "Yes

ma'am, right upstairs in my desk drawer."

"Ok great! So, what you need to do is this; give that bottle a vigorous

shake and splash it all around your office. I'm talking about dousing the

chairs, tables, desk, door handles—just about anything this woman

might lay her hands on. Trust me darling, I have followed the Lord my

entire life and I recognize the voice of an unclean spirit when I hear one.

Something ain't right with this Odessa Starr, darling. I can feel it in the

pit of my *stomach*!"

Call It What You Want

Chapter 5

It was almost 9 am by the time I managed to finally pull myself away from Mrs. Maybelle's extended monologue. Once her engine got revved up, those long flat lips of hers just kept going and going. *Like the Energizer bunny!*

I stepped into my comfortable, "safari themed" office, hung my azure ruched blazer behind the door, powered on the tabletop Feng Shui fountain with an elephant statuette, and then hit play on the mini CD player hidden beneath my desk. The flavorful, jazzy vocals of Jill Scott livened up the small office space, as she began chanting about a woman "getting in the way" of what she's feeling.

I bobbed my head and tapped my foot, humming along with Miss *Jilly from Philly.* As a child, I always wished to be able to sing like her and other famous vocalists. But after hearing an "accidental" recording, of my chipmunk-sounding intonation, I realized that "singing" was NOT my gift and that my singing performances were to be reserved for my showerhead alone!

Call It What You Want

I snagged a cold bottle of water from my mini-refrigerator and a pack of peanut butter crackers, plopped down at my desk, and then began sifting through the huge stack of paperwork. Before I was able to get comfortable, my cellphone chirped twice. I ignored it at first, assuming the text messages to be from my mom, who had become super annoying, after my brother Maxwell purchased she and our stepfather matching Blackberry cellphones. Ever since she learned how to send and receive text messages, she would blow our phones up with random texts- all day long!

However, when the phone chirped a third time, I knew I had to check it out. The back-to-back text messages were from my half-brother, Omar, which read, "*GM sis! I know it's early, but I need a big, big favor . . . is there any way you can lend me a lil' something until next week? I got a new truck, just like the F150 Isaiah drives- only mine is black. It needs some minor work and I am short on funds right now. I promise to pay you back this time sis. With interest!*"

Call It What You Want

I shook my head with my lips puckered in disapproval, knowing damn well that Omar had no intention of paying me back if I did give him another loan. And in the very same breath, I also knew I would feel as guilty as an alcoholic in a wine cellar if I didn't help out my baby brother—as I had promised to always do. I replied, *"Good morning, baby brother. How much are we talking this time?"*

"Only $350. . . I will hit you back with $400 next Friday. I promise." was his immediate response. *"Okay. I'll transfer the money into your account in a few minutes, but I'm gonna need this money back on Friday, Omar. Don't have me make a trip to Springfield to hunt your ass down for my change dude! LOL!"*

"LMAO! I gotchu, sis! Thanks. Love you! Oh, and I am still coming down for the 4th of July. I've got the whole week off!"

"Yaaaay! I can't wait to see you!"

Isaiah would've had a full-blown conniption, had he known that I agreed to give Omar money again. He always made snide little comments about Omar taking advantage of me, simply because he knew I'd do just about

anything for him. I mean, it was true that Omar would borrow a couple
hundred dollars here and there, and damn near disappear off the face of
the earth, sometimes for months at a time. I'd be the first to admit to how
much I hated when he got into one of his "moods" and faded into
silence, leaving me wondering if he was dead or alive. But, I understood
that my baby brother had *issues* . . . all of which could be traced back to
his traumatic childhood.

Omar is my half-brother who shared a strong resemblance to and similar
characteristics with the singer Ray J, including being a spoiled brat! I
was almost 17 when I discovered, not in the most amicable way, that I
was a sister to someone besides my elder brother Maxwell and to
Mister Eugene, my step father's children, whom my mother, Maxwell,
and I had only met twice and heard very little about. I can still recall the
day I was given the news on my new role as "big sister" with astounding
clarity—as though it had happened only yesterday.

My mom had walked into the house one day, looking like she had just
come out of a train wreck, after a long day's work, talking about how

she had some news that was gonna "blow my mind." At first, I thought

she was gonna perk up and announce that she had finally scored big time

on one of the Ohio Lottery games she played on the regular, which

meant early retirement for her and my step-father and a brand-new car

for me- but boy was I wrong!

"What is it mom? Tell me, tell me!" I urged with overwhelming

anticipation, while picturing myself and Symone cruising down the

street in my "imaginary" brand new whip.

"Baby guuurl . . ." she began, beaming, and running her chubby

cinnamon-shaded fingers through her salt and pepper grey hair, "Lord

have mercy . . . you've got a ten-and-a-half-year-old little brother. His

name is Omar Bumper, and he is a *cute* little chocolate thang! He's got

big brown eyes, perfect lips, and that gorgeous thick curly hair just like

you and Ike. Oh honey, the two of you look so much alike, it's scary!"

For the first few seconds after my mother's big announcement, I sat at

the kitchen table as still as a frightened cat. I dunno how my mom

"thought" I was supposed to feel about this news, considering the only time I had seen or heard from Ike, was during special occasions like birthdays, Christmas, and maybe sometimes during Easter or Thanksgiving. But I was sooo NOT impressed! If anything, her breaking news only made me more disgusted and ashamed that I was the partial product of such an irresponsible man.

Ike Nunez, the biological father of Omar and I, is a smooth-talking Dominican, who migrated to the States as a teenager. He met and married my mother Libby, all the while pretending to build a relationship with my elder brother Maxwell, who was fathered by my mom's high school sweetheart.

I was born shortly after my parents exchanged vows, and before I had the opportunity to blow out the single pink and white candle representing the completion of the first year of my life, Ike had kicked me, my mom, and Maxwell to the curb and was residing in opposite side of town, with an entirely different woman!

Growing up, I could not stand being around my narcissistic father. Our relationship was as abnormal as a glaring sixth toe on an otherwise perfect foot! As pathetic as it sounds, all I've ever known of my father were broken promises, creepy yellowish eyes, his long crunchy beard that reminds me of a bird's nest, along with the foul stench of alcohol and Cubans wafting from his breath.

To make matters worse, Ike had a pesky wife by the named Jenene, who looked like a real-life version of a "*treasure troll*" and have always felt the need to dominate each and every conversation ANYONE attempted to have with my father. I could glance at Ike and mention something as simple as the moon or how bright the stars were shining the previous night. Not only would Jenene find a way to slither her *worrisome* ass into the conversation, but we would be subjected to listen to at least 15 minutes of her very sloppy thoughts about how *SHE* felt about this, what *SHE* would do about that. Jenene would get so comfortable with babbling about *HERSELF*, that she'd ease her two daughters into the conversation—one *SHE* wasn't invited to in the first place.

Sometimes I would just glance at her funny looking ass out of the corner of my eye and think, *SHUT THE FUCK UP LADY! Who in the hell*

Call It What You Want

asked for your opinion in the first place? Damn! While other times I'd

take her rude interruption as a sign for me to get far away from both of

them, before I ended up saying some shit that I'd later regret. "That poor

ex-husband of mine's is something else; bless his little heart. Lord

knows that he doesn't know any better than what he was taught by the

wolves that raised him and turned him into a stone-cold alcoholic before

he could graduate from high school . . ." My mom began with one of the

unpersuasive excuses she'd give to justify Ike's irrational behavior.

"But, there is one good thing about Ike that cannot be ignored or denied.

That ole *black-sap* can surely make some beautiful babies! Ooooh, I

CAN'T WAIT for you to meet your baby brother."

"*Oh . . .*" was my only reply, before I pushed Ike's stupid shenanigans

out of my mind and returned my focus on the homework I had been

working on.

The following Sunday, I was annoyed all over again when I learned- last

minute, that Omar and his mother had been invited to our house for

dinner. My mom had obviously picked up on how uncomfortable I was with the whole situation, and knew if she had told me before then about

the planned "meet and greet," I would've found a reason to leave the

house until their little shindig was over. I had no clue as to what was

going on, until I heard a loud knock on the front door around 2pm that

afternoon. My mom was in the midst of preparing what appeared to be a

Thanksgiving feast in the middle of July; and conveniently, Maxwell

and Mister Eugene were out, at Buckeye Lake, fishing.

"Heeey, pretty gurl!" a lean well-dressed woman greeted me as soon as I

opened the door. "Girlfriend, I dunno who looks more like Ike, you or

your brother," she chuckled, tugging at Omar's blue baseball cap to

guide his tucked head in my direction. "Uh . . ." was all I could utter,

while nervously shifting my eyes back and forth between the mother-son

duo.

"Oh, I'm so sorry baby, look at me justa babbling! My name is Diane

Bumper. This here is your brother Omar," she stated, as she excitedly

draped her long arms around my shoulders and pulled me into a tight

embrace and then pecked me on the cheek. Diane was a lot prettier than

I'd imagined her to be. Her face was beautiful like that of an ancient goddess— butterscotch skin, short copper blond hair; with grey almond-shaped eyes that reminded me of a Himalayan cat. She was well spoken and extremely friendly, *genuinely*. After that Sunday afternoon, it didn't take too long for Diane and Omar to become permanent fixtures in our lives. My mom and Diane became as close as Siamese twins, and Omar and I, inseparable!

As expected, our new-found relationship didn't go over very well with Ike or his overzealous treasure troll. Jenene was constantly calling my mom with the most ridiculous and malicious lies that she was able to pull from her ass. She was almost desperate to break the bond that had formed between my mom and Diane. But no matter how hard Jenene tried, it never worked.

During one hot summer evening, my mom, Diane, and I were lounging on the porch, while Omar played curb ball, with some of the neighborhood kids. Mom and Diane were in the midst of discussing something foolish that Jenene had recently said, when I boldly asked

Call It What You Want

Diane why Jenene treated her and Omar so badly. I swear, it was not my intent to pry or even take a step out of my teenage space, and leap into the "grown folks" business. I was merely curious to understand how animosity could survive decades, without any sort of resolution.

Diane explained that Jenene and she had been the best of friends back in the day. They attended the same school, same classes, and even attended the same church. That is, until they became adults and got addicted to street drugs. Diane said, "You know what? To be honest with you baby, I will never understand why Nene hates me as much as she does. If anything, I should be the one with a chip on my shoulder, since she pretended to be my friend long enough to steal my man! Back in the 80's, party, sex, drugs, and alcohol were the only languages we spoke. *Well* . . . at least some of us." Diane paused to fire up one of her Newport cigarettes, probably contemplating over the truth she had just confessed to, while taking a few long drags. As a cloud of grey smoke blew from her mouth and nostrils, she continued, "Ike, Nene, and me were like the 3 amigos.

Call It What You Want

Wherever there was one, the other two weren't too far behind. Nene was

what some would call a 'booster' and whatnot. She used to steal from

high end stores, sell the merchandise for almost half its worth, and share

the money with Ike and me.

Guuuurls, Nene would have us steppin out on the club scene dressed to

nines, with the *stolen* gifts she showered us with.

Couldn't nobody tell us we weren't 'hot shit,' at least not till those

stupid drugs came into the picture. "Not that I am blaming anyone for

the mistakes I made in life, but it was Ike who introduced Nene and me

to cocaine. To this very day, I wished that she and I had both said no to

the drugs and dropped his ass like the bad habit he carelessly pushed

into our souls. Hell, now that I am thinking back on those horrible times,

it seemed as if it only took about 20 minutes for us to transform into a

pair of scandalous '*crackheads*' who cared more about the next high

than we did about washing our asses! Because of our *rotten* addiction to

the "*crack-rock*" Jenene lost custody of her girls- which I thought was

gonna take her straight out of this world. Thankfully Nene's family loved her enough to not let her beautiful girls get lost in the foster

system. They took custody of them and provided those little cutie-pies

with a decent life."

Diane stubbed her cigarette into a glass ashtray that she was tightly

clutching on to, placed it on the porch table, and then took an absent-

minded sip from the orange cup sitting next to her.

"Yeah. . . so, after watching Jenene go through two pregnancies—

without knowledge of the father's identity, because she sometimes

'tricked' for drugs—I made a solemn promise to Allah that if he blessed

Ike and me with a child, I would kick all of my '*crackhead*' activities to

the curb and be the best mother in the world for my baby. I was true to

my word too! The day I found out I was pregnant, I went cold turkey.

I stopped smoking dope. I stopped drinking and partying. I mean I put a

complete cease to everything I once enjoyed for the safety of the little

peanut growing in my belly. But—" she paused long enough to ponder

over her thoughts. "Once I gave birth to Omar, and after the novelty of

motherhood wore out, I found myself slowly easing back into the groove of my old habits. One day, I'd have a little shot of Brandy after putting

Omar to bed, along with a few cigarettes and all that. While over the

next few days, I'd add an extra beer or two to go with the shot of liquor,

along with primo joints.

I prayed, prayed, and prayed, and then finally had an epiphany! I was a

goddamn addict, and, if I didn't get my shit together sooner rather than

later, my son was at risk for the same fate as Jenene's girls. . .''

Diane hadn't even reached the 'thick' of the story, and my mom was

already dabbing her teary eyes with the wet paper towel she had been

clutching between her fingers since the story had begun.

"There is no need to cry Libby; I too had to go through the storm to get

to where I am in life. Allah spoke to me through a dream. He said,

'*Daughter, I love you so much. And you are so much better than this.*

Pass me your burdens, so that you may live life peacefully with your

child who needs you . . .' The following morning when I opened my

eyes, I cleaned myself and Omar up, made a few phone calls, packed all that we owned in a trunk and the backseat of my beat-up Pontiac, and

made a beeline for the house of a dear friend living in Springfield.

"Within a couple of hours of arriving there, I fed Omar, took him to the

park, bathed him, and rocked him to sleep. Then, leaving him behind

with my friend, I checked myself into a drug rehabilitation center. About

a year or so later, I returned to Columbus, with Omar, hoping to rescue

Ike and Jenene from their addiction, as I had been by Allah and my

friend. I hadn't spoken to either one of them during my time in rehab.

But I figured they would understand why I did what I did and appreciate

that I had come back for them! "Well, that wish, dream, or whatever you

want call it was short lived. During my search for Jenene and Ike, I ran

into a mutual friend who gave me the scoop on those sneaky rats.

Apparently, they had eloped after I '*disappeared*' and were happily

living on the north side of town, with a dog, a cat, and a family!"

"*Dagnabbit!*" my mother huffed, "That's awful! She was your best

friend for Christ's sake! They should be ashamed of themselves for what

they did to you!" Diane shrugged her shoulders at my mom's statement, brushed some imaginary lint off her blue denim shorts, and gave a warm smile. "Gurl, please! Allah doesn't make any mistakes. Everything happened for a reason! Shaking those fools loose is what I had to do in order to save my son's life and rediscover Diane Bumper. Hmph! Look at me now— been clean over a decade! Omar is smart as a fox, and I have a special friend who loves me despite my ups and downs, and last but not least, Omar and I have yall— *real family!*"

*

Around Omar's 18th birthday, I noticed the "happy, happy, joy, joy" groove beginning to slowly dissipate.

We were in the process of planning a birthday-cum-graduation bash for Omar, which were only days apart. Everyone was on board with the planning, even Ike, who surprisingly rented a beautiful pool house for the celebration and even wrote Diane a healthy check to cover the food and other expenses. But, as usual, that fish-eyed Jenene had to stir up some shit and, of course, steal the spotlight that was meant to be on Omar. Apparently, *Madame-ruin-it-all* went snooping through Ike's things and stumbled upon the check addressed to Diane for Omar's

party. Instead of asking Ike about the check, as she should have ideally

done, that deranged lunatic jumped into her car and drove to all the way

Springfield, almost an hour away, to question Diane about it.

According to Toney, Diane's "special" friend, Diane never got the

chance to respond to Jenene's crazy accusation of an "alleged" affair

between she and Ike. Nor was she able to explain the reason Ike had

written that check in the first place!

Upon confrontation, Diane clutched her chest and begged Jenene to "just

wait a second," because she wasn't feeling well. Of course, Jenene's

selfish ass didn't care, and she continued to fuss and cuss until

Diane dropped to the floor, losing all consciousness.

Our beloved Diane suffered a heart attack that day and passed away the

following Thursday, June 10th—Omar's birthday 18th birthday.

My baby brother was completely devastated over the sudden death of his

mother. To make matters worse, Ike didn't even make an attempt to

send condolences or heck on his *only son* during this painful time.

Call It What You Want

In hindsight, I guess I can understand why he was a no-show to Diane's memorial services, seeing that he couldn't go anywhere without that treasure troll on his heels. He had sense enough to know that if he had showed up with Jenene in his arms, she would have gotten her ass beat for the stress she put Diane and Omar through.

I'm NOT sorry to say this but uhh . . . I probably would have joined the crowd and popped Jenene a few times on her head, not only for her constant interference in our relationship with our father, but for the pain her egotistical madness caused my baby brother. And had Ike tried to jump in it, I probably would have tried to punch him too! After we said our final goodbyes to Diane, I promised Omar that I'd always be there for him. I would always be my brother's keeper!

Chapter 6

My co-worker, Blaze McFadden, knocked on my cabin door around noon and welcomed himself into my office space, which had been peaceful until he waltzed in with the confidence of someone who had actually been invited. He had been pulling this exact same stunt for the few years we'd worked together, and if I were to claim that I did not

enjoy his friendly pop-ins, I'd be telling a bald-faced lie!

Blaze was a dangerously attractive Philadelphian psychologist with a

great personality and his own noble ways. A debonair, who could stand

shoulder-to-shoulder with some of the most gorgeous men in

entertainment, say for instance Derek Luke, Idris Elba, Michael Ealy, or

even Leonardo DiCaprio, and give them all a run for their money!

Blaze was around 5'9 or 5'11 at most, with an athletic build and smooth

dark brown skin. His eyebrows were naturally arched, accentuating the

charm of his light brown eyes that sparkled from under his sweeping

eyelashes, which looked like they belonged on a giraffe!

His strategically ruffled hair was normally worn in a wild tapered style,

along with a neatly trimmed chin strap beard, complemented by a pair of

thick, kissable lips.

Blaze was so damn fine and he knew it! At the same time, he was

modest and seemed like a one-woman man—someone who prized

genuine and thoughtful conversation over sexual innuendos or secret rendezvous. "Greetings, Miss Lady! How are ya' doing this morning, Queen?" Blaze asked in his thick mid-Atlantic accent. He had a genuine smile on his face that made me feel like my mocha-toned cheeks had faded into a kissed pink color, like spring roses. "Hey, you!" I smiled, "I am doing well, Blaze. Thanks for asking. As you can see, I've been pleasantly occupied all morning with this here business . . ." I replied sarcastically, pointing to the thick stack of papers piled on my desk. He guffawed, and then shrugging his shoulders, said, "Aye, well since you're on a roll, I have a stack to add to it, if you'd like, Miss Lady!" "Ha-ha! No thanks, brotha! I am good with what I have, sir!" We shared a quick laugh, and I asked, "So what do you have planned for the weekend? Something exciting, I'm sure."

"Aww now, Miss Lady, you know that my weekends are always occupied with the club, which by the way, has been off the charts for the last month or so. Taalib, my cousin and business partner, came up with this dope idea to imitate the whole 'Showtime at the Apollo' concept, so we can get more people to the club who will be willing to share their

hidden talents. "Imma keep it real with you though. . . In the beginning,

I didn't have much faith in FAM's views on opening the stage to the

public like that. I was unsure of the type of crowd that would come

through, and I was concerned that people were gon' be expecting a little

'coinage' for their performances or assume that they'd be recruited for a

record deal and whatnot. You know how our folks get down, Miss Lady!

Most of us ain't even gon' think about busting a move without some

kinda compensation!"

All I could do was laugh, because what he said was a 100% accurate!

"Superman," as many of the women around the office referred to Blaze,

was an articulate psychologist during the day who moonlit as a hip

nightclub owner. Most of the office folks, including Mrs. Maybelle and

her husband, had already visited Blaze's upscale club at least a handful

of times. They all bragged about the fancy decor and how well-

organized the nightclub was as well as the lengthy menu of fun exotic

drinks and delicious foods, which sometimes left me feeling kinda 'salty'—I was so tied up with family matters, I hadn't taken the time out to support a friend. . .

Blaze propped his ankle up on his knee, sat back on one of the two, boxed-armed chairs adjacent to my desk, and continued, "Yoooo. . . you would really be surprised by all of the talent hidden in Columbus. I mean, like, the first night of the open-mic had me sittin' at the bar, mesmerized— like whoa! This young jawn, no older than 25, hit the stage and tore down the roof with Donnie Hathaway's joint, *A song for you*."

"Ooooh . . . I love that song!" I cooed. "Yeah, me too! Brotha Donnie would've been proud of the young jawn, because he represented to the fullest, ya' know what I mean? I dunno what it's gonna take to get you to come down to the club and check a brotha out . . . But I'm telling you, Club Marination is where the party's at! *Forreal*."

Leaning forward and releasing a short breath through his teeth, he held up his fingers one-by-one, like bullet points. "For one, we've got the best 'Soul food' in town, a wide variety of interesting beverages, live entertainment, top-notch security, and . . . yeah, let me not forget to mention, Club Marination is home to one of the dopest group of musicians around, since Mint Condition." Giggling, I responded, "Oh, and let me guess, that dope group is Soul Quest, huh?"

"*HELLLL yeah!*" Blaze affirmed, releasing a laugh so loud, it probably echoed through the hall, down the steps, and into the lobby.

Over the next several minutes, Blaze entertained me with a detailed account of his band's last performance, which received a wild standing ovation, and the crowd begging for an encore! I smiled like a proud mother as I listened to him narrate the mini success of his nightclub venture. That is until the sound of his voice faded into a mumble, and my eyes became fixated on his lips, which moved slowly and deliberately, with a few quick pauses in between to show off his pearly white teeth or to slide his moist tongue around the edges of his mouth. *Provocatively.*

"Mmm . . . I guess I am gonna have to make some time to check out this fancy nightclub for myself, since you're always bragging about it!" I

Call It What You Want

chortled, pulling myself back into the conversation and ignoring the

inappropriate thoughts that had tried to creep in. "*Piiish*! It ain't

bragging if it holds the truth, Miss Lady. I'm just saying!" The room

was suddenly filled with an awkward silence, as I observed Blaze slowly

rise to his feet, adjust his "Malcolm X" necktie, and glance at the leather

band attached to his wrist. In what must've seemed like "slow motion," I

gave Blaze a millisecond-too-long once-over.

Stealing a swift peep at his shoes, my eyes trekked up his pants, until my

gaze, accidentally, locked for at least fifteen seconds on the relaxed

bulge in his private area. The thought of what lay behind his zipper

essentially made my taste buds tingle, which I know was totally out of

line on my end-*being a married woman*. Guilt forced the voice of

Symone to invade my dirty mind. I imagined her eyeing me with a silly

smirk on her face, chastising me, as if she were my mother, "Guuuurl . .

. you' betta stop eyeing that man's stuff before he thinks you want some

of it! You should know by now-these jokers think with the head that

'*skeets*' not the one that '*thinks*!'" In all honestly, it was not my intention to be sizing up Blaze up the way I did. I especially didn't mean to be gawking at his crotch like some kind of pervert. I was merely admiring how his brown suede oxfords coordinated perfectly with his black linen dress pants, the midnight blue dress shirt tucked neatly around his waist, and that cream colored necktie pulling everything together and creating nothing but pure finesse . . .

"Aye, you alright, Miss Lady? I asked if you wanted to walk down to Wendy's with me for lunch . . . My treat!"

"Huh?" was all I could managed. I was as confused as I was embarrassed! I swear, had the complexion of my skin been a few shades lighter, my flushed face would've told a great tale of how utterly ashamed I was of my wandering eyes, which were scrutinizing the wrong area, of the wrong man! But then, what made the situation even more awkward was the boyish smirk on Blaze's face verifying that he had not only noticed my curt browsing of his person, but that the brotha enjoyed it! "Sooo . . . is that a yes, Miss Lady? You're gonna join me for lunch?" "Oh. . . Yes! It's a yes!" I huffed, following a nervous chuckle,

Call It What You Want

"Just give me a few minutes to freshen up, and I'll meet you in the lobby. . ."

*

"Ahem!" Mrs. Maybelle cleared her throat loudly, stopping Blaze and me in our tracks, as we strolled towards the main doors, tittering about something he'd been telling me on our way to the reception. "Where are you two younglings headed to in such a haste?" she quizzed, with roaming suspicious eyes. Blaze was saved from answering any questions by his vibrating phone. Whereas, I was forced to provide a clear and concise explanation of our plans, as if we were high-school teenagers. "Oh, we're just walking to Wendy's for lunch, since it's so nice outside. Would you like us to bring you something?"

"Uh-huh! I sure do, sweetheart! I love them Wendy's cheeseburgers!" She bellowed hungrily, as she seized a 'Mickey Mouse' wallet from her burnt orange oversized tote, fished out a 10-dollar bill, scribbled her order on a yellow post it, and handed it to me, grinning toothily.

Call It What You Want

As I exited the counseling center, I noticed Blaze standing by the bottom
of the steps, with a frustrated frown etched across his face.

His left hand moved agitatedly, while his right hand held his phone to
his ear. I galloped down the steps and pointed to my car, mouthing,
"Meet me over there when you're done. . . I have to get something out
of my car." He nodded. Then, turning his back to me, he took a few
steps in the opposite direction. I overheard him say, "Yooo . . . you are
really trippin' woman! We've had this same conversation on more than
one occasion, and each time, I've told you the exact- same- thing. I do
not wish to see you anymore; you know what I'm saying? No means *no*,
and I would appreciate if you would stop calling me. Respect me, as I
have respected you. And move on!"

During lunch, Blaze and I chatted about a little bit of everything under
the sun. I told him about Matthew and Isaac's upcoming summer
vacation to Ocala with my parents and watched his eyes widen with
excitement, as I gave him a mental tour of my uncle's 57-acre estate,

complete with a beautiful photographic pasture and an enormous farm

that housed multiple horses, sheep, and a gang of ornery goats.

He said, "Dayum, now that's *doooope*! I hope your twins recognize their

blessings, you know what I'm saying? Because, growing up in West

Philadelphia, I can guarantee you there weren't any horses, sheep, farm

houses, or green pastures in our neighborhood. It was straight hood; free

lunches, rec centers, public swimming pools, and daily cookouts—that

was about all that us 'poor' kids got back then!"

"Mmhmm, trust me. . . My brother Maxwell and I weren't quite as

fortunate as the twins either. Our mother and stepfather, Mister Eugene

struggled like folks in a burning city to provide us with a good life!

Then, once uncle Tommy and my mother's twin sister, Leena, 'moved

up' in the world, they made sure to look out for everyone in the family,

especially my parents and my kids, who they send for each summer.

My aunt and uncle are such good-natured people. I aspire to be just as

great and generous, offering all that I have to those in need. They've been married almost 40 years. I hope Isaiah and I can have the kind of love that they share. Love that lasts forever and ever!"

"Ah, I see you have all kinds of greatness running in your bloodline; eh, Miss Lady? Seeing the apple doesn't fall from the tree, I am certain that you will have just as many blessings poured into your life as your predecessors." Once again, Blaze had me blushing like a school girl! "So, how's your family, Blaze? It's been at least a couple years since I last saw your little angels, but I'm sure they are as striking as your beautiful wife." Blaze shook his head, then snickered, "Aww, so it's like that, Miss Lady? You just gon' give Keema all the credit for our daughter's good looks, eh? Okay, I see how you are . . . Nonetheless, Macy is now 14, and Luna recently celebrated her 12th birthday. Keema and I have been blessed with a set of honor students with strong aspirations. One wants to become a surgeon and the other, a scientist! I am so proud of my beautiful black princesses and have made it a habit to express as much to them each time we speak. . .

Call It What You Want

They've been talking about studying at Spelman after high school, which neither Keema nor I have a problem with. I told 'em, 'if this is the move yall wanna make, go for it. But, trust and believe your pops will be moving south too!

I ain't tryna' be one of those overbearing fathers. But those girls simply mean the world to me. I wouldn't know what to do if something were to happen to them and I had to wait for a flight to go rescue my daughters, ya know what I mean? We are living in some unpredictable times."

"*Mm-hmm!*" I nodded eagerly. "Regardless of how old they get, as parents we will always see our children as our babies!" I replied.

After ordering Mrs. Maybelle's lunch and starting off for the office, I turned to Blaze and said, "So how has Keema been doing lately? She's an elementary school teacher, right?"

With a hesitant pause and a slow release of air, Blaze replied, "Yeah. . . Keema is still teaching elementary. . . at a private school in Cincinnati. We're, uh. . . in the process of getting divorced. Our final hearing is scheduled in a couple of weeks."

Call It What You Want

"Wh-aa-at?" I stammered, whirling around with big round eyes like saucers. I frantically searched Blaze's eyes to detect if he was joking. His silence confirmed his seriousness, and it kind of saddened me that I had initiated such a painful conversation. Patting Blaze on back, I said, "Awe man, I am so, so, sorry to hear this . . . Had I known about this. . . I would have never-"

Blaze nodded then replied, "Nah, it's all good. Keema and I are at peace with our decision to separate. With the help of marital counselling and meditation, we realized that we were better off as friends, like we used to be back in the day, than as husband and wife. I will always love Keema, you know what I mean? She is mother of my girls and will always be one of my closest friends. I respect her, she respects me. . . It's all good, I promise!"

"But what about the girls, Blaze? How are they feeling about their parents separating? You know divorce has proven to be more difficult for children than for the actual couples. . ." I protested with pouty lips.

"C'mon, Miss Lady, put a smile on that beautiful face of yours! Keema and I had a long talk with the girls, and they are completely on board

with our decision. I must admit, the separation was kind of rough for a

brotha' at first. I was used to coming home to a house full of laugher,

enjoying home-cooked meals, and embracing a soft warm body at night.

Eventually things got better. Keema and I made the transition work.

There is no arguing or unnecessary drama between her and I at all. Like

I said, it's all good . . . Trust me!" The inquisitive part of me couldn't

help but wonder why Blaze and Keema had decided to file for divorce in

the first place. Was it due to financial issues? Infidelity on either side?

Or was Blaze on some Dr. Jekyll and Mr. Hyde shit—cool around

friends and colleagues and a total monster behind closed doors? His

admission of a pending divorce made me reflect on the brief

conversation of his that I had overheard before we left the office. Was

the person on the other end of his phone a factor for the separation or

what? There were so many crazy— NOSEY—questions running

through my mind, but I was too afraid to plunge into such a fragile

situation. "So tell me Miss Lady, how have you been able to keep your marriage so strong and full of life? Is there a secret potion, a love prayer

to this thing, or what? You've gotta share your secret, because I've got a

lot of love to give, and hope to one day meet and marry that special

someone that I'll be with for the rest of *our* lives. You know what I'm

saying?"

At first, I laughed. Because not only had his question caught me

completely off guard, but he, along with a bunch of other people, had no

idea how often I questioned the strength of my marriage! Isaiah and I

loved each other dearly, but our marriage was not always the "happy-

happy kind" that others made it out to be. "Well, Blaze . . . with all

honesty, I can say this; no marriage is perfect. It comes with its fair

share of challenges, some much more perplexing than others. However,

the way people deal with those challenges varies from person to person.

"There's this quote by an unknown author that I've learned to appreciate

and have often shared with my clients struggling with marital issues, *'A*

good marriage requires time and effort. You have to work at it. You have

to cultivate it. You have to forgive and forget and be absolutely loyal to one another.'" There was momentary silence between us, and I assumed he was pondering on the quote. As we climbed up the stairs leading to the counselling center, I turned to look at Blaze who was already looking at me through his metal framed Ray-Ban sunglasses. In a soft tone, I said, "Blaze . . . if you don't mind my asking . . . what happened to your marriage?" He turned his head to the side for a quick second, then met my gaze with a warm smile. "Nah, I don't mind you asking. I figured it was only matter of time now that you would anyway. But umm, Keema left our marriage because she was in love with another woman. . ."

Chapter 7

"*W*ell, it's about time the two of you made it back! I am so hungry my stomach is squeezing my spine!" Mrs. Maybelle began complaining the moment Blaze and I appeared in her line of sight. Blaze chuckled and said, "Ah, c'mon Mrs. Maybelle . . . now wouldn't you have been disappointed if Kayla and I came back with a dried up cheeseburger, three-day-old fries, and watered down lemonade? Our trip was a little longer than expected, only because we were making sure your meal was proper-like, ya' know what I mean? Fit for the queen of the C&O counselling center."

Mrs. Maybelle blushed like a blooming flower, as we all did with Blaze's flattering comments. She beamed and replied, "Well young man, since you put it that way, all is forgiven! Thank you both for looking out for the 'Queen', as you so generously put it . . .I-" The ringing phone on the desk temporarily caught the receptionist's attention, giving Blaze and me the opportunity to exchange a few quick words before going our separate ways for the day.

Call It What You Want

"Miss Lady . . . my secrets are safe with you, as yours are with me, correct?" Blaze asked with his usual smoothness. I smiled and, offering him a fist bump replied, "Of course, my friend. Your secrets are always safe with me. . ."

"Alright then . . ." he smiled again, "In case I don't see you anymore today, I hope you and your husband have a good weekend . . . and I will see you next week."

"Oh yeah, we definitely will!" I giggled, reflecting on the sexy things I was planning on doing with my husband. With an approving nod, Blaze gave me a quick wink, waved goodbye to Mrs. Maybelle and me, and disappeared around the corner near the breakroom.

I stood next to Mrs. Maybelle's oval-shaped station and waited for her to wrap up her phone call. I had her change balled up in my hand, and I wanted to speak with her to see if I had missed any important calls during my lunch break. "Lawrrd have mercy!" Mrs. Maybelle declared after she had verbally confirmed a client appointment for the following week. Snatching the headset from her head, and tossing it on the desk, she continued. "I am so ready for this day to be over, darling; I dunno what to do with myself! These clients are really testing my patience, and I just received a call about my husband Emerald having fallen asleep in a bar with his shoes kicked off, as if he were at home. My God, I swear, if it ain't one thing, it's like nine other things going on in my life! *Ugh*!

"Any ole' ways . . . that hateful client of yours who we spoke about earlier is *here* and has been sitting over in the lobby with her feet propped up on a chair for the last 30–45 minutes. I dunno what her problem is, and at this point honey, I really don't even care. But, I will tell you this. . . that crabby-patty needs some serious prayer, like YESTERDAY!"

"Huh? Now wait a minute. Why is she here so early? I thought her session was scheduled for two o'clock, or did I misunderstand what you told me earlier?" I enquired, glancing at the time on the computer screen, which read 1:36 pm. "Uhn-uhn . . . you're absolutely correct. Odessa Starr *is* scheduled for two this afternoon.

Call It What You Want

I tried to explain as much to her and I also printed out the itinerary that had been emailed to her, with the confirmed appointment date and time. "Hmph! Little good that did, because that only gave her another reason to try to bite my head off! *Umph, umph, umph*, you should've seen how she came high-stepping into the center, flipping her nose into the air, throwing around demands like she was the 'Queen of the Nile.' After she said what she said to me, I didn't utter another darn word. I just looked at her while she mumbled some kind of gibberish under her breath and used my index finger to point her toward the lobby or out the dang-on door! The devil is a lie if he thinks Imma let him get my nerves all tangled up! Oh *uhn-uhn* not today Satan!" Mrs. Maybelle leaned in a little closer, looked into my eyes and said, "Sweetheart, I'm gonna tell you like I did earlier—be careful with this woman, okay? I dunno what her story is, and it ain't any of my business . . . *really*. Nevertheless, it doesn't take a rocket scientist to see that she is horribly DISTURBED. She's got a chip on her shoulder big enough to be seen from miles away. I don't trust that rattlesnake one bit! If she starts acting up while she is in your office, all you've gotta do is send me the signal, and I will have the cops up those steps to escort her mean-spirited butt off of the premises-LICKETY SPLIT!"

Chapter 8

After a quick run to the bathroom to freshen up, in addition to darting into my office to anoint my scattered space, I returned to the reception fully prepared for what was to come. Now I will admit, Mrs. Maybelle had definitely made me a little apprehensive about the meeting with my new client. But after reflecting on the eons I had spent dealing with my crazy, ridiculously malevolent mother-in-law Bertha, I managed to convince myself that getting acquainted to this new "challenging" client was going to be a breeze! Grabbing the file from the box bearing my name, conveniently kept behind Mrs. Maybelle's desk, I glanced at her. She was on the phone and looking toward the waiting area, so naturally I followed her gaze. Between the oversized television mounted on the wall, two women waited patiently to be called for their 60-minute counselling session.

Call It What You Want

To the left of the television mounted on the wall, sat a thin Caucasian woman with fuchsia colored hair styled into a mohawk. Dressed in dark gothic attire, she sat with her shoulders slouched, shaking her thin legs up and down, nibbling away at her chipped black nail polish, and intently scanning the space around her as though she was expecting someone or something to appear from thin air.

The woman on the right was an African American with a hefty frame; her skin was the color of dry sand, with light-colored freckles sporadically spread across her nose and cheekbones. She had a round, pregnant belly, humongous breasts propped beneath her chin, and her crimson-red hair was skillfully styled into a pixie cut. She smiled as though someone was speaking to her on the inside, as she used her thumbs to speedily tap the buttons on her cellphone she appeared immersed in. However, her smiled died faster than wisps of smoke dissipated after a candle flame had been snuffed out, as I approached the waiting area.

Call It What You Want

Slowly looking up from her cellphone the woman with the red-hair shot me an unblinking death stare so withering that it made me flinch.

My gut instincts hinted that she was the woman responsible for ruffling the receptionist's feathers—and probably had every intention of doing the same exact thing to me, if I allowed it. As much as I appreciated my African heritage and gladly embraced the sacrifices made by our ancestors, it was sometimes a great struggle to deal with the far too complex attitudes of black women, especially the hot tempered ones who lacked any filters. It was nearly as tough and painful as pulling out a tooth without anesthesia!

Before rolling the dice, I took in a few deep breaths, and then let it go. "Miss Starr?" I called, shifting my glance between the two women, hoping the one on the left would respond first. The red-haired woman heaved an exasperated breath, rose to her feet, and sauntered towards me, a Grinch like smile etched on her heart-shaped face. "Good afternoon, Miss Starr. My name is Kayla Ward, and I'll be working with you today. Is it okay if I address you by your first name?" I asked, returning a friendly smile while trying to ignore the awkward the air

between us. "*Yap*! You can call me Odessa, no need for formalities," she

replied with an arrogant sneer, accepting my hand with a limp and lazy

grip. "Great! So, my office is on the second floor. We can either take the

stairs or the elevators that are located right next to the reception. Which

works best for you?"

"The steps are fine," she responded drily, as I caught a glimpse of her

wiping the hand I had shook on the back of her long black maxis skirt.

Please don't misunderstand me, dear readers; I sincerely respect the

sensitivities of those who are wary of physical contact owing to certain

phobias and/or religious beliefs. But, I could not ignore that the odd

vibes of Odessa's evil grimaces and rude gestures were both peculiar

and deliberate! She was being a "smart ass" for no apparent reason- *I felt*

it deep within my soul. . .

"So, how did you learn about the C&O Counseling center? Were you

referred by a friend, relative, or a separate organization, hmm?" I

enquired in a congenial tone as Odessa and I marched up the steps

~ 81 ~

Call It What You Want

leading to my office. "Yeah… well, I was sorta like… indirectly referred by a good friend of mine. I rather not mention their name though—you know, with the whole privacy act thingy, or whatever. Besides, I don't think people go around braggin' about spending time with a 'shrink' unless they're crazy or are looking for some type of extra attention or whatever. I ain't into either… I am perfectly sane, blessed, and highly favored and just need to get a few things off of my chest. *Nothing more, nothing less!"*

"*Mmm* . . . I understand where you're coming from Odessa." I lied. "But to clear up any misconception you or anyone else might have about counselling services, good mental health is extremely important for everyone, including therapists. It is not a *bad* thing. Counselling services help individuals like you and I to view our circumstances from a different perspective. It actually improves our quality of life."

"Um…yeah . . . so, I dunno' about all of that, Doc. But uh…I am certainly ready to do this and get it over with..." Odessa shot me a quick side-eye glance and said, " Oh, and by the way, um…I ain't tryna be

Call It What You Want

funny or rude, but, uh... you're much prettier in person than the picture

posted on the center's website. *Gur*l... they've got your face looking all

fat and fluffy. And the makeup around your eyes was so thick, I

wondered if you were tryna' hide a black eye or somethin'. You might

wanna have your people update that raggedy mess as soon as possible!

It's NOT a flattering look sis. *I'm just sayin'. . .*" At that very moment I

fully understood how and why Odessa irritated the shit out of Mrs.

Maybelle. Because for the entire two, three, or perhaps four minutes of

her being in my presence had been nothing but sheer torture! In fact, I

had become so uncomfortable with the awkward glares and negative

vibes that I played with the thought of faking an unexpected migraine

attack, just to have a legitimate reason to cancel the session and get

Odessa as far away from me as possible. Apart from Bertha, my she-

devil mother-in-law, Odessa Starr was by far the only other person I had

ever encountered who wore negative energy around her neck like a

colossal medusa-medallion! Never the less, as a licensed professional

trained to deal with real-life people with real-life issues, it was my obligation to see Odessa through the paid 60-minute session, regardless of how difficult she appeared to be . . .

Chapter 9

"It's nice to meet you, Odessa, and once again, I'd like to welcome you to C&O counselling center. If you don't mind, I'd like to get a little background information—why you're here and what your expectations are about this interview," I told the woman who had managed to kindle up a raging sandstorm from her initial request for availing psychological services. Releasing an inward groan and shifting her weight around in the boxed armchair, Odessa's eyes shot around the room suspiciously.

"Um . . . so . . . I'm here today because I am stressed the hell out, confused, and completely DONE with being mistreated by my unborn daughter's father. I mean, we used to be crazy about each other at one point of time. Whenever he'd call to say hello or show up at my place unannounced, I'd instantly get butterflies. I was that 'down ass chick 'that he wanted me to be—willing and ready to cater to his every whim. But now that his true colors have surfaced, I am realizing that the confident and sexy demeanor of his that I fell madly in love with was simply a front for his stupid and arrogant ways!" Stroking her swollen belly and releasing a weary breath, Odessa continued, "As I'm sure you've noticed, I am pregnant and due to give birth to my baby girl in a couple of months. My goal is to get all the things in my life in perfect order, so that when my daughter is born, I can direct all my energy to her—and OUR happiness . . ."

"Aww!" I smiled, my eyes quickly scanning Odessa's swollen abdomen peeping out of her pink tank top like a perfectly round' basketball. "I bet this is a very exciting time for you, Odessa. . ."

"*It is*." She blushed, brushing imaginary lint off her pink shirt. "You'd think that her punk-ass father would be equally excited, since he was the one always talking about how anxious he was for me to have his baby."

"Mm hmm . . . I'm sorry Odessa, but do we have a name for the man we're talking about? That is, unless you feel comfortable with me referring to him as 'your child's father.'"

Call It What You Want

"Oh . . . uh . . . um, let's just call him King for now . . ." Odessa replied
hesitantly. I nodded, scribbling the name "King" on my notepad. "Okay,
so if you don't mind, can you please explain the nature of your
relationship with King, prior to your pregnancy, hmm?" Odessa sniffed,
then started wiggling her feet, nervously. "I mean, I dunno, it's kinda
hard to explain . . . King and I weren't actually in a 'monogamous'
relationship so to say, prior to my pregnancy. . . if that's what you're
asking. However, we are crazy sick in love with each other— but for
whatever reason, he's being an ass about it. So, uh, I guess the best way
to describe our relationship, then and now, is *complicated* . . ."

"Ah . . . complicated," I repeated with an approving nod. "Tell me more
about this 'complicated' relationship, so you and I can perhaps identify
the problem, alright?"

"Oh, yes ma'am!" Odessa agreed eagerly, bolting upright in her chair.
She cleared her throat at least three times, then folded her hands neatly
beneath her belly— as though she was prepared to deliver a well

thought-out lecture on an Obstetrician Vs Midwife debate, as opposed to

sharing her private thoughts with a mental health therapist.

"Okay, sooo . . . King and I met a couple of years ago at this popular

cocktail lounge around the corner, near my then-apartment on the

Eastside. My homegirl, Nisha, was goin' through some stuff with her

boyfriend and wanted to know if I'd meet up with her, so she could vent

or whatever. Naturally, I agreed and told her to meet me at the lounge,

since that's where I was plannin' to grab dinner for that particular night.

It was a little after 7 pm when I walked into the lounge, and seein' that it

was the middle of the week, during late October, the only people in the

bar besides the employees were the boring 'uglies,' who didn't have

much else to do with their time but post up in a bar, reminiscin' about

how their lives USED to be. . . So, I'm sittin' at the bar, chillin' with a

double shot of Hennessey, playin' an online game of spades on my

cellphone, when I spot this FINE dimple-faced man in my peripheral

vision.

Call It What You Want

He must have noticed me checkin' him out, because he immediately strolled over to where I was sittin' and plopped down on the chair next to me, as if he'd been *summoned* or somethin." Odessa's face crinkled in laughter as she clapped her hands excitedly. "Gurrrl, this man was so damn cocky," she continued, "Instead of sayin' hello or formally introducin' himself, as any other sexy black man would've done, this smooth operator leaned close enough for me to get a whiff of his spicy cologne, shot a quick glance directly at my eyes, and said, '*Waiting for me, eh?*' I busted out laughing like, *'boy, paaaleeeeze! I don't even know you to be waiting for you, so cut out the games, Playah- Playah!* He snickered and was like, '*oh you know me very well, baby, because I'm the man of your dreams . . .*'" Once again, Odessa hooted over the memories of her earlier days with her lover, King. I think even I chuckled a few times along with her, as I've always believed that 'beginners' love' made for the most intriguing stories. "Mm hmm, so what happened next?"

Call It What You Want

"So, Nisha ended up cancellin' our plans for that night. She sent me a long text about how her boyfriend had hidden her car keys or somethin' like that. As much as I love my homegirl, her cancellin' on me was one of the best things she could've done that night. I had a cutie sittin' next to me, who was as thirsty for my attention as I was for his, and I didn't want anyone to disturb our groove.

King and I felt an instant connection. Shit, to be honest, it seemed like I had way more in common with him than any of the other guys I'd dated!"

"Such as?"

Odessa giggled like a piglet, clasping her mouth in an attempt to conceal her noticeable overbite. "Oh Jesus, I am so glad that you asked, Doc! Let's see ummm . . . King and I vibe to the same Westcoast Hip-hop and R&B music. We enjoy some of the same TV shows, like Grey's Anatomy and CSI. And last but not least, we share this DOPE 'animalistic' sex drive that is just OFF THE CHAIN!"

"What do you mean by "*animalistic*?"

Call It What You Want

Odessa guffawed, slapping her knee speedily, as though she was beating a Djembe. "Calm down, Doc, you don't have to take the word 'animalistic' literally. We don't screw around with animals or anythin' crazy like that, if that's what you're thinkin. For the lack of better words, King and I share a strong appetite for sex. I'm talkin' group sex, gay sex— at least for me. Masturbation, oral, anal—I mean, there are no limits for us in that zone. We're completely 'open-minded' and free in terms of our sexuality, you know what I mean?" I nodded, taking a moment to process everything she said. "But apart from the surface stuff, King and I were goin' through some changes in the 'love' department when we first hooked up. I was mourning the loss of a two-year-old relationship with a master manipulator, who used me for money and a place to live occasionally, and King was goin' through some shit with his snooty wife, Pigatha, who obviously didn't appreciate the type of man she was married to—"

"Whoa!" I interjected rudely, probably flashing a disturbed look. "Are you implying that the man you're in love with is married?"

Call It What You Want

Odessa shot me an unenthused glance and shrugged nonchalantly. "*Yeah
. . . that fool is married, Doc. But trust me; he doesn't love her nearly as
much as he loves me. Not only has he told me this on several occasions,
but God has confirmed it, also! King told me that he ain't been happy
with his wife's dumb prudish ass for a very long time. She hasn't done
half of the freaky shit with him that I have—excitedly! Hmph! My man
even told me that his wife doesn't like giving him 'head' because '*his
dick is too big*!' Now how freakin' pathetic is that?" Odessa rasped,
shaking her head with a shudder. "Welp! I'm sure you've formed a
lopsided opinion about my involvement with a married man, which is
fine by me. Opinions are like assholes— everyone has one, but they
think each other's stinks. . ." She sniffed and continued, "Call it what
you want, but I look at the situation like this—if 'Pigatha' was handlin'
her 'wifely' duties *properly*, I wouldn't have been invited to fill in for
her simple ass in the first place! After all, he pursued me . . . just as my
lord and savior, Jesus Christ, directed him to do.

Call It What You Want

Whether you believe it or not, God had spoken to me about my man—
way before he appeared in my life. This is probably why we fell in love
as fast as we did. . . I believe in the power of *prayer*, and even though
this situation might appear to be a little 'janky', it's all a part of God's
perfect plan . . ." I jotted notes on my pad, as I normally did during early
counselling sessions. And, as much as I tried to NOT form negative
thoughts about Odessa Starr, her views, her shifting brown eyes—even
the way she snaked her neck whenever she opened her mouth—irritated
the shit out of me!

People had their own way of communicating, I know. . . But, after
spending only a few minutes with Odessa, I was certainly NO FAN!
"Yeah, so anyway," Odessa persisted, popping a piece of hard candy
into her mouth and smacking her lips like a thirsty dog, "after spendin'
half of the night in the cocktail lounge, kissin' and fondlin' each other,
King and I decided to go back to my place. We had sex in every room of
my apartment, includin' the bathroom! No porn acrobatics or anythin'
like that—just delicious, spontaneous, wild sex! In a matter of weeks,

Call It What You Want

King had me so hypnotized by his persuasive spirit that I let that fool talk me into joining the 'swingers' club'."

"Swingers' club?" Are you speaking of one of those 'secret society clubs' where people go to have sex with total strangers?"

"Yap! Pretty much, Doc! The first few weeks of our time in the club was all about King. He'd pick me up from my apartment every Tuesday and Thursday, drive about an hour to the club—for me to watch him fuck the shit out of two, sometimes three, women at a time! This may all sound weird to you, but my man is talented *like that*, especially after smokin' a blunt or snortin' a few lines of that "magic powder" stuff. . .

"Magic powder—are you referring to cocaine?" Odessa smirked, then nodded. "Yap! He sniffed that shit, and sometimes rubbed it on his '*you know what*' because he said it increased his stamina or whatever. Oh, for the record—since I've noticed how you've been takin' notes and all— during our visits to the club were the ONLY times we got down with the cocaine. We ain't no damn addicts or anythin' like that—we just like to sometimes step out of our comfort zone and have a good time. That's all," Odessa stated defensively. "But anyway . . . once I became comfortable with the new environment, our roles were reversed, and I became the 'showstopper'! Every Tom, Dick, Jane, and Ashely wanted a taste of Odessa's sweetness, includin' the club's millionaire owner who invited me to a 'ménage a trois' with him and his wife. It was all fun and giggles during the time. But as it's been said—the same things that make you laugh will later make your ass cry the blues! Because of that stupid club and the things that I was 'coached' into doin', the man I love has flipped on me. He's putting on a front as if he hates me, and he's denying that he's the father of my daughter . . . which is just flat-out wrong!" Odessa grimaced.

"Mm . . . what is it that you were 'coached' to do, Odessa? And, is King questioning the paternity of the baby because of your involvement in the swingers' club?"

"Ugh!" Odessa cringed and rolled her eyes. "This has to be my least favorite part of this entire situation. But I guess it's relevant, and it helps put the pieces of this crazy puzzle together. So, King had called me on

Call It What You Want

one of the days we were supposed to go to the club, feedin' me a lame excuse about how I wouldn't be chauffeured as I normally was, because he had decided at the last minute to bring one of his 'homeboys' to the club, to give him a sneak peek of our underground world -*or whatever*. To my surprise, King and his friend had beat me to the club.

When I walked in, they already had a table next to the bar, a bottle of tequila, a small bowl of 'powder', and two Asian chicks in between their legs—goin' to work! After the chicks finished up poppin' King and his homeboy's 'tops,' his ass gon' slide over to where I was sittin' with a straight face, talkin' about, '*Dessa, I want you to show my homeboy why I love you so much . . . right now . . .*'

I knew exactly what my man was talkin' about, as he had sic'd me on several other men and women he wanted to witness being turned out, by me and this '*good–good'* I have between my legs. But, when I glanced over my shoulder, at my man's friend who was grinnin' like that fat-ass Garfield cat, I was like, '*OH HELL FUCKIN' NOOOO! I'm not gonna screw that slovenly- sloppy dude. Uhn-uhn! ABSOLUTELY NOT!* Don't

Call It What You Want

get me wrong, King's friend was an alright lookin' guy in the face. But he was fat, corny, and too goddamn chatty for my taste! *Yuck*!"

"Okay, so that we are clear Odessa, your boyfriend encouraged you to have sex with his friend?" Odessa nodded. "Yap, and like a big dummy, I *did it*!"

"Oh wow . . ." I sighed. Shrugging like a defiant child, Odessa said, "Yeah well, call it whatever you want, Doc, but people do some of the craziest shit when they're in love . . ." She glanced at the sparkling diamond ring on my finger, smirking carelessly. "I mean, you're a married woman . . . surely you can relate to where I am comin' from, right?" I ignored Odessa's question and proceeded with the interview. "So, what happened after you had sex with your boyfriend's friend?"

"Pfftt! Well, for starters, fuckin' my man's friend was a complete waste of my precious time. I thank God that it only took three pumps and a grind to get him off, because anything beyond that would've probably made me *barf*! After I excused myself to get cleaned up, I returned to the table where we started out at, to find that King and his funky friend had packed up their shit and left me stuck at the club, like a wadded-up piece of gum! Hmph! I didn't get a thank you for your services, kiss my ass, or anything—those ninjas literally went ghost on me... like I meant nothing to them . . ."

"*Wow*! How did that make you feel, Odessa?"

"Oh, I was PISSED!" she fumed. "I wanted to bust the windows out of both those mutha fuckas' cars— especially my man's, who had talked me into that nasty shit in the first damn place!"

"Did King provide you with an explanation for bailing out on you like that?"

"Hell no! After that night, it seemed like King had fallen off the face of the earth, because no matter how hard I tried, I couldn't make contact with that man for shit! He ignored me for a long time—until I found out that I was pregnant and texted him a copy of my first sonogram."

"Wait . . . you told King about your pregnancy via text?" Odessa made a disgusting "clicking" sound with her tongue and rolled her eyes.

Call It What You Want

"Yap! I sure the hell did! What other choice did I have, considering how he wanted to act all stupid and ignore me and shit, huh? I even sent a copy of the sonogram to his email, just in case he tried to play the innocent role and act like he didn't know nothin' about the baby, when the 'child support' folks came tappin' on he and Pigatha's front door. I gave that slime ball a few hours to get in touch with me so that we could discuss our little 'situation' and warned the mutha-fucka that if he didn't do as I instructed, I was gonna find his wife and expose his ole cheatin' ass!"

"What was his response to that?"

"Now, what do you think, Doc? That ninja called me real quick, talkin' bout', '*Yeah, I've been tryna' work things out with the wife and get myself together . . .*' and I'm like, '*oh blah, blah, fuckin' blah! I don't give a shit about any of that, I just wanna know how yall gonna help me take care of this fuckin'baby.*' King had the audacity to laugh in my ear, as if what I said was a goddamn joke. He said some stupid shit like, '*Dessa, you and I both know that ain't my baby . . . so quit bull-shittin'*

Call It What You Want

me. Since I am a nice guy, who cared about you at one point of time, I'll give you 500 dollars to relieve yourself of your little situation. But understand, I am through with you. We are not lovers or friends! I bout' died when I heard that shit! I mean, I literally could not believe my ears. Not only was this fool playin' me like I was nothin' more than a 30-day fling, but he was actually encouraging me to have my child aborted. He knew all about the painful miscarriages I had suffered while dating other men, and how bad I wanted to be a mother. Like, he was just mean to me. *Heartless* . . . I mean like, *dayum*!"

"Does he have other children, Odessa?"

"Yap! My daughter will be baby number four for King . . . and that's only if the *pimp* doesn't have a crew of other bastards runnin' around Columbus, starved of love and attention, because he's not man enough to handle his responsibilities. I mean, King has spun into such a goddamn fraud, he, um, swayed his homeboy from the swinger's club into thinkin' HE'S the father of my baby! Now this fat stankin' lil' baby-dick mutha-fucka keeps callin' and sendin' me stupid texts about paternity tests and shit. This fool actually wants to sit down with me to discuss co-parenting options—if he's found to be the biological father of my baby girl! I mean, this shit has gotten waaay' out of control, Doc . . . all because King refuses to take responsibility for his actions . . ."

"To be fair, Odessa, I have to ask—is there any possibility that King's 'homeboy' could be the father of your child? From what I've gathered, it seems like you were intimate with his friend around the time of conception, unless I'm mistaken of course. If that is the case, wouldn't you agree that the paternity of the child SHOULD be a legitimate concern for both the men involved?" Squirming in the chair like a worm, Odessa rolled her eyes, as though she was offended by my question. In a voice full of anger and frustration, she snapped. "For your goddamn information LADY, I know who the father of my child is… and it sure ain't his fat funky-ass friend!"

"Mm hmm, and in your opinion, the reality of this situation is . . ." I trailed off, unfazed by her elevated voice, or dirty looks.

Call It What You Want

Odessa didn't say anything, but she cupped her face and screamed out in agony. For a few seconds, I watched as she bawled like an infant. Tears seeped through the cracks of her fingers and rolled down her arms, and for the first time since our introduction in the lobby, I felt a twinge of remorse for Odessa Starr. I especially pitied the child in her womb, who would more than likely be caught in the middle of a nasty war between irresponsible adults.

Clutching the box of tissues on my desk, I sauntered over to the empty chair next to her and sat down. In a soothing tone, I began, "Odessa . . . we can take a break if you need time to pull yourself together. Initial sessions are usually the more difficult ones, but as long as you continue to walk through your feelings, and not around them, the process will become easier. I promise!"

Odessa snatched a handful of tissues from the box I was holding, dabbed her teary eyes, and spoke between sobs, "No! No! No! I don't–wanna–take–no–goddamn–breaks! I need to get all this shit off my chest today, so I can focus on my daughter tomorrow. She's- all- . . . I've got! That

Call It What You Want

greasy black mutha-fucka is in denial . . . and too fuckin' stupid to

realize it!"

"What is he in denial about, Odessa?" I asked calmly. "ABOUT US!"

she shrieked with tight eyebrows, tears streaming down her face. "I

know what God spoke to me about *Isaiah* . . . we're supposed to be

together! I don't give a shit about what he says—about workin' things

out with Pigatha or being around for those spoiled-ass kids, who

probably won't amount to anythin' worthwhile anyway.

With me and the baby is where he needs to be... And, if he doesn't

comply . . . there will be some serious consequences—"

"Odessa," I interjected. "You have the right to feel the way you please,

but it's important for you to understand that your issue is not with this

man's wife or his children—it's with HIM! Have you ever thought

about how painful the exposure of this affair will be for his family? Put

yourself in his wife's shoes for just a second and imagine how

devastated you'd feel after learning that your husband has basically been

Call It What You Want

living a double life— right under your nose. Then, let's consider simple

morals and principals, Odessa. Treat others as you wish to be treated—"

"Blah, blah, blah! I ain't tryna' hear none of that uppity bullshit!"

Odessa snapped childishly, dabbing snot from her swollen red nose and

glaring at me from the corner of her eyes. "How in the hell am I

supposed to be sympathetic towards a bitch standin' in the way of my

happiness, huh? I'm the woman who is supposed to be livin' in the 'big'

house, drivin' around town in fancy cars, and enjoyin' elaborate trips

around the world—not that bitch who always has a fuckin' opinion and

whines every time her husband pulls out his dick askin' for some head!

But you know what, Doc? I ain't even gon' trip no more about this mess

after today, because those mutha-fuckas will be stuck with me for at

least 18 years! I ain't gon' just go away like he wants me to.

My daughter and I deserve the 'world' he promised. And as I told him

earlier today, before I walked into your office, this could've all been so

simple—he's the one who chose to make it HARD! Decision time has

now ARRIVED—either shit or get cho 'stupid-ass off the pot!"

Call It What You Want

"So, are you expecting for him to choose YOU over his family? "I asked, slightly annoyed. Odessa rolled her eyes again. "Uh, duh! I've been quiet long enough. *Isaiah* has officially run out of time!"

"Isaiah . . ." I mumbled, suddenly losing track of my train of thought. This had been the second time I heard her mention that particular name, and just like the first time she had said it, she shot me a peculiar glance—one that sent chills running up my spine, causing the hair on my neck to rise.

I cleared my throat and tried to focus again, glancing at the clock to note that less than 15 minutes of the 60minute session were left.

With my head cocked to the side and my lips sealed tight, I watched Odessa like a hawk, as she barked about how God was going to punish her married boyfriend for the dirty deeds he had served her without a hint of remorse. Not one time could I recall her accepting responsibility for the role she had played, and I didn't even bother wasting my time to point that out to her. I just wanted Odessa out of my office and as far away from me as humanly possible! My eyes became fixated on the movement of her hands, as she reached into her oversized fire-engine-red purse, taking out a multicolored "blinged" cellphone and punching in a 4-digit code. The uneasiness I had felt and that Mrs. Maybelle had warned me about regarding Odessa returned—sounder and more potent than it had been earlier! Odessa wiped the tears away from her eyes angrily and shot me a malevolent glare that was so harsh it forced me out of my seat. With tightly curled lips, Odessa growled, "I am sick and tired of being shitted on! Yall mutha-fuckas got me fucked up—Kayla!" In that moment, I couldn't understand why her words felt so *personal* . . . so *direct* . . . so *harsh*, but in my mind, the interview was over! Odessa had to get the hell up out of my office, and I would refuse to EVER counsel her again!

"Alright, that's it! We're done here . . . umm . . . If you'll just gather up your things; I'll escort you downstairs to schedule a follow-up appointment . . ." Muttering something under her breath, Odessa bent forward, trying to pull up her pregnant body from the chair. During the process, her cellphone fell from her hand, slid across the floor, and landed before my feet.

Odessa and I glanced at the phone simultaneously, then looked at each other. In that very moment, I recognized the nervous fluttering in my stomach, coupled with the rapid beating of my heart. A part of me wanted to step over Odessa's phone and make her struggle to pick it up over her swollen belly. But, regardless of how uncomfortable she made me feel, I just wasn't that cruel a person.

With a quick side squat, I retrieved Odessa's phone. As I attempted to hand it to her, my eyes became glued to her phone's screen. A collage of pictures flashed before my eyes, leaving me completely breathless! The nerves in my body tingled as I squinted at the photos of "King"— Odessa's married boyfriend and the father to her unborn child.

Most of the pictures seemed to have been clicked during King's vulnerable moments—asleep, butt naked as the day he was born, with his flaccid penis on display, along with a few pictures of him sitting on the toilet and taking a shit!

Call It What You Want

Before I was able to muster a word or even revert to my thoughts,

Odessa released a mocking hoot, pointing her long pale fingers at me as

if I had been pranked. "Yahtzee, Pigatha! Your HUSBAND is MY

MAN BITCH! Apparently, Isaiah's punk-ass didn't have the balls to let

you know that you've been voted off the island, so I stepped to the plate

like a grown woman is supposed to, ta' let you know that IT'S

TIME FOR YOU AND MY STEP- CHILDREN TO KICK ROCKS

BOO- BOO! Isaiah and I are in love, and I'm expectin' the child your

'barren' ass wasn't able to conceive, MS. HYSTERECTOMY! Shiid . . .

if I were you, I'd make a mad dash to the courthouse to file those good

ole' divorce papers, because guess what, Pigatha'—what's yours is his

and what belongs to him is about to be allll mine! Ha–Ha–Ha!"

Searching for words, I found none. My head was spinning, as if I had

just stepped off a carousel, and I was seconds away from vomiting. I

wanted to punch Odessa in her throat so bad that my hands trembled

desperately.

Call It What You Want

But I knew that if I hit her, not only would I not have stopped until she was bloody and unconscious, but my ass was going straight to jail! Career and everything else—OVER.

I glanced at the gold 5x7 frame with our family photo on my desk, then quickly turned my eyes to Odessa's neck—where I envisioned my clammy hands swathed tightly around it like a noose—smothering the life out of her and her unborn child! Instead of responding with violence—as I am sure Odessa had anticipated—I burst out laughing, as though the joke was all on her! I laughed so hard and loud that I doubled over, slapping my hands against the desk with warm tears rolling down my face. Once I calmed down, I smirked at Odessa's ugly face and presented her with an offbeat, unenthused clap. "Good job, Odessa! What an outstanding performance . . . Now that you've had your five seconds of fame, GET YOUR PATHETIC ASS OUT OF MY GODDAMN OFFICE BEFORE I SEND YOU GLIDING OUTTA HERE ON A GURNEY!" I turned my back to her, taking a few steps forward and pulling the door to my office wide open.

Call It What You Want

With Odessa's "blinged" phone still in my hand, I glanced at her and shook the phone at her teasingly. "I'm sure you want this back . . .huh?" She nodded in affirmation and cautiously moved towards the door. With a final glance at the collage on Odessa's phone, I drew my arm back and tossed her cellphone down the hall like a frisbee. I glanced at Odessa over my shoulder one last time, and with a disgusted grimace, said, "GO FETCH, BITCH!"

Chapter 10

I was mad as hell by the time Odessa scurried out of my office and down the hallway, racing after her cellphone. That was exactly what I had intended for her to do when I flung it out of my sight like trash.

That bitch had me so perturbed, I was whizzing around the office like a tropical typhoon, snatching up my purse and things while muttering one of my calming mantras that I frequently suggested to my distressed clients: "Do not panic… just breathe." BREATHE!

I was moving at such a reckless pace that the heel of my left shoe ended up getting hooked on the leg of the boxed armchair, which moments earlier had cradled the funky ass of that redhead whore, sending me crashing to the floor with a hard and painful thud. My legs were twisted in an awkward "lunge" position. And the Versace shades, that I had just slid on to hide my tearful eyes, flew off as if they had been snatched and tossed to the opposite side of the room. Even the contents of my purse scattered onto the floor, looking like a busted bag of Halloween candies...

I was literally A MESS! My knees and wrists were throbbing up something terrible from my attempt to break the fall, but I managed to spring back up on my feet like a "G," scoop what I had dropped back into my purse, and make a beeline down the hall and the steps, until I had exited the doors of C&O Counselling Center.

For hours, I drove around the city in complete silence, reflecting over the last 14 years of my life that I had wasted on Isaiah's sorry ass! That fool should have been ashamed for the lives he ruined, from the kids and me to Odessa and her unborn daughter.

Call It What You Want

But, knowing Isaiah Maurice Ward the way *I* did, I knew for a fact that he'd rather blame the man on the moon for the terrible decisions he had made throughout his life before he'd willingly accept responsibility for his actions.

I thought about Odessa too, and the things she shared with me that carried too much accuracy for Isaiah to even think about denying it. For instance, I had every reason in the world to believe her claims about she and Isaiah's involvement with the swinger's club, because that creep had tried to pick my brain about it, saying, "How would you feel about checking out the 'swingers club' with me one night? I mean, I don't have to participate or anything like that... I just want to see what the hoopla is all about... and I think it would be best if you were with me, just in case one of those freaks try to jump my bones and shit..." I had zero interest in a 'swingers club' and I expressed as much each time it was brought to my attention. Ironically, the Tuesdays and Thursdays when Isaiah claimed to be in "managerial training" were the same days Odessa

Call It What You Want

admitted to spending time with her "*King*," enjoying consensual sex with complete strangers at the "horney folks" club.

Those very same days were the times when Isaiah also stumbled into our home late at night, reeking of alcohol with a piss-poor-ass explanation that he knew I wouldn't have wasted a fart on getting verified.

"Kayla, before you even start trippin' and shit... I apologize for coming in so late... I stopped by Momma's house on the way home from work, had a few drinks with the fam and played a couple hands of spades... if you don't believe me, you know you could always call her..."

Unfortunately, the situation with Odessa was not the first time Isaiah's "alleged" infidelities welcomed itself to our dinner table.

Back in the winter of 2007, I remember leaving work early due to a nauseating migraine attack. I had actually been feeling that way the entire day—head banging and jittery for reasons unknown at the time. After my midmorning session concluded, I asked Mrs. Maybelle to reschedule my other clients, so I could go home and rest.

Call It What You Want

Isaiah happened to be on vacation during this particular week, so it was no surprise to find him home when I arrived, with our stereo blasting away and the aroma of bleach wafting through the air.

After a warm shower and sliding on a pair of pajama shorts and a t-shirt, I popped a few Advils, then snuggled up in our bed with a recorded episode of *The Young and the Restless*. Just as *Jack Abbott* and *Victor Newman* started going at it for the umpteenth time, the telephone on my nightstand rang. I snatched the cordless phone from its cradle and answered without glancing at the caller ID.

The friendly voice of a woman greeted me as "Mrs. Ward" and introduced herself as Genève Smith. Genève explained that she had been a former employee of Isaiah's from the wireless company he manages, and her reason for calling was to notify me that she had hired an attorney and planned to file a complaint against my husband— wrongful termination and sexual harassment.

"Wrongful termination and sexual harassment?" I repeated in a high-pitched tone as I swung my legs over the edge of the bed, leaping onto my feet. "Is this some sort of a sick joke?" I questioned, with beads of sweat popping up on my forehead and down the nape of my neck.

Genève breathed out a sigh, then replied, "No ma'am... Mrs. Ward. This is not a joke. I am so sorry to have to call you about something like this—I swear. But after speaking with my mother and pastor, I was advised that I owe you an explanation and a huge apology for the things I have done with your husband. I am hopeful you will find it in your heart to forgive me…"

According to Genève, she and Isaiah had been romantically involved for approximately three months. And until the day they were caught *"tonguing"* each other down in one of the company's storage rooms by another co-worker, she had no idea that she had "almost" fallen in love with a married man…

"I swear to God, Mrs. Ward, I mean no disrespect to you or your family. But, your husband is, like, the biggest jerk that I have ever met in my entire life! Even after Charlene busted him out about his marriage to you, he thought I was gonna be down for seeing him on the down-low.

Call It What You Want

Piiish! I looked Isaiah dead in his eyes and told him to go straight to hell! I told him, 'I dunno what kind of chicks you are used to dealing with, but I have entirely too much class and self-respect to be reduced to a pathetic home-wrecking mistress! I am far from *perfect*, but I was raised better than that!'

"He even had the audacity to claim that the reason he had hidden his marriage from me is because he was too embarrassed to admit that you had taken the children and left him high and dry for another man!

I could tell by the wicked look in his eyes that he was lying his ass off, and right when he puckered up his deceitful lips for a kiss—like everything was cool—I slapped the dog shit out of him. Right in front of Charlene too. She was just as disgusted as I was!"

"Whaat? Did he strike you back?" I yelped as I paced around the bed, shaking my damn head, and trying to make sense of what was being said. Genève tsked, then replied, "*Naw*! He didn't hit me back, but that doesn't mean he didn't want to! From what I can recall, he just stood there- I guess shocked or whatever, gnawing on the inside of his jaw and looking like a stupid ass buffoon...

I'm sorry Mrs. Ward, but I told my mom and pastor, that I really believe that if Charlene hadn't been standing by as my witness, Isaiah would've probably beaten the crap out of me and probably left me for dead in that little storage space. That man is the *devil*! He is mean and selfish and doesn't care about no one else but himself!"

With a slight southern drawl, Genève said, "Mrs. Ward, you shoulda' seen the steam puffing out of his ears when I told him I was putting in a request to be transferred from his team immediately. Isaiah was pissed all the way off! Probably because he got rejected and realized he didn't have as much control of me as he assumed. I mean, I'm young and all, but I am not weak-minded or pressed for anyone's company! I know my rights, and I have no problem standing up for myself... which is what I am doing now..."

I held my breath for a few seconds and pondered on the word "*young*"; because if this girl was about to tell me she was under the age of 21—

and Isaiah's funky ass was close to 40—his perverted behind was gonna have worried about more than just "harassment and wrongful termination" charges filed against him! "Young? Just how young are you, Genève?" I asked nervously. "Umm… I just turned 25, *yesterday*," she replied proudly. "And how old you think Isaiah is, Genève?" She paused, then replied, "*Well*, he had told me he was 28 when we were messin' around and everything. But I did a little research on the internet and now know that he's an old man—at least too old for me. You may or may not know this Mrs. Ward, but your husband is a manipulator—*a master manipulator*! Because he couldn't have his way with me, he turned the entire staff against me… including Charlene, who had witnessed his foul! I was forced to work in an environment with people gawking, snickering, and shaking their heads at me—as if I'd shown up smelling like a bum's asshole, wearing two different shoes on the wrong feet! It was almost as if they were 'punked' into not communicating with me. No matter how hard I tried to be nice and mingle with the team, the only thing I received for my efforts were lifeless hellos, eye rolls, and parched goodbyes. After about a month or so, the tension

began dying down around the office. Either that, or I no longer paid

attention to the hostile work shenanigans. I thought things were finally

looking up for me. I nailed my first interview with a new team, and was

hand selected for a second. "Excuse my language, Mrs. Ward, but this

vile, unethical S.O.B summoned me to the office like an hour before I

was to appear for my second interview with the new team, and then

without a legitimate explanation, he fired me!

To add insult to injury, he had me escorted out of the building by two

garanimal-looking security guards. They had already stowed away my

belongings and had the box sitting outside in the rain—on the hood of

my freakin' car! *Ugh…*" I could hear Genève weep on the other end

before she continued. "I... I was so embarrassed, Mrs. Ward. I cried all

the way home."

As soon as the call ended, I bolted down the steps into the kitchen and

without hesitation, snapped, "What in the world have you gotten

yourself into now, Isaiah?" Isaiah spun around and observed my jumbled expression. "Huh? What in the hell are you talking about, woman? I am tryin' to prepare a lasagna meal for my family. Shit, the question is, why in the hell did you come running down the steps sounding like a herd of angry cattle when you're supposed to be sick from a goddamn migraine attack?"

"I did have migraine, and I am sure it's gonna come back shortly, after learning that your sneaky ass has been creeping around with one of one of those young girls at your job! Jesus Isaiah! The girl has even 'lawyered up' to file a complaint against you for wrongful termination and sexual harassment. What in the hell is wrong with you? Am I not good enough? If you want to be free to mingle with whoever, why don't you just say it? So I can go on about my business!"

With an arrogant smirk, Isaiah slowly moved his head from side to side, then sauntered closer to the breakfast bar, where I was heaving with my arms crossed on my chest.

"See, there you go, shootin' your fuckin' mouth about shit you know nothing about, Kayla. How many muhfuckin' times do I have to warn you to tame your insecurities before you fuck around and push me into

another woman's drawls, hmm? Okay, yeah, you've got a little weight

on you or whatever, but so fuckin' what! You are beautiful to me

Kayla—inside and out… My wedding band is always in clear view; you

know what I'm saying? But these thirsty hoes still wanna throw that

thang my way… and when I turn their asses down, they wanna make

contact with you, just to fuck with your mind.

Shiid, smart as you are, I thought you would've peeped game by now…

but I guess you can't do that shit, huh? Because you're too fuckin fixated

on making me out to be the bad guy…"

I almost laughed at Isaiah's ridiculous response. I guess he thought he

could smoothly skip around his coworker's claims by turning the

conversation to my "supposed" insecurities.

Yes, I had a little extra *pocketing* around my belly and backside, which

probably wasn't the most appealing, depending on who was looking.

But, uhh, I don't recall ever having esteem issues. I loved me some me…

hell, sometimes I had to love myself enough for the both of us!

Call It What You Want

In a bitter, sarcastic tone, I replied, "Ahh negro, please! The only person bothered by my pleasantly plump curves is you! Now, let's get back to the sexual harassment complaint, Isaiah. *What happened?*"

"Maaan, do you know how muh-fuckin' stupid you sound, using sexual harassment and my name in the same sentence? You must be outta your fuckin'mind if you think I've gotta pester a bitch for a piece of pussy... like I told you earlier... I get pussy thrown at me on a regular basis Kayla. Genève's big-lipped, wig-wearing, homely looking ass is just mad that I rejected her stankin ass! Shiid, I ain't tryna be funny, but I wouldn't fuck that ugly bitch with another man's dick! Straight up! That bitch is ugly as FUCK-*I swear to fuckin-God*!"

The way Isaiah described Genève with such sick grimace, one would've assumed Genève was the long lost twin of Eric Stoltz as Rocky Dennis in the film *Mask*.

"Look babe, for the record, I didn't do anything with or to that woman, besides try to help her. One day my buddy Brian and I walked out the back door of the office to find Genève's goofy ass standing beside a raggedy Impala, stomping around and whining like a big ass kid, like someone had stolen her goddamn candy. She had the hood to the car raised, and thick black smoke puffing out of it. Like gentlemen are supposed to fuckin do, Brian and I asked the stupid bitch if she needed help. Obviously she did, and almost immediately she started babbling about how she was struggling, lacked family support, and *blah blah blah*. Brian volunteered to have the piece of shit car towed to her apartment through his AAA membership, and my dumb ass offered to give her a ride home, which I now regret…"

I didn't respond, I just shot him a blank, twisted lip stare. The way he used his thumb and index fingers to pinch at his goatee, and how he shifted his eyes from side to side, was clear indication that he was anxious, indecisive, and lying through his perfectly straight teeth…

"I offered my muh-fuckin time, my gas, and my ears, to that skeezer-which she *beat up* from the moment she slid into car, until we arrived at her apartment, 20 minutes later. I parked in front of her place, and while she continued babbling on about how grateful she was for Brian and me helping her out, the bitch reaches over from the passenger seat like she's gonna give me a hug or somethin' and starts rubbing on my dick. I grabbed her hand, like, 'whoa, hold up lady, *what da fuck*?' Babe, her nasty ass started licking on those soup coolers, and grinning with a horny look in her eyes, talkin' 'bout how she wanted to repay me for my services with… you know, with a little *sloppy toppy*. I pushed the bitch away, like, nah, you ain't gotta do that! I'm good, you know what I'm saying? I'm married Genève... *happily married...*"

The lies Isaiah uttered fell from his lips like Domino tiles. If Genève had offered my husband fellatio—as he suggested she did—I would bet my last dollar that he would have leaped at the opportunity to have his thickness shoved completely down her throat. Isaiah was never one to pass up head… and this, I knew for a fact! "Mmm, so then what, Isaiah?" I asked sarcastically. He frowned and threw his hands up in the air in surrender. "Whatchu mean? I dodged that shit babe! I let that bitch know that I wasn't interested in her like that, you know what I'm saying?

Call It What You Want

I ain't that pressed for attention that I would just let ANYONE put their mouth on me...I mean c'mon now, you should know me better than that... And shit, now that I've had the chance to sit back and think about things, Genève is probably one of those low-key prostitutes working for an escort service or some shit like that... a fuckin slut or something..."

"Isaiah, a prostitute? Seriously?" I pushed. "If that woman was about that kind of lifestyle, she certainly wouldn't have the need for a regular nine-to-five, nor would she have had to put up with the grief she claims you have caused! Cut the games man, this is serious..."

I debated with that fool for what seemed like an eternity. And as I should've expected, he refused to assume responsibility for his actions; he couldn't even provide me with a reasonable explanation about why Genève was fired! Instead, he wasted time throwing shade my way, for being " stupid enough" to believe the words of a woman I had never met. Finally, I said, "Isaiah, look I wanna have your back in this situation, especially if you are telling the truth. But right now, you are making things unnecessarily difficult! This woman is slinging around serious accusations that can ruin your entire career, but you wanna sit here and pick an argument with me? C'mon now… that's not gonna help you one bit… you are gonna have to put your pride to the side and FOCUS, sir!"

I paused long enough to be certain I had his full attention, because I knew the next few words I was prepared to drop on him was sure to agitate every fiber of his being, especially if he was being as deceitful as I suspected. I made direct eye contact with my husband and in the calmest tone that I was able to muster, said, "Honey, look, you may not agree with what I'm about to say, but I'm gonna say it anyway: I think we should speak with Genève… face to face about these allegations, before this mess blows up in *our* faces. Remember this just isn't about you, Isaiah. You have a wife and two children, and we will all be affected if she really does go through with a lawsuit."

"Say what? *Shiid*!" he spat with furrowed brows and flared nostrils like an Arabian horse. "Bitch, you must be out of your rabbit-ass mind if you think I'm gonna waste any of my goddamn time linking up with a filthy tramp telling lies on me! To my knowledge, you dunno this bitch from a can of paint, yet you wanna arrange a damn meet-and-greet? For-the-fuck-what-Kayla? For her dumb ass to pump your head up with more bullshit and lies? You're supposed to have my muh-fuckin back, not hers...." Isaiah shook his head, as if I had done something wrong, then said. "Aye... let this be the last time I have to say this to you, Kayla, because you really are pissin' me off and I promised to not put my hands on your muh-fuckin ass again. I *do not* give a flying fuck about Genève's ugly ass, nor am I pressed about her bogus accusations. If she wants to make a fool of herself, that's on *her* dumb ass!

And, if you wanna leave our marriage over some punk-ass hearsay bullshit, then that's on *your* stupid ass too! Do whatever the fuck you gotta do, Kayla! I am done with this almost laughable conversation..." Isaiah took a gulp of the beer he had snatched from the refrigerator and glanced at me with frustrated eyes, then snorted. "A goddamn meeting . . . da fuck?" He continued.

Call It What You Want

"Do I look like one of your crazy-ass muh-fuckin' clients? I ain't gotta prove a goddamn thing to you or that dingy skeezer! Take yo' ass on, let her entertain your nosey ass with more lies if you want to, cause' I ain't got time for this shit! Just keep a brotha updated, so I'll know when I need to make a move, *dummy*!"

Determined to meet the woman accusing my husband of sexual harassment, I waited patiently for Isaiah to storm out of the house—as he typically did after an argument. Once I was sure he had left, I carried the cordless phone into the bathroom, then redialed the last incoming call. After a quick two second ring I received an automated message: *"The number you've called has been disconnected or the number has been changed... no further information is available..."*

Chapter 11

*I*t was a little after 7 pm that Friday evening, when I exited 105b and drove towards the place I had called home for nearly fifteen years: 3603 Scottwood Road. I had been so overwhelmed by the whole "Odessa and child" debacle, that I ended up driving all the way to Cleveland and back

Call It What You Want

to Columbus in what felt like only 20 minutes! As I waited at a stoplight on James Road, my phone started vibrating for the umpteenth time. I picked it up from the passenger seat's floorboard and shook my head, as it displayed a beautiful Sepia-toned headshot of my best friend, Symone. That girl had rung my phone non-stop, like a deranged stalker, during the well-nigh 6-hour-long drive I had taken on the highway, trying to figure out what I was supposed to do next, or how I was even supposed to feel about the man that I had nearly lost all respect for.

As much as I wanted to get on the horn with my friend and wail over how my life had gone from sugar to shit in a matter of minutes, I knew better than to spring something of such magnitude on Symone over the phone. Because she wouldn't have been able to handle that kind of drama, without being just as DRAMATIC! Symone was so protective about my marriage to Isaiah that if she had the slightest idea about what had gone down in my office hours prior, she would have not only broken her neck to get to my house and confront her "brother-in-law," my bestie would have had our house surrounded by "prayer warriors"—

Call It What You Want

while her friends with "masks," whom she supposedly kept in her pocket in case of emergencies, tracked down and executed the infamous Odessa Starr! I was infuriated by the things I had heard about my husband, for sure. In fact, during my long ride on the highway, I had accepted the fact that I had broken my own damn heart by loving a self-serving, undeserving fool, like Isaiah Ward. So, all of the extra drama that Symone would have come with had to be put on hold...at least until I spoke with my husband- *one on one*.

The moment I turned onto our street and noticed my mother-in-law's minivan parked awkwardly in our driveway, deliberately blocking the entrance to our two car garage, the composed demeanor I was trying to become one with, flew out of the window like a solitary sheet of paper! I bit down on my fist and yelped like a wounded animal, thinking, *Oh God . . . why is she here? This is not the day for Bertha Lee/Smith Dixon/Mitchell-Long, or whichever surname she's using this week, to be fucking with me!*

Call It What You Want

I absolutely, positively, certainly could NOT stand Isaiah's mother!

Bertha was an ugly, mean-spirited BULLY, who was always wrapped

up in someone's personal business! She was as tall as the "jolly green

giant" with dark oily skin, black beady eyes, with bristly grayish hair

usually concealed beneath a light-colored old-fashioned Tina

Turner wig.

Bertha's voice was just as annoying as her mere existence. She yakked

in a rambunctious booming tone, sounding more like tanked-up Bernard,

Jim-Bob, or Roscoe than an actual woman. In addition to her ghastly

physical attributes, Bertha was a rotgut alcoholic who slurped on "bum

wine," puffed on cheap cigars and cigarettes, and cursed like a pesky

pirate!

Long before Isaiah started dating, exclusively, he had shared a lot of

disheartening things about his mother. He confided in me that his Bertha

used to physically and verbally abuse his five brothers throughout their

childhood. She would knock those poor little fellas on their heads with

boards, sticks, and poles whenever they got out of line. He even said that

Call It What You Want

she had used extension cords as a form of discipline, leaving welts all over their bodies like slaves flogged by their cruel masters! Isaiah, however, was fortunate enough to have escaped being subjected to the abuse his brothers had faced, purely because he was her "favorite" of the boys—the one Bertha cherished the most.

As you can imagine, I wasn't too thrilled about meeting Bertha. In fact, anytime Isaiah would mention it, I would quickly change the subject, hoping that he would catch the hint that I wasn't interested, and leave well enough alone. Isaiah got the hint alright, but I soon learned that he'd do whatever he had to do to get his way, regardless of the discomfort 'his way' caused others.

During a humid summer evening, Isaiah had showed up at my parents' house and invited me to the movies, to check out Denzel Washington's latest flick. I had agreed eagerly, because I was deep into that " teenage love" phase and loved nothing more but to spend time with Isaiah.

We were on our way to the movie theater, when I noticed that Isaiah fidgeting and clutching his stomach.

Call It What You Want

I asked him about it, and he explained that he had "bubble guts" due to the Mexican food he had eaten earlier that day, and reassured me that after he used the bathroom, he'd be okay.

So, I suggested we make a pit stop by a Target or Walmart store-their bathrooms were normally clean, and we were too far away from my home to turn back. He shook his head and explained that we were going to be stopping by the home he shared with his mother- which at the time I had no idea was less than two minutes from where we were.

The moment Isaiah parked his car in front of a creepy, dilapidated ranch-style home, I was overwhelmed with concern. Their place was located dead smack in the middle of the Short North—a small neighborhood in Columbus near High Street, which had a notorious reputation for drugs, violence, and heavy gang activity. I was scared as shit as I sat in the car with a 'spooked' facial expression, as I recalled the horror stories I'd heard about innocent people being "jumped" or killed in this part of town for simply for being at the wrong place at the wrong time, or even wearing the wrong color!

Call It What You Want

"You know, I just can't leave you out here in the car by yourself, right? So, you might as well come on inside with me..." Isaiah stated calmly, as he unbuckled his seatbelt and prepared to get out of the car. "This ain't the best neighborhood and shit, and I dunno what I'd do if something crazy happened to you while I'm inside takin' a dump. Besides, I think it's about time my momma met the special lady in my life . . . you know what I'm saying, right?"

My anxiety levels increased significantly, when Isaiah and I stepped on the weakened wooden porch and walked through his front door.

For starters, their house STANK real bad! I practically gagged from the overwhelming stench of mildew, stale tobacco, and aged cat litter. And, to make matters worse, my soul damn nearly leaped out of my body when I turned to the left of the living room and locked eyes with half a dozen fuzzy, jet black, green-eyed felines positioned on an old-fashioned floral couch, glaring at me as if a gremlin had just waltzed through the door! Papers, shoes, and clothes were stacked up in various corners of the living and dining rooms.

Call It What You Want

And, from what I could see of the "kitchenette," with dirty dishes piled in the sink and food splattered on the counters and walls, it hadn't been cleaned for days, if not weeks! Shortly after entering the "*funk box*," Bertha came bustling in from a door close to the rear of the house, gawking at me with such a displeased expression that it made me shudder. "Uh, hello . . . um . . . Mrs. Bertha . . ." I greeted instantaneously and timidly. "Uh . . . my name is Kayla, and I'm a friend of Isaiah's. Um . . . so, we're on our way to the Lennox to check out a movie, but . . . um, we had to, uh, stop by here, because he—"
She cut my stuttering words off with a flippant wave. "Yeah, yeah, yeah . . . save all of that drama for Oprah or Dr. Phil! What's ya' goddamn story, girl? I guess you're pregnant huh, and think that I'm gonna help out with another damn abortion eh? Well the answer is *Naw*...Hell naw! I ain't got no goddamn money, and I ain't raising no hardheaded ass kids for yall...*period*" Bertha sneered, sizing me up from head to toe. "Oh, no ma'am . . . I am not pregnant." I answered respectfully, shaking my head nervously. "Isaiah and I are just friends' ma'am. There's nothing like

Call It What You Want

that going on, I promise..." Bertha cut her eyes at me, as if I had spoken out of turn. "*Pffit*! What chu' mean '*nothing like that,*' huh? I know damn well you don't think ya too good for my Izzy, cause, uh . . . I hate to burst your bubble, but *Kelly,* you ain't all that! Don't get it twisted now, my baby is fine and smart and can have just about any young gal that he wants. As a matter of fact, I know of at least three of 'em, who can't get enough of my boy . . . while you're tryna' be funny!" Quite nervously, I replied, "Oh no ma'am . . . It's nothing like that either. I mean I really, really like your son, Mrs. Bertha; he's a cool guy. We hang out all the time . . . but we're just friends. Also, my name is Kayla, Mrs. Bertha, not Kelly. Kayla Nunez . . ."

"*Nunez*?" Bertha shrieked, twisting her face up as though she had just gotten wind of her rotten breath. "What kind of a funky-soundin' name is that? Is ya' mammie Jamaican or somethin'?"

"Uh, no ma'am. My father is Dominican, and my mother is African American."

Call It What You Want

"*Mmm* . . . yeah okay, *Kendra*." Bertha muttered maliciously, as she pulled a few drags from the long brown cigarette dangling from her stubby dark fingers. "*Mm hmm*," She proceeded with a sneer, purposely blowing smoke into my face. "So since ya' think ya' *all of that*, how many of them neighborhood boys have ya let touch on ya, eh? I see you've got that big ole round ass and wide hips. Surely you've let plenty of 'em play in yo coochie pie!" "*Huh*?" I gulped. "Huh? Huh? Huh?" Bertha mocked immaturely. "What's the problem now, *Keele*? Ya havin' trouble understandin' English? Since ya think you're all that and a bag of chips, I wanna know how many of 'em frisky lil' boys you've done the '*oochie coochie*' with. I already know you fast-ass girls can't keep ya' legs closed to save ya' lives, so I wanna know your stats before you start hunchin' around with my boy, then try to run your sorry ass back to me—whining about being knocked up. Imma tell you right here, right now *Kendra*, I've heard the same tired-ass song from several fast-ass girls like ya, about my boys and their 'loose *dangalangs*.'

Call It What You Want

We ain't got no' goddamn money for cryin' babies, and Izzy don't need no pie-faced hoes distractin' him from his goals, you got me, *Keisha*? Don't start none; won't be none…" Never in my life had I been treated with so much disrespect. And, never had I ever believed in monsters and demons until the day I met Bertha. That woman had a deathly scary air about her, so much so that I had second thoughts about having any type of relationship with Isaiah!

But the adoration that I had developed for Isaiah allowed me to trust him when he told me that everything was going to be alright. However, as the years progressed, Bertha continued to come for my neck with bogus allegations and lies anytime she felt like it- and, Isaiah hardly ever had my back!

A few summers back was when the shit really hit the fan. Isaiah's eldest brother Aalim, formally known as Mister, was released after serving a 15-year prison sentence for drug trafficking, and Bertha had planned an extravagant "welcome home" celebration.

Call It What You Want

This was an exciting time for Isaiah, because out of the five brothers he was blessed to have, he and Aalim shared an inseparable bond—even throughout his time in prison.

I was never officially invited to the party, which I hadn't expected to be, since it was being hosted by Bertha at her house. But, Isaiah was so excited about the twins and I meeting Aalim, that I went along with the program anyway, as I didn't want to risk "killing his vibe" by voicing grievances about his mother's vindictive actions. On the day of the celebration, I trailed Isaiah's royal blue Ford-150 into what appeared to be a junior block party, surrounding a run-down two-story house on a cul-de-sac in West Columbus.

Seeing that Bertha was constantly being evicted from the caves she called home, for disturbing the neighborhood's peace, this place was probably the 2nd or 3rd property she had rented that year—more than likely under one of her aliases.

On top of everything rambling inside my mind, there was an old, scrawny, shirtless, dark skinned man dressed in a pair of blue-jeans short

Call It What You Want

overalls, with a pair of red leather cowboy boots and Robocop sunglasses on, standing in the middle of the street directing traffic as if we were attending a funeral. I could help but to chuckle at how ridiculous the man looked, and wonder if he was one of Bertha's many lovers- that she frequently picked up from the men's shelter.

Small children ran through the cul-de-sac freely, firing water guns at each other as though they were in the middle of a gang war, while the inebriated adults, who should have been watching their children, stood around in huddles shooting craps and passing brown-bagged bottles of alcohol and thick marijuana blunts from lip to lip!

You just don't know how bad I wanted to turn around and hightail back to my safe zone-home sweet home! But, I knew that this would have only given Isaiah a reason to start another fight with me, which I was in no mood for. We parked our cars in a field across the street from Bertha's house. And, with my best "poker face" on, I maintained a tight grip on Isaiah's hand as we approached the crowd of rowdy relatives.

The male members of the family greeted Isaiah and I respectfully, with

Call It What You Want

approving grins and bear hugs, while his finicky female relatives

swarmed around him as if he were a candy man, saying, "Yaaass-It's

about time *YOU* made it, Izzy! OMG, Matthew and Isaac look just like

YOU, Izzy! Mmm . . . *YOU* look and smell so good, Izzy! WOW, those

sneakers are so dope, Izzy! Lemme' hold a few dollars, Izzy; we know

you've got plenty of dough . . ."

Since Isaiah's relatives acted as if I wasn't standing close enough to

smell the alcohol and blunts on their breath, I offered a generic "hello"

with a friendly hand gesture, to ensure that I hadn't faded into an

invisible zone. Judging by the dehydrated "oh . . . hey" response I

received in return—followed by being eyeballed from my sandaled feet

to my naturally curly mane—you would have thought I had said

something offensive to one of those clowns or walked up on them

smelling like a rotten-egg-like fart!

Eventually, we entered Bertha's loud and stuffy house, which was

packed with just as many people as the front yard. Overlapping

conversations were resounding all over the place- with Bertha's manly

Call It What You Want

voice being the loudest! As soon as she caught a glimpse of Isaiah and the twins, her phony behind hobbled over to where we were standing and wrapped her arms tightly around the boys, pecking them on each sides of their cheeks as if she hadn't seen them in months. Rocking back and forth on her heels and holding Isaiah's hand as if it was his first day in kindergarten, Bertha bragged about the accomplishments of her "sweet baby" Izzy. "HER" Izzy was just the greatest guy in the world! "HER" Izzy survived a tour in Afghanistan and was blessed with a high-paying job that afforded private schooling for "HIS" twins. Bertha has gotten so deep with her phony baloney shenanigans, that I had to turn my head to the side to keep myself from laughing in her face- especially when she pretended to have supported "OUR" decision to have the boys attend a private school.

From what I had been told by a reliable source, Bertha was outraged when she had gotten wind that Matthew and Isaac would be attending a private school after completing 5th grade. I was told that she had accused me of being "bougie" and had the nerve to say some crazy shit

Call It What You Want

like, *"The dumb fat cow already got my grandbabies speakin' like 'dem white folks. Now she's gon' put 'em in a private school, where those uppity perverted sons of bitches gon' turn my grandbabies into a pair of identical faggots!"* What a horrible thing to say about your own grandchildren...But, I digress.

"Now, these little handsome twins right here got their grannie wrapped around their fingers like bubblegum. They're the sweetest little boys, just like Izzy was when he was growin' up. Don't you remember how sweet your baby brother was as a child, Mister? Ah shit, I mean Aleem . . . Alime or however you pronounce that Mooslim shit you go by now!" Aalim, unfazed by Bertha's insult, nodded his head and chuckled. "Ma dear . . . my name is Aalim—A-A-L-IM, and it symbolizes wisdom. As far as your thoughts about Izzy being a sweet and innocent kid goes . . . nah, I can't say I recall those days! That boy was spoiled, hard-headed, and *baaaaad* as hell! And from the way things are looking... not much has changed." Everyone in the room laughed their asses off at Aalim's response—all except me, because he was absolutely right; the only thing that had changed about Isaiah was his age. "Ah! There you are, sis!"

Aalim bellowed moments later, after finding me sitting in Bertha's

backyard under an oversized oak tree. "I was wondering where you had

disappeared to, sis. One minute you're standing in the house, tryna smile

your way through the pain of being near Ma, then BAM! You were gone

in the wind!" He chortled walking towards me, clutching the blue milk

crate he had obviously planned to sit on.

"Ha-ha! Yep. I'm still here, Aalim, chillin' and tryna stay outta the way

of the drama. How are you doing? Are you enjoying the party so far?"

I asked with an earnest grin. Aalim positioned himself on the milk crate,

then pulled out a white wash cloth from his pocket to blot the sweat

running down the sides of his taqiyah-covered head.

"Yeah . . . it's all good, sis! I'm happy to be home and more obliged that

my folks have gone all out to welcome a brotha back into society. Imma

keep it real with you though, I dunno who half of these people are! I do

appreciate 'em though!" Aalim shook his head, looking at the ground,

and shot me a dimpled smile similar to that of his younger brother. "So,

Call It What You Want

what's the deal between you and Ma, sis? The tension between you two was so damn thick, I could've cut it with a knife! I already know that Ma is not everyone's cup of tea...her spiteful ways has the tendency of pushing good folks away. But I'd like to hear your side of things... what's the deal?" Heaving a deep sigh, I replied, "Aalim, to be honest with you, I dunno why your mother hates me as much as she does. I can't think of one thing I might have said or done to make her feel as if we can't breathe the same air and co-exist. But, she hates me with a passion like that of a fierce cheetah fighting off a hyena. And, as you've seen with your own eyes, she ain't shy about it either!"

"Wow that's deep sis!" Aalim stated, as he shook his head in disbelief. "How long has this been going on, eh?"

"Uh . . . only for FOREVER!" I chortled and continued,

"I used to pray all the time for a sit-down with Bertha to discuss our differences so that I could at least apologize for whatever I've done to make her behave in such a despicable manner with me. But shoot, after almost 15 years of this mess I'm over it!

Call It What You Want

I've accepted the fact that Bertha and I are never gonna see eye to eye. I will peacefully stay in my lane and allow your mother to stay in hers."

"Yeah. I definitely understand that. At the same time, it's kinda' embarrassing to see and hear about Ma acting like a petty-ass school girl at this stage of her life. Ma has some serious issues, and I've told her several times that she needs to seek some counselling or something to help her cope with things. But you already know that she ain't on anything like that. It's sad to say, but Ma' purposely mistreats everyone who crosses her path and don't see anything wrong in it. Which is why my Queen is at the crib, and not here celebrating with me. Ma' don't know how to treat people, you know what I'm saying? And there is no way in hell that I'd bring the woman who has been holding me down the longest, around the family to be mistreated. Nah, hell nah! That shit right there would NEVER happen! Shit is sad sis...sad as fuck!" Aalim was truly a breath of fresh air compared to the funk I was used to inhaling whenever anyone associated with Bertha was around.

Call It What You Want

It was because of his friendly thought provoking conversation that I had stayed at the party longer than what I had originally anticipated.

But, as soon as two "hair-hatted," provocatively dressed women started going back and forth over some "he says, she says" crap, I knew it was about time for me and my boys to get out of dodge.

I quickly located the twins and informed them that it was time for us to go. They begged me to stay an extra ten minutes to finish up the 'Tekken' game that they were playing with a group of their cousins. Reluctantly I agreed...and to kill that extra ten minutes, I grabbed a half-full trash bag placed near the house's backdoor and began picking up half-eaten plates, beer bottles, and the red plastic cups scattered throughout the yard. Once the bag was full, I carried it to the kitchen, where I intended to tie the bag up and have the twins carry it to the row of trash cans across the street, on our way out. Instantly, my ears were drawn to a conversation wafting from the front portion of the house, where Bertha stood on the porch—reared back on her knock-kneed legs, rolling her neck and grunting like a mule, as she diced my character up

Call It What You Want

in front of a complete *dud*. "*Arrgh*! I just can't stand the bitch, Nadine!

Period. *Point blank*! Yaw may think she's all this and all that or

whatever. But lemme' fill you in on a little secret. Kayla's stankin' ass

ain't worth a dime, and neither is her nappy-headed mammie! I know

you seen how that big fat cow pranced her big jiggly ass into my palace,

with her nose balled up like we're all peasants beneath her mutha-

fuckin' feet! Go on and tell me you didn't notice her disrespectful

bullshit Nadine, so I can look into your cocked eyes and tell you that

you're a goddamn liar!"

"*Naw*!" Nadine replied immediately with a slight chuckle. "I didn't see

anything of the sort, Bert. Kayla actually seemed happy to be here, until

you started actin' ugly as you always do whenever she's around." With

a plastic-tipped cigar in one hand and a cup of bum wine in another,

Bertha huffed, "Hear me out loud and clear, Nadine. I don't give a damn

if the funky bitch was happy to be here or not. The point is—she WAS

NOT invited! I'm gettin' sick and tired of Izzy's ass bringin' that bitch

around, when he knows that the mere sight of her gives me a goddamn

Call It What You Want

headache. But, I guess that poor boy of mine just dunno' how to act with it comes to that 'pussy.' He acts just as stupid as his father used to when one of them little whores had his nose wide open; God rest his soul..."

Bertha took a swig from her cup, placed it on the banister, and continued, "I swear to Gawd, Nadine, that bitch Kayla drives me up the fuckin' wall! She's always eyeballing me like she wanna say somethin' slick, but she knows that I'd whack her ass into the next damn century and wouldn't give it a second thought if she did!

I've got a trick for her ass this time . . . *Mm-hmm*. Just wait until I talk to Izzy. Imma fix that snooty bitch once and for all!"

"Oh lord, I'm almost afraid to ask. Whatcha got brewin' now, Bert?" Nadine asked reluctantly. "Shiid...you ain't gotta say it like I'm some sort of trouble-maker, Nadine. I'm just gonna tell Izzy about how she was all 'googly eyed' chitchatting with Mister's slick wannabe Mooslim ass! I bet you any amount of money that she was out there tryna offer him some of that *bare* 'pussy' Izzy used to be so crazy about! Ooh' that ole' fat freaky heifer is sickening!

Call It What You Want

What woman other than those with the 'nasty woman's disease' shaves the hair off their pussy anyway, huh?"

"Well, Bert, I know a lot of women who shave their pussies. HECK, I used to shave mine back in my PYT days . . ." Nadine defended. Bertha waved her hands dramatically and responded, "Oh, goddamn it . . . Never fuckin' mind, Nadine! I shoulda known that your ugly ass woulda found a way to come to Kayla's defense. Imma make sure Izzy beats the donkey-kong shit out of her ass this time. I'm gonna tell him everything I saw. And, if the mood strikes me to slide in a little extra . . . *Hmph*, so be it!"

"Aww now that's just downright wrong, Bert . . . don't do that to Kayla. Izzy may really try to hurt that girl, if you persuade him into believing she was flirting with his brother . . . just leave the girl alone! Sheesh!"

"Shiid," Bertha spat, shrugging her beef back shoulders and shifting her weight to one foot.

"I'm sick of her pluckin' my goddamn nerves— SICK OF IT ALL! Hell, if you ask me, Kayla ain't even all that cute, with that big ole

Call It What You Want

jiggly ass floppin' about like a bowl of Jell-O, and those big funky tities

that she's always showin' off with tight shirts and low-cut sundresses."

Nadine busted out laughing. "Bert, you must be drunk outta your mind

or high off that shit you were smokin' with those boys earlier, because

Kayla is very nice looking, *sexy* if you ask me, and she's as sweet as pie

too!"

"Paha! Yeah . . . whatever!" Bertha huffed. "Alright now, you're gonna

keep fuckin' with that girl and get cho' ass whopped. You know what

they say about those 'quiet' ones! Oh, and don't forget that the girl has a

mother and family, who are probably as crazy about her as you're about

Izzy . . . I'm jus' sayin'."

 "Pfftt! Whatever, Nadine! Izzy would kill that heifer dead if she even

thought about layin' a finger on me! And you don't wanna get me

started up on Kayla's saggy tittie mammie, Lizzy, because she's another

one who I can't stand. Remember that time when Izzy told us about how

Kayla's daddy left her mammie in the dust, to hook up with her best

friend?

Call It What You Want

Well, uh, if 'mommy dearest' knows what I know, she'll stay in her place and tread lightly with this second husband of hers. Because, I can think of several naughty things I'd like to do with that pretty mutha-fucka! Haa! Ain't no shame in my game!"

Nadine, whose physical attributes reminded me of a gypsy because of the earth-toned, ground level dresses, beaded head scarves, and feathered earrings she wore, moved closer to Bertha, standing where I could now see her. "Not that my opinion matters, Bert," she began with explanatory hand gestures.

"I ain't tryna be funny, but Kayla is a helluva lot nicer and more responsible than the other gals your other boys have hooked up and had all those badass kids with. She's so good to those twins, and you'd have to be deaf, dumb, and blind to overlook how crazy she's about Izzy. Hell, he must be tappin' that sweet spot properly, because anytime I see the two of them together, Kayla is grinnin' at that boy like he's a darn superstar!"

Call It What You Want

"Goddamn right- cause my baby *is* a superstar!" Bertha declared, proudly, before they clapped their hands excitedly and laughed like a pair of hyenas. At this point of their tittering, Nadine paused as if she had seen a ghost, after she noticed that I was standing close enough to have heard their entire conversation. I watched as Nadine's eyes shifted nervously. She rocked from side to side, clearing her throat loudly in an attempt to alert Bertha about my presence. But, it was too late; the damage had already been done! The garbage bag I had been in the process of knotting deliberately slid from my hands, releasing all of its filthy contents onto the carpeted floor.

Later that evening, Isaiah and I had a terrible fight. He had stumbled into the house incontestably drunk and agitated over the malarkey Bertha had promised to feed him. After being drilled about the conversation I had shared with Aalim and being accused of flashing him sneak peeks of my 'pussy,' I was chastised for intentionally emptying a bag of garbage on his beloved momma's and ruining her already heavily soiled carpet. I was called every horrible name in the book, smacked, choked, slammed against the wall, and warned to never look Aalim's way—let along whisper a single word to him.

A few weeks later, Karma tapped on Bertha's door, as I knew she would! Apparently, she had an argument with one of her "drinking buddies" who got fed up with her condescending prattle and socked her in the mouth with an empty cognac bottle. In the process, Bertha lost several teeth, and the right side of her jaw was temporarily wired shut!

Chapter 12

I sat in my car, parked in front of the house, for at least 30 minutes, before I could garner enough strength to face "Sir-Creep-A-Lot" and his filthy crew. It was my hope that Bertha, and whichever set of warped-minded peons she had attached to her hip for the day, would leave our house, so that Isaiah and I could talk in private. But as you can imagine, it did NOT go down like that!

I pulled myself out of the car and strutted up our slightly inclined driveway. As I reached for our tempered glass screen door, I thought about the scene from the movie "Waiting to Exhale," where Angela

Call It What You Want

Bassett snapped after learning she had been replaced by a frail, blonde, thin-lipped, white woman. That sistah snatched up each and every item owned by her lying, cheating, narcissistic husband, crammed it into his car, and lit it up like a bonfire!

I felt her pain. I felt her disappointment. I felt her fury! And in that moment, I would've loved nothing more than to have locked eyes with Isaiah and repeat Angela Basset's unforgettable words verbatim, "Get your shit! Get your shit and GET THE FUCK OUT!"

I closed my eyes, inhaled slowly, and exhaled. Then, I whispered repeatedly, "*No weapons formed against me shall prosper! No weapons formed against me shall prosper! No weapons formed against me shall prosper!*" After taking in one last breath of fresh clean air, I turned the doorknob and walked inside. My house was filled with jubilant laughter when I stepped into the foyer. Seated on the brown Italian leather couches were Bertha, Nadine, Isaiah, and his crafty "pill-popping" cousin Memory, who I didn't trust as far as I could see her thieving ass! They were having a good ole time, laughing their asses off, as Isaiah animatedly recounted a childhood story about the time he had been

caught smoking weed with a few of his big brothers in the garage of one

of the many rented properties Bertha had. He recounted, "Maaan,

momma must have smelled the ganja in the wind or some shit, because

she came out of nowhere with one of those thick warehouse brooms and

whacked all three of us on our heads like *whoop, whoop, whoop*! Haa!

Haa! That shit hurt like a muh fucka! And on top of that, my ass got

riffed on by my homeboys for at least a month, for the egg-sized lumps

that broom stick left on my head! I had two muh-fuckin golf ball size

lumps on the back of my head and one dead smack in the middle of my

forehead. Momma had my ass looking like one of those Snorts with the

tubed heads!" I shook my head in disgust; I had heard this horrid story

more times than I could count on my hands, and I *hated* it! I never

understood how getting caught smoking weed at the age of 10 and being

thrashed on the head with a broom handle was something to be proud of.

But, then again… this was a prime example of how weird Isaiah and his

folks were; they'd find humor in the cruelest, meanest things . . . and frown upon those who didn't share the same dark humor. By this time, I was sure that they were aware of my presence, because not only did our alarm system chirp each time the door was opened, but I was sure they heard me moving around in the foyer as I kicked off my shoes and dropped my briefcase to the floor.

I convinced myself that I would be able to ease past the merrymaking quartet without being noticed, since they were evidently enjoying Isaiah's stories. Lo and behold, when I turned around to glance at my reflection in the mirror to make sure that I didn't look as fucked up as I felt inside. Bertha's beady black eyes were staring a hole in the side of my face, a conniving smirk plastered on her ugly face! Taking myself by surprise, I grinned at my monster-in-law through the mirror, then childishly winked at her, even though flashing her a glimpse of both of my middle fingers would have felt a helluva lot better!

She looked as though she was going to barf when I did that, and I absolutely loved it!

Call It What You Want

With a slight chuckle, I shook my head and sashayed through the living room towards the kitchen with ease. I held my head as high as a giraffe's ass, and softly hummed the hook of Jill Scott's "Slowly, Surly" jam. The room that was filled with boisterous laughter and giggles moments earlier was suddenly as quiet as a graveyard. Although I refused to make eye contact with any of their stupid asses, I was certain they were shooting each other confused glances like, '*Wait, what just happened?*' As soon as I made it to the kitchen, I poured and quickly gulped down a glass of the Prunotto Bricco wine I had purchased for Isaiah's birthday. The chatter in the living room resumed—with Bertha leading the prattle, of course. "Hol' up. Wait a goddamn minute now! Please tell me that I ain't the only one who noticed how *SHE* walked into my son's house, with a stankin' ass attitude eyeballing us, like we ain't supposed to be here . . . How many times have I tol' yall that she hates when we visit Izzy and the boys, hmm? Now yall got the chance to see this shit with your own damn eyes! Umph, umph, umph! I cannot stand that ole fat-ass moose. Izzy you need to check her, before I do!"

Call It What You Want

Unfazed by Bertha's ill-mannered comments, I poured a second glass of wine and decided to sip on it, while I typed a text to Symone, letting her know I was "*Okay*" and would get back to her later. "Oh, hell no! Uhn-uhn . . . not today, Bert!" Nadine screeched, interrupting my train of thoughts. "I ain't gonna sit here and listen to you pick on that girl again. You ain't right, Bertha . . . and Izzy, you are just as bad for allowin' your wife to be disrespected in her own damn house! For Christ's sake, the girl is right in the next room. Sho 'nuff she can hear yall, and I betcha' she is mad as hell! *I know I would be!*"

"Blah, blah, blah, Nadine! Go straight to hell, wouldja? Your snaggle-tooth ass ain't got a damn thing to do with this here; this is family business! Betta' shut your ugly-ass pie hole before you piss me off, and I make you 'foot it' all the way back to the west side! Try me . . . if you think this is a game Nadine, cause I've been sick and tired of your fuckin' shit *anyway*!"

"*Pffft!* I've got plenty of money in my pocket, Bert, so I ain't gotta walk no damn where! But you know what, you're absolutely right. You

Call It What You Want

pickin' on that girl ain't none of my business. But Imma say this and then leave it alone. Yall are dead ass WRONG for what cha' doing to that girl. Jesus is always watching and recording. Kayla ain't bothered a soul, but here you are, getting yourself all worked up because she walked into HER house and ignored your mean ass! Like I tol' you the other day, if you don't like Kayla, stop coming over here *Bertha*! I've never seen her say or do anything out of the way to you, yet you're always tryna find something to bitch about!" There was a brief pause in the conversation, after which Nadine continued in an even tone, "Now that I have spoken my piece I'm goin' outside for a cigarette—maybe even two. Memory, sweetheart, you're more than welcome to come with me. I dunno about you, but ain't nobody got time for the foolery that cha' auntie is on . . ." I can't recall hearing a verbal response from Memory. But in the midst of Bertha demanding that Nadine "shut her drunk lips" and Isaiah yelling for his mother to "chill out," I caught the distinctive sound of two sets of flip-flop sandals flapping speedily towards and out of the front door.

Call It What You Want

"Ya' see that shit, Izzy? This is exactly why I don't bring Nadine's retarded ass out in public with me too often. The dirty bitch doesn't know how to act, and she talks too goddamn much! Hell, after today, yall may not see her sorry ass for a while. Imma put her on a punishment for a little while, since she wanna act like a hard-headed two-year-old! Fuck Nadine!" Bertha complained to Isaiah, who had lapsed back into silence. "Now, back to what I was tryna tell you about that damn wife of yours before I was rudely interrupted. I might not have been the best mother to you rock-headed boys—it was hard raising yall on my own. But, I ain't raise nair-one of you to be a simple Simon, ya hear? That wife of yours has made it as clear as day that she doesn't have any respect for you or the family. Oh, wait . . . I take that back cause you know she is crazy about that sneaky Mooslim brother of yours—and I've tol' you how I feel about that whole situation. But uh . . ."

"Aight Momma, enough already! I ain't tryna hear that shit right there, so don't even start with it! *Damn!*" Isaiah yelled, annoyed with the tomfoolery his mother attempted to feed his mind. "Like I told you the

Call It What You Want

last time you tried to bring up some shit about my wife 'crushing' on my brother, whether you like her or not, Kayla don't get down like that, momma. She's a good girl, at least in that respect . . . not that it's any of your business, but I am the only man who has been up in that— believe me! You know what, never mind all that shit Momma, yall just need to go on and bounce. I'm tired, I've got a fuckin headache, and I need to have a private conversation with my wife—"

"Oh . . . so you're throwing me out, are you?"

"What? Momma, no! I just need to talk to my wife without all the extra bullshit and drama."

There was another pause in the conversation, before Bertha's booming voiced turned into a phony whimper. "Fine, Izzy! I guess I'll just go on and leave, since you're being mean to your own mother, who has your back more than your wife or any other hussy would. I was only tryna help your ignorant ass out, since you're obviously blind to your wife's bad manners. But, okay son . . . if you wanna play the role of 'boo-boo the goddamn fool' and allow that girl to run all over you, disrespect your

Call It What You Want

mother, and lust after your brother—you can be my goddamn guest! When I'm gone from this earth and am unable to protect you, remember this—I tried to warn you, son! I have done my part as your mother, and if that wasn't good enough, I am sorry! That said, Imma use your bathroom, then we're outta here... Maybe when you calm down, you will come by the house, so we can talk about this. That is if Kayla doesn't try to add some extra shit to the complaints she is about to beat your ears up with and try to turn you complete against me . . ."

Isaiah mumbled something to his mother, and a few seconds later, he moseyed into the kitchen.

His shoulders were slumped, his hands shoved inside his pockets, and his lips pursed, leaving only a straight line where his full lips were supposed to be. I could tell by the way he clenched his jaws, that he was dangerously annoyed. "So, what's going on, Kayla?" Isaiah questioned in a flat tone. "You wanna tell me why you stepped through this muh-fuckin' door, disrespecting my family and shit, when they've done nothing to you, huh?"

Call It What You Want

I responded with nothing but an unenthused glance and a nonchalant shrug, before turning my attention back to the glass of wine in my hand. "Oh, so you wanna be childish and shit, and act like you don't hear me talking, eh? Is this the game you wanna play, Kayla?" I sighed tiredly and nodded. "I heard you, Isaiah—loud and clear. However, you and I have more important matters to discuss, which unfortunately doesn't include ME catering to your vindictive 'MOMMA,' who you've allowed to disrespect me for entirely too damn long!"

"Nah!" he huffed, rubbing his palms together anxiously. "First off, watch ya' fuckin' mouth! Secondly, you need to take your dumb ass out there and apologize to Momma for hurtin' her goddamn feelings! As a matter of fact, since you wanna be such a smartass about the shit, you can go on and apologize to Nadine and Memory too! This is my muh-fuckin' house as much as it's yours, and you ain't jus' gonna run my folks off because you wanna hold on to some whack ass bullshit from the past! I dunno what kind of bullshit you're on, Kayla, but ya' betta get it right, before I beat your muh-fuckin ass. *Again!* Goddamnit!"

Call It What You Want

I held my husband's gaze for a few seconds, before I threw my head back and burst out laughing. "Negro, pleazzzzze! You can say whatever the hell you want to say to or about me. Trust and believe me when I say this, there'd be a cold day in HELL before I'd even CONSIDER extending any type of an apology to your mother! That MONSTER has been on a mission to assassinate my character for as long as I've known her. I've dodged Bertha's cheap shots and ignored the lies she oh-so carelessly spread through your family about me for years. I've even tried ignored the slick shit she has said about my relatives, whom she barely even knows, as well as sly remarks she has made about my body IN FRONT OF YOU Isaiah! Yet, you think I owe her a fuckin' apology? I know you're fuckin' *lyin*! I don't owe that woman anything more than what she has been giving me—which is ANGUISH and fuckin' HEADACHES!" I declared, slamming my hand on the breakfast counter like a mallet. "I don't deserve half of the rotten treatment I've received from you rotten circus clowns.

Call It What You Want

But as they say, you win some and lose some! I've lost a lot, okay? But my 'winnings' are on the way! And that you can take to the bank, *brotha*!" I asserted with a reassuring nod.

"Mannn, so what the fuck you sayin', Kayla? Just spit out what the fuck you mean and spare me all the 'riddle me this, riddle me that' bullshit!" he demanded. I tilted my head back and swallowed the remaining contents of my glass, before slowly placing the empty glass on the counter and turning my head towards my husband.

Once we locked eyes, I began, "Well, Mr. Ward, your gargantuan, pale-faced, redhead *hood rat* concubine blessed me with an 'entertaining' visit at the office today. She told me all about the sneaky shit you've been saying and doing behind my back. . . You and I are through Isaiah, which I am sure your mother will be thrilled to hear!"

"My, uh, friend?" Isaiah stammered. "What fuckin' friend, eh? Quit bullshitting me, Kayla . . . say what you've gotta say and miss me with all of this nonsense . . ." He barked nervously.

Call It What You Want

"Does the name Odessa Starr ring a bell, sir?" I probed sarcastically and waited for a response. The mere mention of Odessa's name must have struck one of Isaiah's nerves hard. Because his eyes became as big as saucers, and his deep brown skin tone faded to a pale tan-like shade in a matter of seconds. My husband was so shocked by my words that the poor fella didn't know whether to shit or go bowling!

"Mm hmm . . ." I hummed with an assertive nod. "On top of the claims about y'alls scandalous love affair, Odessa wasn't shy about sharing the details of the drugs, gut-wrenching orgies. Oops, pardon me husband. . . I almost forgot to mention the humongous bump in your boo-thang's belly. I guess congratulations are in order, KING. According to your whore, the daughter my "barren ass was unable to give you" is in that repulsive women's oven and is set to make a debut in August. It would be a crying shame if that baby was born on my birthday, huh? I don't think you or Odessa would be too thrilled about that . . . considering I am the 'source' of y'alls damn problems . . ."

Call It What You Want

"Shut the fuck up Kayla, before I smack the shit out of you! That bitch ain't carryin' my goddamn seed! I don't give a fuck about what she says, that bitch is a habitual liar! You are stupid as fuck for believing some bullshit like that!" Shrugging, I taunted, "OH . . . so, you do know who I'm talking about, eh? Thanks for the confirmation! And just in case you didn't receive the memo—YOU AIN'T WORTH SHIT!" I glanced at my cellphone after it vibrated and displayed Symone's *"Okay sis, I love you"* response. I then looked up at my husband and shook my head in disgust. "She also told me your claims about her unborn child belonging to the 'homeboy' you convinced her to have sex with at the Swinger's club you had been trying to get me to visit with you for the longest time. I can't imagine who this 'homeboy' is, nor do I really care to know. But, uh . . . I hope YOU ALL figure things out soon, because an innocent baby is on its way into this godforsaken world, whether yall like it or not. That child deserves to have both parents present in its life, even if yall can't agree on the reckless situation that you all made . . ."

As frustrated as a crackhead without a lighter, Isaiah began having his immature, overdramatic temper tantrum as he always did when his back was up against the wall. "See, bitch! There the fuck you go playin' those stupid ass mind games again! Instead of you havin' my muhfuckin' back—like a wife is supposed to when these lonely skeezers come up with these weak-ass stories— your dumb ass is always quick to jump on their bandwagon just to make me out to be the bad guy out here!" Isaiah groused, trying hard to maintain a firm demeanor. I shook my head, quickly interrupting him, "No suh' . . . Tryna flip this shit on me is NOT gonna work this time, buddy. Odessa's words are more than just a 'bullshit story.' Considering the fact that this woman knew personal things about me that only YOUR SHADY ASS could have disclosed. She even had pictures of your fuckin' dick Isaiah—a dick I can easily identify with my eyes closed!"

"Pictures?" Isaiah yelped, moving closer to where I was sitting. "You're a muh-fuckin liar, Kayla! That bitch ain't got no pictures of my dick— shit, you don't even have any pictures of my dick, *dumbass*!"

Call It What You Want

Isaiah nodded and shot me a confusing smirk. "Aight . . . Okay then . . .
I see what's going on here. Your silly lil' ass is tryna be slick and use
some of that reverse psychology bullshit on me to cover up what you've
been doing behind my goddamn back... Earlier this morning, you said
you were only working half of your shift. But now, it's almost 8 o'clock
at night, and you fall through this muh-fucka..." Isaiah continued,
pointing at the door, "talking outta the side of your neck about a bitch I
couldn't give two shits about. Get the fuck outta here with that stupid
shit, Kayla . . . and grow the fuck up!" he spat, with a dismissive hand
gesture.

"Wait, so you're saying I'm in the wrong, is that it?" I asked, pointing to
my chest. "I know I'm not perfect, Isaiah, but dayum . . . do you ever
take responsibility for the fucked-up shit you've done, huh?" Isaiah
pumped his fists a couple of times and flew around the breakfast bar to
where I was sitting. With sweat beads forming on his forehead, he
barked through clenched teeth, "Bitch, I swear to God, if you don't quit
talkin' to me like I am a muhfuckin child, Imma knock your big fat ass

Call It What You Want

smooth off of that goddamn stool! Just keep on running your mouth,

Kayla . . . I swear I'll beat the shit outta your gullible lil' ass! *Forreal.*"

"Uh huh, that's right, Izzy . . ." Bertha chimed in, slithering into the

kitchen like the ugly black snake she was. "Let that hussy know who

wears the pants in this marriage! I've been sick and tired of you lettin

her get away with being so disrespectful towards me. Hell, instead of

threatening her, you should have already smacked the taste outta' her

smart-ass mouth!"

For a few seconds there, I was completely taken aback by Bertha's

presence. I had assumed she had jumped on her broom and disappeared,

as I heard her say she was gonna do. Obviously, her nosey ass hadn't

left and had probably been eavesdropping on our conversation the entire

time… waiting for the perfect opportunity to interject.

"Look-a-here, Kayla," Bertha demanded, while glaring at me with her

black beady eyes. "I've tried to be as patient with your monkey ass as I

can," she continued. "But every time I turn around, you're either

stressing my son over some insecure nonsense, or you're tryna find

Call It What You Want

ways to interfere in our relationship. Then today, I guess ya' felt bold enough to go all out with the disrespect. Waltzing your big funky jiggly ass into my son's house— flipping your nose up at us like you're somethin' special! Girl you musta lost your goddamn mind talkin' 'bout my son ain't shit, bitch . . . you ain't worth shit! Ooooh, *goddamnit*!" Bertha growled like Yosemite Sam from the Looney Tunes. "I swear to God, if it wasn't for Izzy and my grandsons, I would've paid someone to off your sadity ass a long time ago. Trust me, *our* world would be a whole lot smoother without your triflin ass around, gettin on my fuckin' nerves!"

During the first few seconds of Bertha's "well-thought-out" speech, I had risen from my sitting position and leaned against the breakfast bar with a look of pure astonishment. As soon as my mind registered the part of her speech that included her thoughts on ending my life, red circular dots flashed before my eyes.

Call It What You Want

And before I could fully understand what was about to happen, I was rushing towards Bertha like a raging bull—ready to knock the three remaining teeth in her mouth clean out of her head!

I wanted that old ugly, dirty-footed, black, beady-eyed monster to feel the harrowing pressure of the futile crap she had forced into my life. I wanted to hurt her, make her cry.

I wanted to beat that old bitch to a pulp and laugh in her face as she begged for me to stop. The sweet gratification of defeating and annihilating my enemy, once and for all had taken full control of me . . .

As my clenched fists were inches away from connecting with Bertha's face, Isaiah charged at me from behind, lifted me off my feet, and slammed me flat on my back on the kitchen floor. A sharp pain shot through my head, neck, and back immediately, but the adrenaline rush forced me to get back on my feet, flailing my arms and fists like my life depended on it.

As I punched Isaiah a few times in his face and head, he managed to grab a handful of my hair, tossing me around the kitchen like a rag doll.

Call It What You Want

I screamed, punched, and dug my fingernails into his face, arms, and chest, hoping for Nadine and Memory to hear the commotion and at least break things up, so I could get away. Just as Isaiah drew his fist back like a slingshot, preparing to thrash my face, I shoved my knee into his balls, then watched his eyes roll to the back of his head. He tumbled onto the kitchen floor like a pile of crushed bricks and moaned like a dying horse!

Instantly, Bertha began to scream, and in a matter of seconds, she had seized a rusted switchblade from her dingy lopsided bra and began charging towards me with an ear-piercing shriek, "YOU DONE FUCKED UP NOW, BITCH. NOW YOU'RE GONNA FUCKIN' DIE TONIGHT!"

Standing less than three feet away from me, Bertha swung the blade wildly, barely missing my face. As soon as I felt a slight burning sensation where she had nipped my shoulder, I gripped Bertha's hand, grasping the blade clenched firmly in her fist, until it fell on the floor.

Call It What You Want

Then, I twisted her arm behind her back, forcefully slamming her frail body against the refrigerator—face first.

"Bertha, I want you to listen to me, and listen good . . ." I began, maintaining a tight grip on her arm and yanking on it a few times, just to let her know that I wasn't playing anymore of her games. "If you ever, ever, ever, ever come near me or my children after today, I swear to God I'll go to the end of the earth just to make sure you suffer! STAY THE FUCK AWAY FROM ME...DO-YOU-UNDERSTAND-ME?"

Bertha whimpered and squirmed, which only made me yank her twisted arm higher up her back. As snot and tears ran down her ugly aged face, she was no longer the foul-mouthed bully she portrayed herself to be when she had an audience. And I was no longer the passive, obedient daughter-in-law who accepted her verbal abuse like a gift!

"I'm gonna ask you one more time Bertha, or I'm gonna break this arm of yours . . . DO-YOU-UNDERSTAND-ME?"

"Ooouch! Oh my Gawd . . . Yes! Yes! I understand you bitch! Izzy or somebody, help me, please!

Call It What You Want

This lunatic is gonna kill me..." she cried out in pain. Glancing over my shoulder at Isaiah, who was still lying on the kitchen floor in a fetal position—clutching his nuts and still moaning like a dying horse—I returned my attention to Bertha's exposed grimy nape and said, "You can have your lying, cheating, slack ass, piss-poor excuse of a son back. I'm done with all of you fuckin earth disturbers! *Done*! Let this be a lesson you never forget. . . DON'T EVER COME FOR ME UNLESS I SEND FOR YOU, BITCH! *Period*."

Chapter13

A few weeks later, during a Saturday morning in mid-June, my homegirl Essence Grey showed up at my house unexpectedly. While I was in the process of throwing out some of the old junk in our garage, her squeaky clean rose-gold Mercedes S600 pulled in and parked in our driveway, thumping Prince's classic song, *"When Doves Cry"*. I beamed in excitement as I waved at Essence, knowing full well that she was going to give me a piece of her mind for being out of touch. We had not spoken since the twins had left for their vacation to Florida—damn near

Call It What You Want

a month before— which was odd because we normally chatted up several times a week. Essence and I had only been friends for a few years. But, our sisterly vibe was so strong that it felt as though we had known each other our entire lives.

My homegirl was modest, brutally honest, and just as foxy as she was intelligent. She was a few inches taller than my 5'3" frame, with flawless chocolate-colored skin, deep dark brown eyes, short wavy hair, and a stunning figure that commanded immediate attention from men and women alike. And, at 43 years of age, Essence had the face of a fresh "tenderoni", a master's degree in business management, three successful beauty shops, under the name of Grey's Salon Loft, alongside a popular weave boutique in Atlanta, Georgia, managed by her only child, Lana.

The funny thing about my relationship with Essence was that I had actually been acquainted with her ex-husband, Lance, for years before I got introduced to her.

Call It What You Want

Lance, a flamboyant "asshole" of the first degree, had been a long-time friend of Symone's husband, Ron, and oftentimes attended their family functions—emptyhanded, solo, and desperately thirsty for attention. Lance was just as attractive as Essence— tall, slim, fair skinned, with hazel-shaded eyes and dirty blonde dreadlocks that were usually pulled away from his face into two thick French braids or a neat ponytail. However, dude was proudly unemployed… and as shady as the real Slim Shady himself!

This pompous clown was too flashy for his own good. He carelessly cruised through the streets of Columbus in a gold-rimmed, money-green Monte Carlo, with a banging stereo system, drawing unnecessary attention to himself. He covered his scrawny body with nothing but the best urban gear—Gucci this and Polo that, and he almost always had sparkling jewelry dangling from his fingers, wrists, and neck—like one of those "hot boys" that the hood chicks loved to salivate over. As much as I tried to keep an open mind when it came to Lance, I did not trust that hazel eyed crook as far as I could see him.

Call It What You Want

My concerns were not just based on some simple surface stuff; they were compounded by the fact that I had heard more than one blatant lie fall from Lance's potato chip-thin lips, and I absolutely despised liars! And, my concerns were further escalated during a cookout at Symon and Ron's home, when I had walked into the kitchen and caught him touching Symone inappropriately while her husband was in the same room with his back turned!

On the other hand, Isaiah was a *huge* fan of Lance. All Lance had to do was walk in through one of Symone and Ron's doors for my grown-ass husband to become as hyped up as a crazed cheerleader, beaming with enthusiasm, "Awe shit, there's da man with the masterplan! Yeeeeaaaaah!"

A couple of weeks before the year 2009 was set to make its debut, Isaiah came home from a night-out with Lance and Ron. He was all buzzed up as expected, bragging about the plans he had made for us to have an "epic" New Year's Eve celebration, at a black-tie gala at the Columbus Convention Center.

Call It What You Want

Initially, I was psyched with excitement, grinning and tossing mad-props to Isaiah for his new-found spontaneity. But as soon as he said, "*Yeah, I'm just grateful to my dawg Lance for the hook-up. He's got connections with some real big shots, babe…*" I felt sick to my stomach. It did not help to learn that Symone and Ron were attending the gala too. After the hanky-panky shit I had witnessed between Symone and Lance, the last thing they needed to do was get caught in public, touching and flirting with one another—like they did when they thought no one was watching…

To my surprise, Lance's invitation to the New Year's Eve gala came with more perks than I could have ever imagined. In addition to Isaiah and Ron being decked out in dark tuxedos and neckties, Symone and I were decked up in sparkly black gowns and high-heeled shoes, which were all gifts from Lance. We were chauffeured in a white stretch limo and provided VIP seating, with unlimited access to delicious cocktails and scrumptious hors d'oeuvres.

Call It What You Want

I was very impressed by Lance's kind deeds... But as the old saying goes—no matter how much a snake sheds skin, it is still a damn snake! When we were being escorted to table number five, as indicated on our invites, I caught a glimpse of Lance conversing with a thin, chocolate toned woman whom I assumed to be his wife, since Symone had made it a point to repeatedly remind me that we would finally get the chance to see what Mrs. Grey looked like in person.

This chocolate beauty must have informed Lance that we had arrived and were approaching the table, as right after her glitter-painted lips moved purposefully, followed by a nod in our direction, Lance hopped on his feet and whirled around to face us—grinning from ear to ear like a proud father.

"Ooooooh-weeeee! Now that's what I'm talkin' 'bout, family . . . look at my peoples looking all *dapper* and shit! This is how the real G's do it, you feel me?" Lance squawked, greeting our husbands with tight handshakes and "gangster" hugs.

Call It What You Want

While Symone and I stood in line behind our husbands, as if we were waiting to kiss Prince Hakeem's ring and Lance flapped his lips about the $1500 he spent on his cufflinks, Symone nudged my side, motioned at Essence with her eyes, and whispered, "*Mm hmm* . . . I see Lance decided to bring his wife out of hiding after all. What do you think about her cause, uh, I don't think I am too impressed?"

"Girl, paleeeeze! I'm glad to see that the '*Mrs.*' actually exists! Because I was beginning to think that yall were lying about the 'playa from the Himalayas' being a married man . . ." I responded jokingly yet seriously.

"I mean, wow, look at how beautiful she is, Symone," I continued. "Lance should be proud to carry a snazzy duplicate of the great Lauren Hill around his arms! They complement each other very well—cute couple!"

Symone shot me an unenthused glance and then released a mild grunt.

"*Mmm* I dunno about all that, Kayla. Lance says he was raised in the Bronx, so I guess she's a little 'rough' around the edges like Lauren Hill . . . but they look NOTHING alike, Kayla."

Call It What You Want

Just as my best friend's negative thoughts rolled out of her mouth, Essence swooped past the men, approaching us with a friendly smile and extended arms.

"Hey now! It's about time I got the chance to meet the two beauties my husband speaks so highly of! Oh, by the way, my name is Essence Grey and I'm married to the 'light bright' over yonder!" she quipped, pointing at Lance. Immediately, I cracked up laughing, as I accepted Essence's embrace and complimented the pink glittery body-con dress she was wearing, which hugged her curvaceous body to a T. "It's nice to meet you, Essence. I am Kayla, Isaiah's wife, and this is my best friend, Symone, Ron's wife." Symone refused Essence's friendly gesture and offered her a dry limp handshake instead. She then mumbled a cheeky reply, "I hope Lance has told you nothing but good things about us . . ."

"*Mmm,* no worries, Boo! It's all good. Trust me girl, had Lance told me otherwise I would not be standing here, talkin' to you right now. I don't do drama and can't stand negativity of any kind, which I'm surprised he

Call It What You Want

forgot to mention to you all . . ." Essence answered in a sharp tone, ending their odd exchange with a stealthy eye roll!

For what seemed like an eternity, Lance filled our ears with tales of famous entertainers he had either ran into at one point of time or regarded as family. Biz Markie, a rapper from the 80s, was his paternal first cousin; Steve Harvey was "almost" his stepfather, and the singer/ musician D'Angelo was a homeboy whom he claimed to have attended high school with in his hometown of Richmond, Virginia.

While Lance might have been telling the truth about his connections to the mentioned celebrities, I found it odd and disrespectful that his long-drawn-out speeches never included his wife, who sat directly across from him. I do not recall the word "we" ever escaping his braggadocios lips. All I heard was, "me, me, me, me, me, and me, me, me, me, me . . ." Everything was always about Lance—E-V-E-R-Y-T-H-I-N-G!

I excused myself from the table, claiming to be heading to the ladies' room, which instigated a chain reaction from Essence and eventually Symone. The guys, along with Symone, appeared to be intrigued by

Call It What You Want

Lance's long-winded stories of "me, me, me," whereas Essence and I had become quite blasé by his self-obsessed bosh. "Girls, I am so, so sorry for my overtalkative husband . . ." Essence began, once we were far enough from the guys to speak without being ear-wigged. "It's like the drunker he gets, the longer his freakin' dialogs become!

I swear to God; he is the ONLY man I've ever known to get a freakin' woody from just talkin' about himself! Don't get me wrong, I love my Lancy dearly, but he can be so damn embarrassing at times!"

I chuckled, playfully patting Essence's arm. "Girl, pleeeze! Don't even worry about that. We are used to listening to Lance's over exaggerated 'tales from the hood'. My husband is a big 'talker' too, especially if the topic concerns something he's passionate about—which is himself! So, I know how to tune them out and focus on something else, with NO problem at all!"

"Paahaa! You too, huh? I thought it's just me!" Essence chortled.

At the bar, Essence, Symone, and I ordered drinks, and stood around chatting, laughing, and observing people. Essence and I had our heads

Call It What You Want

thrown back, cackling and hi-fiving on different topics, as though we had known each other well beyond the few hours we had been acquainted. Meanwhile, Symone was acting in a standoffish manner, chuckling here and there but not really saying too much. "Symone, you cool?" I asked, attempting to pull her into our conversation. "Yeah . . . I'm good, *BESTIE*. I'm just thinking about some thangs . . . that's all." "Ooookay . . . and what is it that you're thinking about, Symone?" I asked, annoyed by her immature behavior, especially by the emphasis she put on "bestie".

"I'll just talk to you about it later." was her curt reply, before she turned her attention to Essence. "Uh, Essence . . . I do have a question for you though . . . how long have you and Lance been married again?" Essence chortled, waving her hand dismissively. "Gurl, I've been with my handsome 'light bright' for over 20 years now. We were married for about seven years before we split up the first time. We called ourselves 'dating' again after the divorce had been finalized or whatever, and my crazy ass let him talk me into a trip to Vegas, where we got married a

second time by a drunken, pigeon-toed Elvis Presley impersonator!"

"Pahaahaa! Not a pigeon-toed . . . Essence!" I burst out laughing

hysterically. "Girl, yaaaasss! And the dude was as drunk as Cootie

Brown too!"

"Aww, how cute is that...I'm sorry, but how many kids did you say yall

have?" Symone pressed on in the same sarcastic tone. Essence folded

her thick lips inwards, then shot Symone a murderous glance, releasing

one of those "don't push me to the edge" chuckles. I was certain

Essence was going to slap Symone's condescending attitude clean from

her soul! *And couldn't deny that she probably deserved it. . .*

"Yo . . . first of all, I don't recall mentioning anything about our

children, Symone. But since for whatever reason, you feel the need to

dig deep into our personal business, Lance and I have a beautiful 24-

year-old daughter Lana Grey—a graduate from Spelman—who manages

my boutique in Atlanta. In total, Lance is the father of eight, unless I've

'intentionally' lost count or really just don't give a fuck. Any more

Call It What You Want

questions, Symone?" Symone wanted to debate with Essence—I could

see it in her eyes. But I was not going to let that happen when we were

supposed to be enjoying ourselves at the extravagant event. So, I slid

between the two women, draped my arms around their necks, and started

crooning along with the song "No One" by Alicia Keys, in my strikingly

unmelodic voice.

Symone obviously had an issue with Essence, which I suspected had

everything to do with whatever it was she had going on with Lance.

However, the tension between the two simmered the moment we hit the

dance floor, and it stayed that way for the majority of the night… I was

the last to learn that we would not be returning home that night from the

gala. When I told Isaiah that I was tired and ready to go home, he told

me we were joining the other two couples for an overnight stay in the

penthouse suite at the Hyatt that Lance and Essence had on reserve—

which was only few minutes away from the Convention Center.

I was too tipsy to be annoyed by yet another one of Lance's sneaky

gestures. So, I kept my mouth shut and simply went with the flow of things. As soon as we arrived at the elegant penthouse, I thanked

Essence and Lance for their generous hospitality and made a beeline to

one of the two king-sized beds!

After what seemed like a catnap, I was startled by slurred mumbles and

frantic shakes. Screaming in my face as if the hotel was on fire, Symone

yelled, "Kayla, get your ass up and put your shoes on. Some shit is goin'

down in the hallway, and I don't want to have any part in it! Here I'm

tryna get my life right with the lord, yet I'm surrounded by a shitload of

negativity! I've called my dad, and he's on his way to pick us up... I'm

never, ever doing anything like this *again*!"

I sprang up on the bed, my head spinning like a flywheel and drool

running down the side of my mouth. I blinked a few times to moisten

my clouded contact lens and gather my thoroughly perplexed thoughts,

then whined, "Symone, I'm drunk . . . pleeeze...just let me sleep it off . .

. Where is everybody . . . ain't they drunk too?"

"I know you're drunk sweetie, and so am I! But something has

happened, and I've no idea where our husbands are. Lance and *your*

Call It What You Want

little buddy are M-I-A also. So, there is no telling what the two of them have gotten into! *Lord Jesus*! I had a feeling something crazy was gonna happen tonight. I should've gone with my instincts and stayed home with my babies! It's a crying shame how people start acting all weird and stupid once they've gotten a freakin' buzz. And for that very reason, after tonight, I'm done with all this worldly crap!"

As Symone rambled on, sounding more nervous than usual, the rumbling in the hallway became louder and more audible, accompanied by the sounds of scurrying feet and a chattering crowd. A fight or struggle was definitely in full effect. My only hope was that it had nothing to do with our husbands, especially my sometimes "bully" of a husband! Grabbing a high-heeled shoe from the bag she used to gather up our things, Symone wrenched the door open, as though she was expecting a masked murderer to be standing on the other side— waiting to attack her. But as quick as she removed that shoe from her bag, it fell to the floor, and she clasped her hand on her mouth in disbelief.

Call It What You Want

I followed Symone's gaze and damn near lost my breath when I saw precisely what and who had captured her attention. Stark naked as the day he was born, Lance's massive limp Johnson swung around like a baton, while Essence had him locked in a tight chokehold, pounding her tiny fist into his face, as if she was kneading dough! Essence shrieked as heartbroken tears streamed down her face. "I fuckin' hate you, Lance! This marriage is fuckin' over, you scandalous son of a bitch! *Finished*!" While some of the spectators shook their heads and twisted their lips with revolted expressions, others gossiped amongst themselves, filmed, and snapped pictures of the thoroughly embarrassing scene. Lance had been caught with his pants down in a room with another woman, while he *thought* his wife was fast asleep—only four doors down the hotel's hall!

I honestly thought I would never hear from Essence after that crazy night at the hotel. But she surprised me with a phone call a couple weeks later, which I found strange because I could not remember giving her my personal number. She asked if Symone and I would be willing to meet

Call It What You Want

her for lunch or dinner one day, so that she could apologize to us for her behavior at the hotel, in person.

Certainly, I did not have a problem meeting up with Essence. I liked her from our initial introduction, and I was anxious to hear her side of the story. However, although I did not mention anything about Symone to Essence, I was unsure of whether she was gonna be up for the meeting, as she had seemed to not care much for Essence's company during the gala. But, much to my surprise, Symone agreed to the lunch date and admitted she had inadvertently treated Essence unkindly.

She explained that she and Ron had gotten into a heated argument right before they were picked up by the limo on the night of the gala, therefore she took her frustrations with her husband out on Essence. She claimed to have prayed for an opportunity to apologize and make things right with Essence, which seemed plausible at the time. But for some odd reason, I just could not regard Symone's words to be sincere...

The next day, we all met at an Applebee's restaurant on the east side of Columbus. Essence told her side of the story, which baffled us even

Call It What You Want

more than we had been after witnessing a naked Lance being

manhandled by his wife! "First off, I know yall really don't know me all

that well," Essence began explaining, "And I'm sorry the two of you,

and your husbands, had to be introduced to the crazy side of the

'Scorpio' that lives within me. Lance and I have been through a whole

loooooot of shit over the years, and unfortunately, that was the day I

became utterly fed up with his tricky bullshit and fuckin' snapped!

I have thanked the Lord a million times for making me leave my pistol

at the house that night. I probably would've killed Lance's trifling ass

that night, just for thinking it was cool for him to fuck another woman

while he thought I was four rooms down the hall—drunk and asleep!"

Essence took a sip from her drink and continued, "Anyway, before

Lance and I got remarried, I had told him I wasn't cool with all the shit

he had put me through when we were married the first time and wasn't

down to go through it a second time. I mean, I'm talking about baby

momma drama, STDs, vandalism of our properties, and knockout drag

fights with his delirious lil' side bitches.

Call It What You Want

I even had ninja's back when we were being stalked by a 'few' of the dummies he had got himself involved with... filed restraining orders and everything, just in case I ended up 'popping' one of those dumb-ass bitches. I told Lance like, 'Dude, if you really wanna be with me, I'm gonna need you to get rid of all of that fuckin' drama and treat me like a queen is supposed to be treated. You know what I'm saying, ladies?" Symone and I sipped our drinks, nodding in unison. "Lance whined about how miserable he had been during our time apart, and he promised he'd be a much better husband than he had been the first time around..." Essence tsked and shook her head.

Looking in her eyes, I could tell she was still bothered by the break-up, but she maintained her no-nonsense demeanor to shield her broken heart. "Well . . ." Essence continued, "Needless to say, I fell for the bullshit Lance fed me and remarried his lying ass. For the first 90 days, life was good for us. We spent a lot of time together— shopping and traveling. He even started preparing fancy meals and shit, wooing the hell out of me! But as soon as his shady ass got comfortable, we were right back at square one!"

"Oh no!" I whined, nodding my head sympathetically. "What did he do, Essence?" She harrumphed, then replied, "This mutha-fucka went out with his boys one night and didn't return home until the following evening! Ooooh, I was so fuckin' mad at Lance, I couldn't even look at him! He claimed to have been working or whatever, but I didn't believe any of that bullshit! He was back to his old tricks, and I was determined to bust him out once and for all..." Chuckling at the thoughts running through her mind, Essence proceeded, "So, the white chick that yall may or may not have noticed, balled up in the corner with a towel covering her naked body on the night of the gala, wasn't just some random chick looking to get broken off by a 'brotha'. Sundae is one of my clients, whom I had hired to test Lance's loyalty . . ." I gasped and jerked back so hard that I almost fell off of the stool. "Dayum, Essence, girl you are coldblooded!" Essence chuckled and shook her head. "I ain't gon 'say all of that Kayla. I just ain't the one to be played like damn 4th grader.

Call It What You Want

If Lance didn't want me, he should've just let me be, you know what I'm sayin'?" Symone and I nodded again. "Sundae was supposed to just flirt with Lance a little bit, you know, make him think he was gonna get a little pussy or whatever. As yall see, Lance's nasty ass walked right into the elaborate smokescreen, with a boner and at least three magnum condoms on deck! I strolled into the room just as she was about to slid his dick into her mouth and literally tried to beat the souls out of the both of 'em!" Symone was the first one to burst out laughing, waving her hands for Essence to pause her story, she said, "Now wait a minute, Essence. You mean to tell us you beat your friend up too?" Essence laughed and nodded in affirmation. "Yeah . . . kinda sorta. And that part was a sheer accident, I promise! Seeing her on her knees preparing to please my husband made me feel some kind of way. Something inside me just snapped! Shit, until Sundae called my name and begged me to stop punching her, I had actually forgotten that I was responsible for creating the ruse in the first damn place!"

Call It What You Want

"Wow! That is crazy, Essence. How are things between you and Lance now?" I asked. "Dang it, Kayla. You must've read my mind, because I was about to ask the same question . . .." Symone chimed in. Essence chuckled, taking another sip from her Hawaiian blue cocktail. "Well. . . I haven't actually *seen* Lance since that night at the Hyatt, but I have spoken with him several times—through collect calls from the county jail where he's being held without a bond!" I gasped and clutched at my chest, thoroughly taken aback. "What the hell! Why is he in jail, Essence?"

She rolled her eyes and spoke flatly, "From what I understand, he got flagged down by the 'boys' on the freeway for speeding. Once they checked his plates and ransacked his car, Lance and one of his boys were arrested and charged for being in possession of drugs and more than a dozen unregistered firearms. He claimed he had nothing to do with the guns or the drugs, or whatever, but his goddamn fingerprints were lifted from both! For years, I had been advising Lance to get out of the drug game, but he is so damn cocky and stubborn—that fool thought

he was invincible . . .”

“I know this might come across as a stupid question, but I’m gonna ask

anyway,” Symone interjected shyly. “Are you gonna stay with him

while he serves his time in prison?” Essence threw her head back and

roared with laughter. “Ooooh heeeeelllll no! Honey, I’ve already filed a

petition to have our second marriage annulled! I will always have love

for Lance Grey— he is the father of my daughter, and he was once my

husband and best friend. But that’s about all I’ve got on that whole

situation! Lance and I as a couple will NEVER, EVER happen again!

Now that my marriage is over, I’m gonna take the time to get to know

ME again and figure out what I am gonna do with the rest of my life.

But don’t get it twisted though—this doesn’t mean I’m plunging into

that whole celibacy bullshit. A sistah must get the ‘poonanny’ played

with on the regular. But as far as a relationship is concerned . . . naaaah!

It’s a big *NO* from me, dawg!” Essence asserted with her best

impersonation of Randy Jackson from American Idol.

Call It What You Want

"I can do bad on my own!" she declared smugly. My heart wept for Essence as she continued to talk about the love and respect she had lost for her husband. At that time, I had prayed that I would never have to walk in her shoes. But only a few years later, there I was, standing in those same ugly shoes—angry, humiliated, and too ashamed to admit that my life was not as perfect as it appeared to be on the surface. I was not prepared to disclose the way I had "snapped" the night I had confronted Isaiah, leaving him lying on the floor with his nuts practically sitting on his stomach, and his momma thrashing about in the pool of her own fishy smelling piss that I'd obviously scared out of her. But, Essence deserved to know as much about my "real life" as Symone did, and I was about to give her and ear full of it!

Chapter 14

"*He*eey Boo!" Essence squealed, sauntering into the garage where I was standing next to the Honda Accord that Isaiah and I had been saving for the twins to drive once they obtained their driver's license. Essence was cutely dressed in running gear—colorful sneakers, compression pants, a pink halter top, and a white Old Navy cap. I, on the other hand, looked like a complete bum, with my dense bushy hair pulled into a ponytail, which probably had all kinds of gook stuck in it from all the cleaning I had done that morning, bleached cutoff shorts, a dingy tank top, and a pair of beat-up sneakers that should have made it into the dumpster years ago! "So, what cha' got going on in here, friend? You've got stuff boxed up like yall are moving or something . . ." Essence observed, her eyes scanning the semi organized garage and resting on me, awaiting a response.

My head dropped to the ground immediately, as I felt guilty as hell for not even taking some time out of my crazy life to reach out to the one friend who would understand what I was going through—more than anyone else in my small circle. I just hadn't been in the mood to speak to anyone who would eventually ask me about Isaiah, which would only force me to admit that I hated him, followed by at least 20 legitimate reasons for my feelings! To make matters worse, Symone and I had been bumping heads with each other ever since I told her about Isaiah's outrageously scandalous affair with the redheaded whore. As usual, she

neglected to listen to what I had to say about it, but conveniently

managed to make OUR situation about herself by expressing how

disappointed SHE was with Isaiah, and how SHE would have handled

things if she were in my shoes—which only irritated the shit out of my

soul and made me regret bringing the shit up in the first place.

We ended up having a terrible argument. And even though we made up

the very next day, it did not change the way she had made me feel.

That being said, I did not want the same thing to happen between

Essence and me. So instead of reaching out to my friend to let her know

that the world as I had known it had completely fallen apart, I chose to

hide the matter from Essence, as I *thought* I was doing with the rest of

the world. . .

"Umm . . . so yeah, I was planning on calling you sometime this

weekend to let you know that we'll be moving soon. Um . . . uh, that is,

the twins and I. I found a nice place out in Pickerington, which I'm

hoping to close on by the end of next month. It's a humongous condo

Call It What You Want

with three bedrooms, four baths, a finished basement, and a working

fireplace—just like I have always wanted—"

"Yo! What the heck are you talkin' about, Kayla?" Essence asked with

an astonished look on her face. Tossing her head from side to side, she

shrieked, "Are you tryna tell me you're leaving your husband, after like

71 years together, eh?" I nodded, trying hard not to giggle at the extra

digits she had jokingly added to our marriage. With my eyes lowered, I

confessed, "Uh, I'm not just '*leaving*' Isaiah. I've filed for divorce."

"You did what!" Essence gasped and cried out in sheer disbelief. "Why

Kayla? What the fuck happened that quick? Yall were happy, all lovey-

dovey and shit when yall brought the boys to the shop last month to get

their hair braided, and now you're talking divorce? What the fuck,

Kayla? Is the mother-in-law fuckin' with you again, huh? What

happened?" For the next 30 minutes or so, while Essence sat quietly

puffing on her "ganja stick", I narrated all that had transpired in my

office on the eve of Isaiah's birthday— from the moment Odessa

stepped into my world to when I tossed her home wrecking ass out.

Call It What You Want

Once I finished the story, Essence smacked her lips and shook her head in disgust. "*Umph, umph, umph*, that dusty, albino looking bitch is at it again, huh? Oh my goodness, I knew I should've beat her ass back in the day when I had the damn chance—" Slightly confused by Essence's response, I said, "Wait, you know Odessa?" Essence rolled her eyes and exhaled a cloud of smoke. "Do I know her? *Pffft*! That big goofy bitch used to work in my Northside salon a few years back. I didn't like her then, and now that you've told me this, I can't stand her mutha-fuckin ass! That bitch is so bloody full of her ugly self—conflict and turmoil are as significant as oxygen to her stupid ass! The only good thing I have to say about Odessa is that she's a phenomenal stylist. I mean, she can slay some hair, and with a few strokes of her make-up concoctions, she can make Whoopi Goldberg look like Halle Berry's twin! But, the buck stops right there. Ole girl is SICK in the head yo! *Sick . . .*"

"Tsk . . ." I shrugged. "Yeah, well obviously she's just the type of chick Isaiah likes. He has obviously kept her around for some time. I guess she's anxiously waiting for her turn to be the next Mrs. Ward."

Call It What You Want

Essence rolled her eyes and chuckled. "Yeah, what-the-fuck-ever! That girl is fuckin' bonkers, Kayla! LITERALLY. It's like she lives in her own bizarre world, where she and whoever's man she has her dirty hands on at that time are the only ones who exists. One minute, you'll catch her rapping about some self-righteous bullshit, talkin' about the Lord thee, thy, thump, and shit. Then, as soon as you turn around, the freakin' sociopath is runnin' around town like a dog in heat, tryna get pregnant by somebody's son, brother, uncle, or goddamn grandpa! Just trifling!" Essence paused and shot me a serious glance, then continued.

 "I don't wanna scare you, Kay Kay, but I hope you've visited your gynecologist since finding out about Isaiah and Miss *Sticky-thongs*. Odessa is a '*nutt-bucket*' for real! I know over a dozen dudes who've run up in that, and at least 2 of them caught gonorrhea from her nasty ass!"

"Oh, heavens yes! Girl, I took care of that IMMEDIATELY, and I'm happy to report that *Yoni* and I are good!" Essence gave me an approving nod and released an exasperated breath.

Call It What You Want

"It's crazy, because this isn't the first time Odessa has managed to get herself tangled up in someone's marriage. She pulled this same crap when she worked at my salon, which happened to be one of the reasons I fired her and barred her from stepping foot into any of my establishments!"

"Barred her? Well dayum!" I laughed. "What did the 'garbage-pail kid' do to make you do that, Essence?"

"Gurl, it was Labor Day weekend in 2007 when my daughter, Lana, and a couple of her friends from Atlanta had come to Ohio to spend some time with me. Out of the blue, I receive a frantic call from Chance saying, 'E, you may wanna stop what you're doing and come to the shop real quick, because I think Odessa is about to get her ass WHOOPED!"

Chance Ellis was Essence's best friend and business partner—a stylish male fashionista with more panache than any of the women I knew or rolled with. Just like the musician Prince, Chance was tiny in stature, standing about an inch over five feet, with a gorgeous pecan complexion and dark wavy hair that he usually wore slicked back into a neat ponytail, complimented by a pair of hypnotizing, emerald green, almond-shaped eyes.

Essence flopped one thin leg over the other and continued, "According to Chance, this white chick, who looked like Winona Ryder's doppelganger, walked into the salon, asking for Odessa. Chance said he hadn't thought nothing of the woman's request, as he assumed her to be one of Odessa's regular clients. He paged 'big red' to the front desk and carried on with his work or whatever. Gurl, he said that as soon as Odessa laid her eyes on the woman, she started showing her natural pale ass, with a grandiose performance of trying to humiliate the poor white woman in front of everyone in the damn shop. She called the woman all types of names and even used her funky fingers to jab the woman in her forehead, like she was a damn dog or something—"

I interrupted Essence with a loud tsk. "Oh, hell no! That woman should've punched Odessa in her damn throat right then and there! I'm sorry but uh, people can say whatever they want. When you feel bold enough to put your hands on someone, you're begging for urgent

Call It What You Want

BEATDOWN!" Essence sniggered and bobbed her head in agreement. "Shiid…you can say that again! I can't even tolerate a person raising their voice at me, let alone tryna flex and all that shit. Uhn-uhn, this chick ain't puttin up with that kinda shit—*not at all*!"

We shared a quick laugh. "So anyway, by this point, I was watching the shit go down from the surveillance video being streamed to my cellphone, while grabbing a smoothie from Starbucks." Essence continued, "Yo, that white chick didn't flinch a bit or even bat an eyelash as Odessa worked overtime to demean her. I mean, ole girl stood as stiff as the goddamn Statue of Liberty, with one of those creepy 'yeeeah, uhn huh—just keep on playing with me' smirks on her face, which would have scared the shit out of anyone with any type of fuckin sense! Once ole girl had gotten enough of Odessa's shenanigans, she flashed a smile as wide as the darn sun, and from what Chance told me, she thanked Odessa for her feedback, apologized for any inconvenience she might have caused, and marched out of the shop just as smoothly as she had slid in."

Call It What You Want

"Oh wow! I can already tell that things didn't end well. . ." I sighed and shook my head. Essence laughed and took a few hits of her ganja stick after relighting it. "*Pffit*! You damn right about that sis! After the white chick left the shop, Chance said Odessa asked him for a quick one-on-one so that she could explain what had just happened. He agreed and took her into his office. He said, as soon as he shut the door, the big dummy plopped down on the floor, bawling her stone-cold heart out about how she had been used and abused by yet another 'married man'. And, just like she claimed to be pregnant with your husband's child, she said the exact same thing about the white chick's husband, which turned out to be a boldfaced lie!

Chance said she babbled on for at least an hour, yakking on about how 'his wife just doesn't understand the love we share . . . This is all God's plan . . . we're supposed to be together . . .' and a bunch of other weird shit. Ooooh girl, I wanted to slap the shit out of Odessa just for being so fuckin STUPID!"

Call It What You Want

"Wow!" I exclaimed. "That's just crazy! It all sounds like the same stuff she told me about her 'King' before I knew it was my husband she was venting about . . ."

"Yo, like I said earlier, Odessa is one sick chick! I tell ya—she is SICK, SICK, SICK, SICK!" Essence reiterated with a confident nod. "Oh, but wait, there's more to this story, which will certainly put a smile on your beautiful face, my friend."

I sighed and rolled my eyes. "Girl, pleeeze! I don't think there's anything about that grimy woman that can ever put a smile on my face . . . that's unless she trips and gets lost in a deep, dark black hole!"

Essence clapped her hands at my response and cackled like a hen. With her eyebrows raised and a grin flashing on her face, she remarked, "Let's just say—Odessa got exactly what she had ordered the day she made the mistake of thinkin.' she was gonna pluck that white chick's husband away from her. Later that day, while Odessa was strutting her stuff across the parking lot and tittering on her phone with one of her little hoodrat friends, the dumb bitch forgot to pay attention to her surroundings and got caught slippin! Gurl, the white chick whom

Odessa thought she had humiliated and shit, crept up on her trifling ass

like a slick-ass thief in the night.

The white girl pulled her leg back as far as she could, and *FLOOOP!*

She kicked Odessa straight up in her red ass! Pahaahaa! I'm telling you .

. . ole girl kicked that bitch so hard up her ass, her momma and grand

momma probably felt that shit! Then she jumped on top of her, and

pounded her fist into Odessa's face, until a few my other stylists

intervened…and saved her dumb ass!

"By the time Lana and I made it to the shop, the parking lot was packed

with the police, nosey onlookers, and an ambulance where Odessa was

stretched on the gurney, looking like the *Hamburglar* from them

McDonald's commercials. She had big ole crocodile tears streaming

down the two blackened eyes that the white chick had left her with…"

"Dayum!" was all I could manage to say, shaking my head in

incredulity. Essence rolled her eyes. "Tsk . . . Ah yeah, that white chick

beat Odessa's ass real good, which is exactly with that stank-bitch deserved. But dig this—I overheard her telling the cops that she had

been jumped by a group of teenage girls, who had mistaken her identity

for one of their peers... Hmph! You should've seen how quick I flew

over to that ambulance and killed the big fat ass lie she was trying

to sell. Not only did I tell Odessa to her face that she was a goddamn

liar, but I whipped out my phone and let the cops watch her get that

dumb ass of hers spanked by the white woman, whose husband she had

been sleazing around with for only God knows how long. When the

video ended, I squinted at Odessa and pulled a Donald Trump on her

crazy ass—*BITCH YOU'RE FIRED!*' Get cho' shit outta my shop and

scram!" I laughed at my animated friend and shrugged. "Well, I guess

Odessa will fit right in with Isaiah's dysfunctional family, because they

loooooooooove that type of drama! Aye . . . as long as they're all far, far

away from the twins and me, I don't give a damn about them or

anything they do."

After a while, Essence and I made our way inside my cool house, where

I cut up some fresh fruit and prepared grilled cheese sandwiches for the two of us. Essence had the munchies after smoking up her entire ganja stick, whereas I was simply hungry because I had not eaten anything since the previous day. Between taking bites of her sandwich, Essence asked, "So besides the mess going on with Isaiah, what else has been going on with you? How is work? How is Symone? How are your parents, especially Miss Libby, hmm? God, I love that little lady to pieces!" I beamed at the mere mention of my mom, who was still unaware of the shit Isaiah had put me through, and as long as I could help it, she would not hear a word about our drama until the divorce was finalized.

"Work is cool . . ." I stated honestly. "And, Symone is alright. I'm supposed to be meeting up with her in a couple of hours for lunch at Easton. You are more than welcome to come along, if you like . . ." Essence shook her head and rolled her eyes. "Gurl, I appreciate the offer and love you dearly, but uh . . . I am not in the mood to deal with Symone's judgmental ass today, or even tomorrow.

Call It What You Want

I know that's your girl and all, but she gets on my mutha-fuckin nerves with all of that bible-babbling shit! She's alright. . . but she's *not* real!" I went on to tell her about my upcoming vacation and how excited I was to see my baby brother Omar, who was coming in from Springfield and planning to spend the entire week of the 4th of July with Maxwell and me.

"Oh, and before I forget, Maxwell wanted to make sure you were aware of the cookout/pool party at his house for the holiday. I think Max has a little 'thing' for you, Essence. Unless yall got something going on that I don't know anything about . . ." I teased, nudging her playfully. Essence blushed. "Girl, as quiet as it has been kept, Max has been tryna get with me for a while now. He's is sexy as shit, but uh . . . gettin' involved with him would be a serious conflict of interest. For one, he is just as much a player as me! And seeing that I don't have too many people whom I truly consider a "friend" besides you and my baby Chance, I am not about to jeopardize our relationship over a meaningless fling!

Call It What You Want

You know what I mean? By the way, what did your family have to say about the shit that Isaiah done got himself caught up with, eh? I am sure both of your brothers wanna whoop his ass for playin you like that..."

"Maxwell is aware of what happened, and yes, he was pretty fired up about it. But I haven't said anything to Omar yet, or mom for that matter— just because I don't want her to worry anyone. My mom would worry herself half to death about me and my marital issues while she's supposed to be enjoying her vacation. Plus, she is crazy about Isaiah, has always been . . . and I am sure it's gonna break her heart when she finds out WHY he and I are no longer together.

Ugh, I hate lying to my mom or anyone else for that matter, but until my mom and the boys return back home in August, I don't have no other choice but to act like shit is sweet between Isaiah and I, and deal with the consequences later . . ."

Suddenly, Essence's phone vibrated on the dining room table, flashing a picture of Chance. I asked Essence to tell her bestie that I said "hello" and then excused myself from the dining room to retrieve my own phone from upstairs. When I returned from the quick trip to my bedroom, Essence was wrapping up her call with Chance, while walking towards the foyer. As soon as she ended her call, she turned to me for a quick hug. "Well sis, I'm gonna get outta here now. I've gotta stop by the bank for Chance and run a few errands before it gets too hot outside. You know, I can't think straight when it's too hot, especially when I'm high!" We laughed in unison. "Okay honey." I smiled, accepting her embrace. "Thank you so much for dropping in to check on a sistah and listening to my drama. I apologize for being out of touch; I guess I needed a little time to process things, you know what I mean?"

"Oh I get it, trust me. Don't let that albino bitch worry you none, her days numbered. It's time for that funky bitch to learn who NOT to fuck with . . ." I waved my hand dismissively, "Girl, I am not worried about Odessa Starr, nor am I worried about Isaiah Ward. As long as they stay the hell away from me, everything will be alright. They can have each other, for SURE!"

Call It What You Want

Essence nodded and smiled. "I hear you sis, but that bitch got it coming!
Period. Essence started out the door but stopped in her tracks to face me.
"Oh yeah, I meant to ask . . . do you want to go out tonight? I've got
tickets to the 90s theme talent show going down at Club Marination.
You should come on out and hang with your girl for a while–join me for
some sistah-girl shenanigans. Chance and I were supposed to attend the
show together, but his mom is back in the hospital, and as one would
expect, he wants to be with her."

"Awe. That poor woman has been struggling for as long as I've known
Chance. Tell him I send my love. Nope, never mind I'll call him later to
see how he's doing. I love Chance and his mom, Mrs. Mae."

"Yep, she is an absolute sweetheart! But what about tonight Kayla? Are
you rollin' with me or nah?" I winked at my friend and giggled. "Oh
yeah, I'm definitely rollin' witcha' homie! Club Marination it is!
What time do you wanna meet?"

"Meet?" Essence guffawed, glancing at me over her sunglasses. She
pursed her lips, shaking her head from side to side, and said, "Chile

please . . . your fashionably late' behind won't be meeting me

ANYWHERE! I'll be here to pick you up at 8 o'clock on the dot!"

Chapter 15

After Essence left my house, I jumped into the shower, washed my hair, slicked it up into a jazzy ponytail, and threw on a multicolored sundress, with a pair of sexy gladiator sandals. Within an hour's time, I was speed-walking across Easton mall, charging toward the Mexican bistro where Symone and I had agreed to meet for lunch.

It was no surprise for me to find Symone seated at one of the rear tables in the bistro with her eyes glued to her smartphone. That girl was addicted to her mobile device and was even more infatuated by the fact that she could use it as a tool to pry into other people's private lives— especially the folks she attended church with and found suspicious for one reason or another.

"Ooooh bestie, I love that dress, and your shoes are cute too! You look so chic!" Symone squeaked, tossing her phone into her purse and rising to her feet. She tightly wrapped her arms around me and kissed my

Call It What You Want

cheek. I blushed and thanked her for the compliment, then quickly returned the favor by admiring her freshly braided cornrows and the cute little burnt orange sundress she was wearing. "So, what's been going on with you, Symone? How are the girls and my brotha Ron?" I asked after we sat down at the table and placed orders for sharable appetizers and a pair of frozen margaritas.

Through pursed lips, Symone replied, "Guuuurl, so much has been going on with my crazy family, I dunno where to begin!" Rolling her eyes dramatically, she continued, "Kayla, your 'goddaughter' Trinity has really been testing my patience lately. I'm so sick and tired of her mannish behind pippin' through my house looking, speaking, and smelling like that ole punk Justin Bieber, I can't think of anything besides tossing her out of my house! I already know that you aren't gonna agree with what I am about to say, since you've condoned the little trysts your "*buddy*" Essence has had with women. But, that lesbian crap is downright disgusting. And it should *not* be a part of my daughter's life!

Call It What You Want

It's not like Trinity is ugly or weird or anythin' like that. My baby is as pretty as ever. She's also smart, and very ambitious! Not in a million, trillion years would I have ever thought my baby would develop into one of those damn bull-dikers—running around town, chasin' after 'tits and clits' like a damn BOY! Ewwww . . . *Yucky*!" Symone spat, shaking her head in disgust. "She must've inherited that 'lint-licking, bush-bumping' crap from the sperm donor's side of the family," She continued, "Because as far as I'm aware, no one on my side of the family entertains that gay-blade, LGBTQ crap! We all may have other issues and everything, like most families do. But as far as that nasty 'cooch on cooch' business goes? Noooooope—we don't get down like that! Never have, never will!"

I immediately felt annoyed by the manner in which Symone had quite conveniently pulled Essence's business into our conversation. She was always trying to say little slick stuff behind Essence's back. But when they were face to face, it was all smiles and fake conversation...

Call It What You Want

"So, a few days ago, I decided to sit Trinity down for a sincere heart-to-heart. The discussion was going real smooth until I asked her if she'd consider dating this fine young man named Lenny, a drummer boy from the church, before she fully committed herself to the queer community . . ." Symone shrugged her shoulders and snickered. "Gurl, Trinity was furious with me! She started screaming and hollering all kinds of crazy stuff, and even had the nerve to get all puffed up in the chest like she was gonna swing at me or something! I looked that child of mine dead in the eyes and told her, *'You betta deflate yourself down, SIR/MA'AM, while you still have a chance! Your momma is a saved woman, but that doesn't mean I won't beat the skin off your black ass if I need to!'"* Symone slapped her hand against the table and released a long, hearty horse laugh. "Shoot, Trinity almost awoke the old me! And you know how the old me always enjoyed a good fight . . ." I stared at her blankly, trying to figure out exactly what she found to be so damn funny about taking jabs at her 17-year-old college-bound kid just because of her sexual orientation, along with her ridiculous thoughts of fighting her!

Call It What You Want

Trinity was a darling and looked a lot like her mother when Symone and I had first become friends, back in the day. They shared the same golden-brown skin tone, curvaceous model-like figure, naturally curly hair, and the exact diastema between their front teeth. Nevertheless, this mother– daughter duo was as incompatible as pancakes and ketchup! There was always bickering and arguing going on between these two, mainly because Symone wanted to control Trinity's life and Trinity wasn't having it! "Moving on from Trinity and her ridiculousness . . ." Symone continued.

"The big guy and I've been at odds with each other for almost two weeks now. I love Ron, *God knows I do*. But sometimes, Kayla, I just can't stand him! Ugh!"

"Oh no! What's going on between you and Ron now, hmm?" I asked sympathetically. Symone's response was temporarily interrupted when a bouncy blonde waitress returned to our table with our food and drinks in hand. But as soon as the woman left, Symone picked up right where she had left off.

Call It What You Want

"To make a long story short, Ron got mad at me after I made a teeny-weeny suggestion about him losing at least 100 pounds—"

"SYMONE!" I gasped in pure disbelief, interrupting her mid-sentence. "You better tell me you're joking girl, because that is downright mean and RUDE! Oh my goodness!" Symone harrumphed and remarked snobbishly, "Well, for your information, I didn't bring up Ron's weight to hurt his little sensitive feelings or whatever. I was simply tryna bring awareness to his expanding circumference, so that he could do something about it.

C'mon now, Kayla . . . I would expect for you, him, or anyone else close to me to pull me to the side and let me know that I am eating everything in sight and beginning to look and breathe like a dang-on walrus! After a little research, I discovered that he qualifies for weight-loss surgery through our insurance, which would be covered a 100 percent!"

Symone paused, quickly scanned the room, and then leaned in close so that I could hear what she was about to say next without being overheard by eavesdroppers.

Call It What You Want

"Look Kayla, you might think what I said to my husband was callous or whatever, but I swear to you—it wasn't like that! Just hear me out . . . and please don't judge me. I am horny as hell—alllll of the time! It has been so long since Ron has been able to love me to a 'real' orgasm that I've forgotten how it feels to *cum* naturally. He is almost 350 pounds, Kayla! I can *barely* see his petite 'shabonka' these days, so you can understand when I say that I CAN'T FEEL IT EITHER!

"I'm sorry to say this but, uh . . . if it wasn't for 'Donte' and the case of AAA batteries I have stashed in the back of my lingerie drawer, I would've already cheated on Ronald's sexually incompetent tail, granting one of these Mandingo warriors full access to my sweet poonanie!"

I shook my head compassionately, for Ron's sake, as I listened to Symone's harsh judgments of the man who loved her passionately and unconditionally.

From the moment Symone had introduced me to Ronald Butcher almost 15 years ago, I became an immediate fan!

Call It What You Want

Ron was respectful, as sweet as aged wine, with an amazing sense of humor, which was perfectly complimented by the great depth of knowledge and insight he had about worldly matters.

On top of Ron's unique personality and noble ways, he looked like a doppelganger of American Idol's 2003 winner Rueben Studdard, with his large frame, sleek goatee, boyish smile, and all. I do not think the fella could *blow* like Rueben, but he surely looked a lot like him.

The thing that impressed me the most about Ron was how he had swooped into Symone's life, basically freed her from the "bounce that ass" mentality she once worshiped, and introduced her to Christianity. This man did not care about Symone's promiscuous past, or the fact that she was a 20-year-old mother of a toddler who was supposedly conceived during a drunken "flirt and squirt" session with a guy she claimed to have only known by the nickname "*Fresh*".

Ron adored Symone—flaws and all. Having a family was his main ambition, and within a couple of years of dating my best friend, he married Symone and adopted her daughter Trinity.

Call It What You Want

Needless to say, Symone had a damn near perfect life with a damn near perfect man. So what if ten inches of "beef" was not bursting from his britches and he had a little extra weight on his body!

Ron loved Symone and treated her like royalty, regardless of his, and her, shortcomings—especially when compared to my husband who was *well endowed* and equally talented in the bedroom but a disloyal verbally, physically, and mentally abusive "momma's boy" who cared more for himself than anyone else in this world!

"Uh . . . hellooooo? Earth to Kayla!" Symone snapped her fingers a few times in an attempt to pull me out the daze I had slid into and back into our conversation.

"What in the world are you thinkin' about, hmm? I asked you a simple question, and here you are—sitting looking like you're lost in space! *Sheeeeesh*! I know you ain't buzzin' off your margarita that fast—at least not after two sips! What's wrong with chu' woman?" I was too embarrassed to admit that I had not heard a single word she had uttered after listening to her wisecracks about Ron's "mini-member," so I played it off with a silly giggle. "Please forgive me friend. I guess I am in need of a nap. I've been up since like 5 o'clock this morning, rearranging the house. Now what was it that you asked me, hmm?" I probed with a silly side-eyed smirk.

Symone heaved a deep sigh and replied with a confident smile, "I was just asking when you were gonna abandon this whole 'stubborn' attitude and make some time to speak with your husband. Ron and I have spoken with him several times, and in spite of all that has transpired, Isaiah is missing you like crazy, Kayla!

Just this past Thursday, he came by the house, drunker than a boiled owl, beggin' us to convince you to talk to him. I'm sure you couldn't care less about what I'm about to share with you . . ." Symone paused, tossing a cheesy nacho into her mouth and gobbling it up before continuing. "But, uh . . . apparently, Isaiah's little 'Jezebel' has been steadily stalkin' him for the last month or so. He told Ron and me that she follows him all over town, rings his phone non-stop, and sends him all kinds of bizarre texts. The crazy loon even had the audacity to show up at his office, tryna cause a scene! I advised Isaiah to push his pride

aside and file harassment charges on that zany woman! Ain't nobody got

time to deal with an irrational fatal attraction who refuses to take NO for

an answer. I watch the *Investigation Discovery* channel, *Fatal

Attraction*, *The First 48*, and other shows like that, and I've seen how

those kinds of cases can easily turn deadly . . ." Snapping her fingers and

nodding, she continued, "just like that! That crazy woman hasn't

contacted you, has she?"

"HELL NO!" I snapped with an "I wish she would" attitude and tone.

"Odessa has no reason at all to contact me! Once this divorce has been

finalized, she and Isaiah can hold hands and cha-cha slide all the way to

hell as far as I'm concerned . . ."

"Divorce?" Symone gulped, her eyes bulging out of her face. "Kayla!

How can you even allow that godawful word to fall from your mouth,

when you haven't even given Isaiah the proper chance to explain his

side of the story, huh? I ain't tryna take sides or anything, Kayla, but

you're not being fair, and you damn well know it!

Call It What You Want

Everyone makes mistakes, including you, big head, but it doesn't mean they have to spend the rest of their life paying for it!"

"Huh? Ugh! Whatever Symone. Let's just change the damn topic, please." I shrugged, clearly annoyed.

Symone sat back in her chair and stared at me, as if she was trying to read my mind. A moment later, she shot back up and proceeded to defend the man who had slit my heart in half without a second thought. "Well for what it's worth, Mrs. 'I don't give a crap', Isaiah takes full responsibility for the little 'situation' he had going with *Jezebel*... However, he is adamant that he is not the father of the baby she is carrying. I think you should at least carefully consider all of the facts before moving forward with a divorce. Kayla, that crazy woman fed you a bunch of crap, just to get back at Isaiah for cuttin' ties with her. Yes, he was wrong for entertaining her, but you know most men get a little weak in the knees when it comes to lust. According to Mark 7:20–23, '*It is what comes from inside that defiles you. For from within, out of a person's heart come evil thoughts, sexual immorality, theft, murder,*

Call It What You Want

adultery, greed, wickedness, deceit, lustful desires, envy, slander, pride

and foolishness. . .'"

"*Uggggh*!" I grunted with a dramatic eye roll. "I am not tryna hear any

of that bible stuff Symone. Regardless of what you or your bible says,

this divorce is gonna happen! Odessa can have Isaiah or hash it out with

the other women he's been screwing—not my monkeys, not my

goddamn circus! I'm tapped out, Symone . . . *DONE*! Life goes on, and

so do we!"

"Hey now, you don't have to get all snappy with me, big head! In case

you forgot, I am on your side. We all know you're hurting, Kayla. Heck,

if I were in your shoes, I'd probably be ready to stick my foot deep into

someone's tail, for interfering with my life the way Jezebel has done.

But what you must understand is, God frowns upon divorce, my friend.

You recited those holy vows yourself— for better or for worse, till death

do you part, and guess what? This might be one of those *'worsts'* that ya

signed up for. Yall can fix this, honey. I knew that yall were meant for

each other waaaaay back in the day, when you were crushing on that

Call It What You Want

dimple-faced man! Isaiah's heart belongs to you, as yours belongs to

him." Symone tittered, as she obviously found humor in the "wooing"

stages of my relationship with Isaiah, while I tapped my foot anxiously,

wishing she had never mentioned his name in the first damn place.

The more she defended my deceitful husband, the more frustrated I

became— until I finally snapped.

With a "timeout" hand gesture, I forcefully stopped Symone dead in her

rambling tracks. "Okay, okay, Symone . . . I've had enough of you

sitting up here, trying to make up every goddamn excuse in the world to

justify Isaiah's fucked-up actions! Since you seem to know so fuckin'

much about OUR situation and how it should be handled, do you really

think you know the whole truth, huh?"

"Uh, I . . . um . . ." Symone stammered before I cut her off again.

"While that lying, trifling, scandalous son of an UGLY bitch sat posted

up in your house, gassing yall with bogus tears and unapologetic regrets,

did he happen to mention the part where he and his fire breathing

Call It What You Want

mammie tried to 'jump' me in our kitchen the night I confronted him about his dealings with Odessa, huh?"

"Whoa–whoa–whoa, what!" Symone stuttered with a flabbergasted look on her face. "What in hell do you mean they tried to 'jump' you? Are you tryna say they tried to attack you—physically?" I nodded in affirmation. "Yessss! That is exactly what I'm saying. If it weren't for the fact that I am NOT as 'soft' as they apparently thought I was, God only knows what kinda damage they would've done to me that day. Shit, it's a miracle they didn't end my life all together!"

"OH HELL NO!" Symone fumed, shaking her head angrily. "He didn't mention anything about a freaking fight! Ooooh . . . now I'm fuckin' pissed!" She asserted through her clenched teeth.

In great detail, I recounted everything that happened on the eve of Isaiah's birthday, when I confronted him about his affair with Odessa. I told her how he had vehemently denied having any knowledge about Odessa's existence until I informed him that she had pictures of his naked ass, including his limp dick.

Call It What You Want

I broke down the fiery exchange between Bertha and I that had led to me being flung around the kitchen like a rag doll and slammed on the floor as though I was participating in a WWF competition. Then, I explained how I had fought back against the demented mother–son duo, leaving Isaiah with his nuts lodged in his freakin' chest from being kneed, and his big bad wolf of a mother flopping around on the kitchen floor in her own urine, like a fish out of water!

Angry tears oozed out of my best friend's eyes and dropped on the wooden table. With a trembling voice, she exclaimed, "Jesus! That is horrible, Kayla! I sure wish I had known all this ahead of time, because there's no way in hell I would've been sittin' here defending that fool had I known about the stunt he and his Momma pulled! That's just wrong . . . dead ass WRONG!"

"Yeah . . ." I huffed! "But that ain't even the whole story, Symone."

"Huh? What do you mean?"

"Well, I had planned on coming to your house that night, just to cool off and hopefully get some rest. But I knew your place would be the first one Isaiah would look into, and I didn't want to bring any heat to you or your family. So I ducked off at a friend's house until the next morning. Symone, you won't believe it, but when I returned home the next day and walked into the house, it looked like it had been hit by SWAT! *Literally!* Our chocolate Italian leather furniture had been flipped and tossed to the opposite side of the room. And do you remember those oval glass tables we found on sale at Value City just last month?" Symone nodded.

"Tsk . . . girl, I dunno know if they slammed a hammer on 'em or what, but they murdered those damn tables— along with the African oil paintings I had been collecting for the last decade or so. I mean, those monsters tore up EVERTHING—EVERY-FUCKIN'-THING!"

"Oh my Jesus! That is messed up, Kayla! Real messed up!" Symone acknowledged angrily. "You're damn right about that! Oh, and to add insult to injury, I found a little 'burner' phone that the sneaky bastard had obviously been using to communicate with Odessa, along with the other thirsty hoes he had being screwing on the side.

Call It What You Want

His nasty ass must've had over a hundred pictures of half-dressed or butt naked women, grinning and posing in compromising positions. Odessa must've been one of his favorites though, because he had quite a few pictures of her pasty ass, showing off a 'Batman' belly ring dangling from her navel, along with her furry puss-pocket cocked open, flaunting a clit as long and thick as Shaquille O'Neal's freaking thumb!"

"What the? Oh my Goodness!" Symone shrieked, covering her mouth and forcing a gagging sound from her throat. "That's disgusting Kayla, please tell me you're lying!" I rolled my eyes and continued, *"Pffft!* I can't just make this stuff up, Symone. Isaiah is one foul son of a bitch! So much so that he forgot to delete the three-minute video I found in the phone, of his face buried between another woman's thighs. . ."

Symone shook her head, clasping it with her hands, and yelled, "What in the world, JESUS! Are you sure it was him, Kayla? I mean, you do know pornography can be downloaded to phones and other devices . . . maybe—" I cut Symone off, raising my hand and slowly shaking my head. *"Uhn-uhn!* I'm POSITIVE that the man in the video IS my

Call It What You Want

husband. The real question is—whose yoni was he munching on? At first, I thought the woman was Odessa, because of the colorless body and the pink areolas I was forced to look at in her many pictures— until Isaiah pulled his face away from the woman's ass, turned towards the camera, and gave Odessa a verbal que to '*come taste this pussy*,' which his obedient concubine did without any hesitation!

It was the most sickening shit I've ever seen in my life, Symone!

At the same time, it was all the confirmation I needed to understand that our marriage IS over! I am done with all the fighting, crying, and trying. I'm done with Isaiah—1000 percent DONE!"

"Wow! I mean, I just . . . I just don't know what to say, Kayla . . ." I moved my hand in a sweeping gesture and heaved a heavy sigh. "Aye, it is what it is, ya know? All things happen for a reason, as it's been said, '*People come into your life for a reason, season, or lifetime.*

When you figure out which one it is, you'll know exactly what to do for each person.' I understand it now and I'm *good*! They can have his nasty ass. I don't want him. . ."

Call It What You Want

"Aw man . . . I'm so, so sorry to hear this, my friend! Isaiah should be ashamed of himself for what he has done. I can't wait to tell him this— DEAD TO HIS FREAKIN' FACE!" With a nonchalant shrug, I responded in a flat tone, "Symone, you don't have to say anything to that creep. I'm not mad, nor am I bitter. Our marriage has run its course. It's over now, and I've made my peace with that."

After finishing off our drinks and nibbling at the appetizers we had ordered, Symone and I ended the depressing dialog about my failed marriage and left the Mexican restaurant to indulge in some overpriced Easton shopping. We cruised through the mall for over an hour, dipping in and out of stores—purchasing things we had no need for, before making our way over to our favorite spot: the candle store.

The moment we arrived at the fishbowl-like shop, we were greeted by intoxicatingly fragrant scents, friendly employees, and a bunch of anxious customers. Luckily, we were able to maneuver our way through the small crowd, find our preferred scented candles, and check out within ten minutes.

Call It What You Want

With several shopping bags in our hands and whispered chatter about the transgender cashier whose perfectly applied make up made Symone and I look like a couple of wooly headed boys, my thoughts were suddenly halted by a distant, shrill snicker that forced me to stop moving and gasp in search of the breath lost.

I had heard that same wicked laugh multiple times, and each time it happened to whizz through my ears, my mind envisioned a beastly hyena, prowling and salivating through an ugly wide mouth with razor-sharp teeth—ready to devour whatever or whoever crossed its path.

As chills trickled down my spine and my brain struggled to contemplate my next move, a thunderous "PHARRRRRRRRRRRPP" escaped my body, releasing a distinctive smell that could not have been disguised as anything else, even if I tried to play it off as so.

Symone cleared her throat loudly and shot me a disapproving frown, peeping at my behind to confirm I had not shat myself. "Ooooh girl, I think that margarita is getting to your stomach. The bathroom is right over there, if you need to use it before we leave…" Symone suggested, eying my backside a second time.

Time slowed down to a funeral's pace as the daunting laughter inched more and more into my personal space. In my mind, I warned Symone of the monster that would be appearing within the next few seconds and suggested that we should hide.

But, by the time I was able to part my lips to speak up, Bertha strutted past the candle shop with an animated smile etched on her face and multiple shopping bags dangling from her long dingy arms.

For the first time in years, my monster-in-law actually looked like she had taken a bath! She was garbed in a fashionable attire—a candy-apple red sleeveless sundress, matching sandals, and a polka dot oversized tote bag. She had even deserted her disheveled wig, wearing her natural hair that was dyed platinum blond and cut in a low tapered style!

"Uhn uhn! Kaaayla, is that . . ." Symone stuttered with a confused look on her face.

Call It What You Want

I tsked and nodded before she could complete her question that did not require an answer. "Yep, *Mm-hmm* . . . it's exactly who you think it is, Symone."

"Well, no . . . I mean, I know that's Bertha's ole despicable tail alright, but the redhead with her . . . is that . . . you know . . . hmm?"

I stepped outside the candle shop to steal another glance at Bertha and her newfound friend, then turned back to face Symone, who had already snapped several pictures of the duo with her smartphone. "Affirmative, my friend. You are looking at Shrek and his beloved Donkey!"

Chapter 16

"*Yo,* Kayla your mother-in-law is off the fuckin chain with her old and shiesty ass! I'm telling you, she's very lucky that I wasn't in the mall with yall when she came cruising through with Odessa. I would've cussed both of those jackasses out, and punched the '*certified homewrecker*' straight in that gigantic forehead of hers! *Ugh!* I hate that dirty albino bitch! This vendetta that Bertha has against you is going a little too fuckin far. Somebody's gonna get *hurt* fuckin around with that

that bitter ass woman, and it better not be you! *That woman is the devil. Pure evil*!" Essence remarked, as we drove to the club, discussing how Symone and I had caught a glimpse of Bertha and Odessa gallivanting together through the mall as if they were the best of friends.

I shrugged and sighed, glancing out of the passenger window. "Isaiah's whole freakin family is nuts, and I am sure Odessa will fit right in with reckless hooligans! As Long as they stay the hell away from me, I really don't give a shit about them, or anything they do. I'm over it Essence."

Club Marination was "jumping" like an old-school house party when we finally arrived. Cars were snugly lined end-to-end on Front Street and, from what I could see of the neighboring parking lot, displaying a neon green sign that read "CLUB PARKING ONLY"—it had definitely reached full capacity!

"Whoa! Gurl, this place is really packed tonight! My friend from work told me it gets pretty darn busy down here on Saturday nights, but *sheeeeesh*! I didn't think it was gonna be like this!"

Call It What You Want

I exclaimed, pointing to the long line of people standing behind the red-rope divider.

There must have been at least seventy people, anxiously waiting in line to be cleared to enter the club by two bald Arnold-Schwarzenegger like security guards wearing tight black muscle shirts and dark sunglasses, with more people rapidly approaching. I glanced over at Essence and said, "Ooooh gurl...I dunno how long you're gonna be able to stand in line with those stilettos on. I hope you've got some flip-flops in the trunk, because we might be standing for a good while." I complained jokingly.

Essence smacked her lips, blowing smoke from her ganja stick out of the window. "Gurl, pleeeze! You've been around me long enough to know that I always keep a 'connect' nestled beneath my bra strap. So, standing in that line, or any other line for that matter, just AIN'T happening!" Essence flicked the ash from her ganja stick and handed it over to me— as if I had asked for it! "Here, hit this shit a couple times and relax. Fuck Isaiah, his messy ass mammie, and fuck Odessa's bitch ass too! In fact,

Call It What You Want

fuck anything that has brought stress your way within the last month, my friend. Tonight, we are gonna have some fuuuuuun! *Sucka free fun.*" Essence persuaded with a silly wink. Essence stationed her gold Lexus in the "Staff Only" section of the parking lot located near the rear of the nightclub. After spraying the interior down with a bottle of Pink Sugar fragrance mist—to disguise the scent of the "herbal essence" we had been smoking—she made a call from her cell, singing in a scratchy Macy Gray tone, "We're heeeeeeere, baaaaaaabeeee!"

Sliding the cell into her bag and tucking her pistol between her breasts, Essence turned to me, poked me in my arm playfully, and giggled, "You alright over there, Kayla? If you're too high, we can sit here and chill for a few minutes. . ." The couple of tokes I had taken from her ganja stick had suddenly given me the giggles. So, instead of providing Essence with a clear and concise answer, as I am sure she expected, I nodded and busted out laughing! My grandmother always told me, laughing was the best form of therapy and she was absolutely right! I had laughed so hard, I almost had an orgasm!

Call It What You Want

Shortly after my "laughing fit" had reached its end, we were greeted by a straight-faced dark skinned brotha' by the nick-name of "Big-B," who immediately reminded me of the actor Ving Rhames. After a quick introduction, Essence explained that Big-B was her ex-husband Lance's cousin, whom she still regarded as family and maintained close contact with. As Big- B chaperoned us through the club's back door and towards the plush VIP section, I was grinning like a child in the middle of the FAO Schwarz toy store in New York City and swaying my hips to the beats of "It's all about me" by Mya.

Club Marination was one of those big fancy clubs—reminiscent of the lavish nightclubs in Las Vegas—bright flashy lights and all! On top of the mesmerizing cathedral ceilings, the walls of the club were skillfully decorated with framed posters of numerous music legends—Bob Marley, Nat King Cole, James Brown, Earth, Wind & Fire, Gil Scott Heron, Boney James, Kenny G, New Edition, Mint Condition, and a slew of other famous artists.

Call It What You Want

There were two vibrantly illuminated bar areas, with harmonized red leather high-back bar stools, which were stocked with high-end liquor bottles lined against a mirrored wall.

There was also a large patterned dancefloor, lit up by colorful disco lights that boogied with the music, and an end-to end stage, where standing microphones, a piano, and a drum set were positioned.

By the time we arrived at the VIP area, I was thoroughly pumped and ready to dance, especially when Sean Paul's jam "I'm still in love with you" erupted from the club's speakers.

Leaving Essence behind to chat with Ving Rhames' doppelgänger, I hit the dancefloor without a lick of hesitation, smiling and rhythmically rolling my hips to the boisterous beats of the banging music.

The tokes I had pulled from Essence's ganja stick had me feeling bold, free and extremely brave. In fact, when the DJ introduced the singer Brandy Norwood's "*I wanna be down*" challenge, which involved random people in the club singing, freestyle rapping, or reciting one of the three verses from her remix composed by rappers MC Lyte, Yo-

Call It What You Want

Yo, and Queen Latifiah, the *high* 'pushed my boldness a few steps further.

Squealing in excitement, I waved my hands wildly to grab the DJ's attention. Much to my surprise and joy, he noticed, and instantly motioned me to come up on stage. Bubbling with enthusiasm, I made my way to the stage, grabbed hold of the mic, and, as soon as the beat dropped, I popped out of my shell like a pearl, setting the challenge off with the first verse rapped by Mc Lyte.

"Yeah…I get exotic with tha' melodic tune I get hypnotic with tha' moon, but you got to put me down soon, I flip a sideshow if you come my way—up, down, and around, even sideways; I'm about as ready as the Lyte can get; we can go all out; I ain't afraid of the sweat, but yet I bet you got the techniques to freak a girl inside out; what's that all about (oooh yeah). Can I've some of that; you got to put me on; word around town is your nine-men strong; I wanna be put on in tha' worst way since the first day; I think it was a Thursday… (oh baby) you be that brother that I wanna sink my teeth in, make me wanna ask where tha' hell you

Call It What You Want

been; I like the way you be with all that personality, but I got flava' too; You needs to get with me…"

I noticed Essence near the edge of the stage beaming and grinning twinkly, as I showed off my rapping skills. And once I passed to mic to the next woman, who was waiting eagerly for her chance to flow with the next verse, I stepped off the stage in into my friend's arms as she hugged me and screamed excitedly.

"KAYLA! Gurl, you *slayed* that shit! Like—OMG! I am so freakin proud of you! I ain't gon' front though, I was scared as shit when I spotted you walkin' up on the stage—gigglin' and shit. I was thinking to myself, '*Oh gawd, I done got my homegirl high, and she's about to embarrass the hell out of me and her!*' But *shiiiiiiiiid*! Once you started bobbing your head, and your arms started swinging to that dope ass beat, I knew you were going to tear that shit up, like a mutha-fuckin boss!" Essence grinned and flashed me her phone." See. . . I've got most of it recorded. I'm gonna send it to Chance? Haa! He is gonna lose his freakin mind when he sees this shit!"

Call It What You Want

Eventually, we strolled back over to the VIP area, where we chatted, sipped on cherry wine, and nibbled from the basket of the delicious fried shrimp and calamari rings we had ordered. The talent show started shortly afterwards, and it was absolutely phenomenal!

We clapped, cheered, and sang along with the talented people who showed off their exceptional singing and dancing skills, especially this one all girl group who came in the club looking like the group TLC, and performed their hit, "What about your friends".

During a short intermission, Essence filled me in on some of the recent drama that had been troubling her life. She explained that she had run into a "little issue" so grave that she had to break the lease on her Hilliard apartment and move to the opposite side of town.

"What in the world have you gotten yourself into this time, eh? And you better not tell me you had another fight with that stupid-ass neighbor of yours and got yourself evicted, Essence!"

"Tsk," Essence huffed. "I've never been evicted a day in my life. That shit right there is for those trifling, irresponsible hoes—not Boss like

Call It What You Want

me! Anyway, I had to move up outta' my apartment, because I was being stalked by a goddamn one- night stand, gurl. . ."

"Whaat!" I gasped, offering her my full attention. "What the hell happened?"

Essence quaffed down her wine and placed the glass on the table, so that she could use her hands to add emphasis to her story—as she always did. "So, I kinda' got myself involved with this big, black blue-eyed Haitian guy named Malik, who I met last month during a hair show in Toledo. Gurl, this man was so freakin' fine, I just had to have him! We chatted up during the after-party, had a couple of drinks, and danced— you know, the whole nine yards. He asked me if I'd accompany him to his hotel room to spend some time with him, since he was only in town for that one night.

Don't judge me Kayla, but Guuuurl, I went back to that man's room, and damn it was on! He strapped with a nice juicy *thanga-thang* like I like it. And the brotha' was as skilled as a freakin' porn star, gurl— flipping and flopping my body all over the room like it was nothing!"

Call It What You Want

She paused, giggling like a child. "To show my gratitude for how good he made my body feel," she continued, "I left the brotha a healthy tip on the nightstand, along with my business card—which I utterly regret, now." I shook my head and laughed loudly. "Oooooooh, Essence gurl, you kill me— leaving those cash tips and all for your 'boo-thangs,' after humpin' their damn brains out. I'd feel like a damn floozy if I messed around with someone, fell asleep, and woke up with a wet ass, an empty bed, and loose dollars tossed on the nightstand— especially when your *Iggggnaaaant* behind has left men with sums less than the price of a pack of darn cigarettes!"

"Aye, well...some of these ninjas do the same shit to women—if not worse—they don't give a rat's ass about anyone's feelings beyond their own. Sooo....why should we care about theirs? It is what it is, you know what I mean?" I nodded, taking a sip from my exquisite glass of wine, patiently waiting for Essence to finish her story.

"Anyway gurl, so Malik called me up about a week or so after we had messed around, saying he was coming to Columbus on business and

Call It What You Want

wanted to hang out—or whatever. I declined his offer immediately,

because, for some reason, I just wasn't feeling it, ya know? Of course, I

didn't *say* that to him, which I probably should have. Instead I lied

through my damn teeth, telling him that I would be in ATL during that

time, but would make time to hook up with him some other time…

"So, a few days later, I had arrived home from the shop around 8:30 or 9

o'clock at night. I had stopped by Roosters to pick up some wings, along

with a bottle of Cîroc, which I had planned to enjoy alone—with my t-

shirt and panties on, along with my recorded episodes of Basketball

Wives. I strolled into my apartment, placed my chicken wings on the

stove, and put my liquor inside the freezer. And as I was making my

way up the stairs to take the shower I noticed the reflection of the

television in my bedroom—flashing on the wall next to the bathroom.

I paused for a minute, and was like *now wait a damn minute…did I leave*

that TV on? Granted, there had been plenty of times when I've

carelessly rushed out of my place, leaving on the lights, radios, and all

that you can possibly imagine—but I wasn't too sure about this time.

Call It What You Want

I took a deep breath and tried to push the scary thoughts running through my mind. But *baaaybeee,* when I reached the top of my damn staircase and turned the corner leading to my bedroom, I spotted this creepy blue-black mutha fucka sprawled across my goddamn bed—with nothing but a pair of white low-cut socks covering his long dinosaur feet! Guuurl, I bout' lost it..."

"No way! You are lying!" I shrieked, laughing out loud. Essence shook her head and harrumphed, "Nah, I bullshit you not, Kayla. The ninja even had the nerve to slide to the edge of the bed with his arms extended, talkin' about *'Yes, my love, you finally made it home to your king. I've been waiting for you all day...*"

The way she strained herself to deepen her voice and mock Malik's French accent really sent me into a laughing frenzy! I laughed so loud and hard that Essence couldn't help but join in!

"Laugh all you want, you punk—that ninja scared the crap outta' me! I damn near broke my neck runnin' out of the apartment—fell down the steps and everything!"

Call It What You Want

"Hahahahahahhaaaahahaa!" I roared even louder, clutching my cramped stomach. "Aye, but I learned a few valuable lessons that day…" Still sniggering, I asked, "Oh really now? What did you learn, my friend?" With a silly smirk on her face, Essence replied, "For one, I've gotta' keep my gun on me at all times, and two—never trust a black man with blue eyes. THEY ARE THE BLOODY REINCARNATION OF THE DAMNED DEVIL HIMSELF!" We laughed in unison.

Chapter 17

The club's music faded out, as the DJ's voice reverberated through the sound system. "Yoo! Yooo! Yoooo! Are yall enjoying the show so far, eh?" The crowd responded with loud excited roars. "Aight then," he continued, "With that being said family, coming next on stage to croon you beautiful SINGLE ladies into a world of ecstasy are four of the smoothest, dopest, and most humble brothas I've met in Columbus thus far. Please family, GIVE A WARM WELCOME TO CLUB MARINATION'S VERY OWN SOOOOOOOOOOOULQUUUUUUEST!"

Call It What You Want

The crowd thundered in wild excitement, and Essence and I followed

suit—clapping and jumping in our seats like a pair of anxious teenagers!

"Ooooh girl, I've heard this group is the *bomb!*" I chirped, turning to

Essence. "I work with their manager, Blaze, who boasts about them allll

of the time!" Essence nodded. "Uh-huh, and I heard they are FYNE as

hell too!" A melody of the 90s' R&B group Blackstreet began thumping

through the speakers, making the crowd cheer even louder, and sway

their bodies from side to side. Within a few seconds of the introduction,

four medium built, smooth skinned kings, garbed in all-white short

sleeved linen pantsuits, matching dress shoes, and white fedoras, glided

onto the stage, serenading the crowd with their perfect finesse! "Before I

let you go, before I let you go, can I get a kiss goodnight, baby?" they

sang in unison. Like every other woman in the club that night, Essence

and I moved our hips, swaying from side to side, snapped our fingers,

and sang along as if we were at an actual Blackstreet concert.

I had been a fan of the group since they had hit the scene with the hot

number "No Diggidy." So, a little rendition to send me down the

Call It What You Want

memory lane—of the more peaceful days of my life—was exactly what
I needed! In perfect pitch and impeccable range, the darkest fella of the
group nailed the first verse of the song—looking straight at the crowd,
without a hint of fear or hesitation. *"Lately I've been*

thinking…something is going wrong, cause' you've got an attitude, and
you're not in the mood like ya used to…"

Instantly became weak in the knees! So much so, that I had to grab hold
of a chair to maintain my balance. The voice behind the mic was that of
my colleague Blaze, my extremely handsome and down-to-earth buddy,
whom I had been vibing with for years. His voice was as smooth as
melted chocolate and as passionate as a teenage love affair.

The way he gently swayed his hips to the beat—flexing his large hands
in a persuasive manner, pursing and licking his lips with passion— sent
warm pulsating sensations surging through my entire body! Blaze's
voice, his vibe, and his energy had me completely mesmerized.

"Goddaaaaayumn! Those are some FYNE ASS brothas,

Call It What You Want

Kayla! You can call me the whore of Babylon if you please, cause all four of 'em can get a taste of this juicy poonanie tonight! You hear me? *Mmm-hmm*, especially the chocolate-drop over there with the heavy equipment hiding behind his zipper! *Mm-hmm*!"

"Essence!" I chuckled, playfully nudging my friend's arm. "You are so damn nasty!" Still giggling in glee, she bantered, "Whatever Kayla, don't even try to act like you didn't peep at the thick print in his pants, Miss 'Dick Spy!' Your x-ray vision probably noticed it before me!"

I burst out laughing, because she was right. As quiet and careful as I tried to be, I took a gander at Blaze's seemingly well-proportioned package *every time* he was around me. But, I'd never admit that to anyone—not even if I was caught looking at it!

"Gurl, that's my colleague, Blaze. You know, the one I told you owns this club and manages SoulQuest?"

"Oh yeah...is that right, eh?" Essence cross examined me through squinted eyes and twisted lips. "So, you're telling me that you've been working next to a fine Mandingo Warrior, who is as SEXY as Morris

Call It What You Want

Chestnut, with a voice as smooth as that of Luther Vandross, and you've not had a single thought about fuckin' the soul outta him, huh?"

"Whaat!" I blushed, guiltily. "Everybody doesn't wake up with nasty thoughts about stuff like that like you Essence . . ." I lied with a semi-straight face. "*Mmm*, and if that's the case, tell me why your ass is blushing like a freshly blossomed petunia, eh? I was born at night, but not last night—Chicca! What yall got going on, hmm?"

"Absolutely NOTHING Essence!" I laughed. "Blaze and I are just friends; he's a really cool guy, funny, and a great listener. Trust me, if something beyond that was going on, you'd definitely be the first one to know!"

What I told Essence was the honest truth. Blaze and I were *just* friends. He and I shared strong an attraction to one another—which I purposely hid from my friend, no lines had ever been crossed. Our friendship was purely *platonic*. He had been the perfect confidant since things had gone sour between Isaiah and me. Thanks to our nosey colleague, Seong—who works in the suite adjacent to mine—Blaze had been informed

Call It What You Want

about what she had overheard from my office the day Isaiah's *"garbage pail kid"* decided to pay me a visit. Blaze had called my cellphone repeatedly that evening to check on me.

However, it wasn't until after the "kitchen brawl" that I had answered his call—bawling and babbling *at that*— he convinced me to drive to his home immediately. Blaze listened to me, prayed for me, and even allowed me to lie in his arms and cry until I had eventually fallen asleep. When I opened my eyes the next day, I was on his couch, fully dressed and wrapped up in a Strawberry Shortcake blanket, like a burrito, while he lay asleep on the floor beside me, wearing the same T-shirt and basketball shorts that he had been wearing when I had arrived. . .

"Mm- hmmm…" Essence uttered, with a side eye glance. I chuckled. "What's that look for, Essence? You know I'd never lie to you! I promise . . . Blaze and I are just *friends*! As a matter of fact, how about I text him and invite him over to our table—where you can speak to him on your own . . . "

Call It What You Want

Essence had been away from the VIP area for a good five minutes or so when I felt a light tap on my shoulder.

Slightly irritated by the fact that someone thought it was cool to touch me without permission, I inhaled and released a deep breath, then spun around, flashing probably the meanest mug ever!

For all I knew, the person poking at my shoulder could have been Isaiah or one of Bertha's dusty henchmen, sent to chastise me for the egos I had bruised the day those two clowns had tried to "jump "me in my own damn house. Isaiah and his "dusty squad" were cruel like that; they'd treat you like dog-shit as long as it was permitted. But the moment you decided to return the favor and treat them as you had been treated, those freaking behemoths would lose their minds in the name of *vengeance*!

My insides flinched as my eyes rested on a broad chested frame with chocolate arms shooting towards the ceiling, gesturing an unarmed position.

I blinked a couple of times, trying to figure out what I was supposed to do next—especially if those chocolate arms decided to grab or strike me.

Call It What You Want

But, when his voice wafted past my ear like a cool breeze, I knew that everything was gonna be alright. "Wasup Miss Lady? I thought I had noticed you getting your 'boogie' on out there on the dance floor. But then I thought, *'Naaah, if my friend was in my club, certainly she would've reached out to a brotha'*. Then, when I got your text, I was like, woooow—my eyes WERE NOT playin' tricks on me! Miss Lady *is* in my club tonight!"

We shared a quick laugh, then he said, "So how have you been? You look great, by the way." I blushed as I slithered out of the chair and fell into Blaze's warm embrace. I was quite tipsy at the time, so I am sure that I probably leaned into him a little closer than I would have any other time- especially if anyone else were around.

Blaze tossed out a few flattering compliments as he sized me up from head to toe, including the fact that he was very impressed by the way I looked outside of the business attires he had become accustomed to. I had always kept myself together. But, on that particular night, I had

Call It What You Want

gone above and beyond to look as sensual as one of those plus-size models Mrs. Maybelle had always compared me to.

My voluptuous body was draped in a black, scalloped V-neck skater dress, which perfectly complimented my *Double-D twins*, slender tummy, and my perfectly round behind—along with a pair of leopard-printed heels, which—thanks to the pole dancing classes I had fallen in love with—added emphasis to my thick chocolate thighs.

Together with my long tresses left free and wild, like the singer and songwriter Kelis had worn hers in her first single "Caught out there," I undoubtedly looked as delicious as the forbidden fruit!

And, judging by Blaze's desirous demeanor, he felt the same way too!

"Soooooo, when were you gonna tell me you're a dang-on singer, Mr. Dave Hollister? Dude, you've got a beeeeeeautiful voice—I could listen to you sing alllll day, every day! I'm surprised that you aren't signed on to someone's record label, and ballin' out of control like Usher—talkin' about how you just 'manage' SoulQuest. *Hmph*!

Call It What You Want

That is a HUGE understatement, Blaze, and you know it!" I joked, playfully poking his arm. Blaze bowed his head to the side, releasing a modest chuckle, then tried to flash a serious expression, which made the both of us burst out laughing.

"See, there you go, Miss Lady! You've got a brotha' up here blushing so hard, that I can't even get my story together!" We laughed in unison. "But nah, seriously…" he continued with a genuine smile, "What I told you is the truth. I do manage SoulQuest, and I never speak much about my hidden talents, because, uh, I don't care much for being in the spotlight. The only reason I performed tonight is because the lead singer's wife gave birth to their second prince early this morning. He had to be with his family, the show had to go on. I had to do what needed to be done, you know what I'm saying?" I nodded and smiled.

"Well, you did an awesome job Blaze! Bravo brotha!"

"Thank you, Miss Lady. I appreciate the compliment. But enough about me, who did you come to the club with, if you don't mind my asking?"

Call It What You Want

"Blaze, you should know by now that you can ask me anything. I don't have anything to hide. I'm hanging out with my homegirl Essence tonight, who left for the ladies' room over 15 minutes ago. Knowing her the way that I do, she has probably gotten side tracked flirting with someone..."

"Ah, okay. . . cool. I'll just sit here with you until she returns. Can I get you a drink or something?" Blaze asked, as he helped me slide back into the high back chair, then seated himself beside me. "Oh no thank you. The only thing I'll be drinking on for the rest of this night, is this warm water, that has been sitting here for the longest! Don't judge my homegirl and I, but we probably went through at least two bottles of wine tonight. I have definitely had enough." He nodded, waved to the waitress and ordered two glasses of ice water with a few slices of lemon on the side.

"So, how are things with your husband?" Blazed asked the moment the waitress left our table. "Have yall been able to sit down and talk things out, as I suggested? I emailed you a list of amazing marriage counselors throughout Columbus. I do not know them personally, but I have heard a lot about their work."

"Nah." I replied with a bleak head-shake. "It has been almost a month since I have spoken with or even looked into the eyes of that man. He sends long annoying text messages when he's drunk and in his 'feelins' and calls my phone from time to time, just to leave voice messages, calling me every name besides the one given to me at birth. I haven't given that man an ounce of my energy, Blaze. I have filed for a divorce and the farther he and his dysfunctional relatives stay away from me, the better off we will all be! Speaking of which . . . earlier today, my best friend Symone and I had the pleasure of spotting his *mother*—and the alleged baby momma/side-chick cruising through the mall, laughing and giggling, as if they were the best of friends. It was crazy seeing the two of them together like that, but I guess I shouldn't have been surprised. I am almost certain his mother supports their relationship. That woman hates me with a passion, and is always searching for ways to hurt me."

Call It What You Want

"Woah, so your mother-in-law and the mistress are cool like that?" I nodded, "Apparently so..."

"Damn, Miss Lady..." Blaze sighed with a sympathetic nod. "I'm sure that felt like a smack on the face, eh?"

"*Ugh!*" I grunted, trying to shake the thoughts of my husband and my wretched in-laws away from my mind. "I'm so sick of all of this drama with these people, that the thought of them sometimes makes me sick on my stomach! I think I just need to get away for a while— far enough to where I can actually BREATHE without having to hear, feel, or even run into any of those circus clowns! I'm just tired Blaze. I'm sick and tired of every *goddamn* thing that concerns *those* people! I am far from perfect, but I damn sure don't deserve to be treated like this!"

Blaze held my gaze for a second. Then, he placed his hand over mine and gripped it tenderly.

"You're absolutely right, no one deserves to be treated that way, Miss Lady. And uh, if you are serious about getting away for a while, I can make that happen for you."

Call It What You Want

"Huh? What are you talking about, Blaze?"

"I'm going to Philadelphia in the morning . . ." He paused long enough to glance at his watch, before returning his focus on me. "Actually, in less than six hours, I'll be flying to my hometown of West Philadelphia to attend a surprise birthday party Monday, for one of my cousins. I'll be there until Wednesday morning. You're more than welcome to join me, um. . . that is If you are serious about *'getting away'*."

"Aww Blaze, that's so sweet of you, but I don't wanna' be more of a burden to you than I already have been. Besides, I have to work all next week. My vacation doesn't begin until the following week." I nudged Blaze's shoulder with mine and giggled. "And do you know how much I would have to pay for a last-minute flight? My goodness!" Flashing a warm smile at me, Blaze replied smoothly,

"All you've gotta' do is say *yes* and pack your bags. I'll handle everything else . . ."

"C'mon. . . You're kidding me right?" He laughed and shook his head. "Do you trust me?"

Call It What You Want

"I mean, yeah . . . you've never given me a reason to feel otherwise—"

"Good. So let me take you away for a little while. . .I promise you won't regret it." Needless to say, after Essence met and chitchatted with Blaze, then later dropped me off at home, I showered, changed my clothes, packed a suitcase, and drove to Blaze's house—to stash my car for the next few days!

Chapter 18

*A*fter the night at the club, the next few days of my life felt as though I was walking in paradise. Blaze was *all* I needed to put the drama of Isaiah and his family behind me—if only temporarily—and bring some light back into my gloomy life!

Blaze was very attentive towards my needs. Besides the fact that he'd frequently asked if I was alright, when he caught me deep in thought, pondering on the problems I had to face back at home. He kept me laughing. And when he would playfully grab hold of my hands from time to time or even throw his arms around my shoulders as we mingled with his family and friends— as if we were a couple, I felt *safe*.

Call It What You Want

On our first day in Philly, we visited several of his relatives. Unlike the rolling eyes, twisted crusty lips, and the overall negative energy I had become accustomed to whenever I had been forced to breathe the same air as my malevolent in-laws, Blaze's kith and kin were warm and affectionate and as sweet as sugared candy.

They hugged and kissed me as if I were someone they had known all their life but hadn't seen in years. In fact, Blaze's folks were so hospitable and affectionate that although the question was never asked— I *think* they thought I was Blaze's girlfriend! The Monday after we arrived was the surprise birthday party of Blaze's first cousin, Octavius Brown, a professor at the University of Philadelphia.

As soon as Octavius walked into the Sheraton's ballroom and everyone yelled "SURPRISE," I swear to God I had to take a double look at the middle aged man. He nearly looked like the identical to the popular actor Lawrence Fishburn, when he played the role of Morpheus in *The Matrix*—dark suit, bald head, gap teeth, sunglasses and all!

Call It What You Want

The birthday party was exceptional and was probably one of the best
and most well-organized parties I had attended in all the 38 years of my
life. In addition to the 80's-themed décor, the mouthwatering canapés,
and the best soul food to have ever kissed my lips, the fact that
Blaze's folks knew how to have a good time added to the charm of the
party.

We ate, drank, laughed, and danced all night long! And guess what?
There wasn't a lick of drama to report! The very next day, we joined the
family for a fulfilling breakfast at Blaze's Aunt Jody's home. She owned
a beautiful home in the suburbs of Philly, and she was a certified chef
who made sure we had the best breakfast spread available in town.
Aunt Jody didn't serve just a basic breakfast meal with sausage, eggs,
bacon, and toast; instead, she had two long tables completely laid out
with assorted fruits, yogurt, pancakes, muffins, bagels, biscuits,
breakfast pizza, and my absolute favorite, apple and maple breakfast
bread pudding! While enjoying friendly conversation, Blaze and his
peeps decided to take me on a grand tour of the city— which was

Call It What You Want

absolutely thrilling! We rode in a huge red tour bus with a competent

driver, who recounted some of the historical events that shaped Philly

and stopped the bus at many of the historical places, such as the

Liberty Bell, Reading Terminal Market, Independence Hall, and the

Philadelphia Museum of Art, for up-close and personal viewing.

After the tour ended, I let Blaze talk me into an indoor skydiving

excursion, which was something I had never thought I would do. But I

did it . . . and what a wonderful experience it was!

Later that evening, we attended a cook-out at Thaddeus' place.

Thaddeus was one of Blaze's childhood friends who was also an

exceptionally talented vocalist. It was quite amusing to watch Blaze,

Thaddeus and a few of their buddies harmonizing tunes—with strong,

silky smooth pipes—like the *Isley Brothers*. I was having a really good

time—until my phone vibrated, and I noticed it was Symone calling for

what seemed like the tenth time that day.

 I found it odd that she and Isaiah had been calling my phone *incessantly*

since I had left Columbus Sunday morning. Isaiah would ring my phone

Call It What You Want

and get sent straight to voicemail—of course. And then seconds later, taking cue from it, Symone would call, and I would have to send her call to voicemail too. . .

As strange as it may sound, their back-to-back calls made me nervous and made me wonder if the two of them were in cahoots against me. I figured Isaiah had most likely convinced himself that we were gonna sweep his little situation with Odessa under the rug — and keep moving forward with life, as we had done so easily with all the other scandalous stunts he had pulled over the years. And, *undoubtedly* Symone had jumped on his bandwagon, taking his unapologetic tears and bullshit talk to heart and was trying her best to "pray" him and me back together— even though I had made it quite clear that a reconciliation between Isaiah and I would *never* happen.

"Heeey *Bestie*! I've been calling you for hours! I know you ain't that dang-on busy, punk! You're at a retreat for heaven's sake, surely you can answer the phone when I call!" Symone blurted before I even had the chance to say hello. "Sooo . . ." she continued, "Your husband is

Call It What You Want

here at the house and wanted to speak with you real quick. Hold on a minute while I get him." My body went completely numb when I heard those words come out of Symone's mouth, coupled with what she had thought she had whispered to Isaiah, but I clearly heard, *"Here boy, I did what you asked and got her on the phone . . . Please don't make me regret this Isaiah! BE NICE! Or she'll never take you back . . ."*

Just as I suspected, my best friend had sided with my husband and put me in a situation where I *had* to talk to him even though I had no desire to do so. "Uh, hello? Kayla . . . Babe, how are you doing? "He asked smoothly. "Hey . . . *Isaiah* . . ." I responded unenthusiastically, then waited for him to proceed with his usual nonsense. Isaiah guffawed, *"Goddamnit* Kayla! You ain't gotta sound all dry and shit when you talk to me . . . *Sheeeeesh*! Cut a brotha some slack, wouldja? I've been calling you every day for almost a month. It wouldn't have hurt you to call me back and shit. In case you forgot, I'm still your husband. Regardless of what you *think* has happened with Odessa's funky ass, I still love the shit outta you, Kayla. *I swear to God I do*."

Call It What You Want

Yeah right and what a fuckin' tragedy that is! I thought instantly.

"Yeah so uh, I hear you're in Washington DC for a retreat and everything. Must be nice — especially when your entire trip is free, Right?" He continued, as if things between us were cool. "What time do you think you'll be flying back in tomorrow? I can pick you up from the airport if you need a ride . . ."

It took a few seconds for me to realize what he had just said to me. But once it all registered, I realized that Symone had run her big fat mouth about my whereabouts after she had sworn to the nine Gods that she wouldn't. And that made me *livid*! I was so infuriated by Symone's betrayal that I started stammering and stuttering like a fool, failing to provide Isaiah with an immediate response.

To play off my befuddled state of mind, I said, "Hey Isaiah, can you hold on for just a second? I've got a call coming through on the other line . . ." and quickly muted my phone. I needed some time to not only remove myself from the backyard party but also get my rambling thoughts in order before I ended up saying something that I would later

Call It What You Want

regret. As I walked around the side of Thaddeus' house towards the front porch, which I was hoping would be free of any distractions, I frowned thinking about Symone and shook my head in disgust. I loved Symone dearly and would have done just about anything for her—the sister I never had. But I was beginning to feel like our friendship was little one-sided.

The last time we had been together at Easton mall, Symone had pretended to understand my pain and frustration about Isaiah's cheating shenanigans, especially after we had spotted Bertha strolling around the mall with Odessa like they were Cagney and Lacey!

Something had *changed* in Symone. . . but at the time I just couldn't figure out what it was.

In retrospect, I was glad that I had been in the right mind to follow my instincts to sell Symone a fictitious story about my whereabouts for the three days I planned to be away from Columbus. Had I told her the truth— that I had taken a few extra days off work to fly to Philadelphia with a friend and distance myself from the overwhelming drama in my

Call It What You Want

life—she would have broken her neck to run and report it to Isaiah, just as she had reported *my lie*! The only person who knew of my exact location, and who I was spending time with, was Essence—the only person proven to have my back!

I reluctantly unmuted the call and started talking to Isaiah in the calmest voice I could muster. I didn't want him to know how annoyed I was with him or Symone's shady ass—whom I intended to serve a fat piece of my mind once I returned to Columbus.

"Okay, my apologies, Isaiah . . ." I began, plopping down on one of the porch chairs, and crossing my legs. "Now what is it that you were saying?" Isaiah heaved an exasperated sigh and arrogantly replied, "Man, miss me on all that formal shit, Kayla. You don't have to speak to me like I've ruined your goddamn day! C'mon babe . . . I know you're still mad at me for some of the silly shit I've done, but if you'll only calm down and give a brotha a chance, I promise I can make things great between us again. Like it used to be . . . You know you love me as much as I love you babe . . . quit playing games!"

Call It What You Want

"*Hmm . . .*" was all I could manage, even though there were at least a handful of wretched, ominous, and blasphemous things I wanted to scream at him! "Yeah, so like I was telling Symone and Ron, I wish you would've let me know about your plans for DC. It's pretty obvious that I wasn't invited, which is cool *I guess*. But you know how I feel about *our* home being left unattended and shit especially with those badass dirty kids who just moved next door to the Smiths!"

"Umm, well . . . I guess I didn't really think about any of that Isaiah, considering that we have an alarm system," I responded sarcastically.

"I guess you do have a point there. Yet and still . . . you never answered my question though, what time are you coming back tomorrow? I can pick you up from the airport, and maybe we can grab something to eat, so we can talk and shit . . ."

I slid right to the end of his statement, purposely skipping the part about the time of my arrival a second time. "What is it that we need to talk about, Isaiah?" I asked, with full knowledge that there were many things that needed to be discussed between us, beginning with how and when we were gonna tell the twins about our pending divorce. I think I had

somehow convinced myself that seeing or even speaking to Isaiah was

something that I would have been able to keep on the back burner—

forever. I *loathed* him just that much!

Isaiah paused as though he had to think about his answer before

responding, then said, "I . . . uh, we need to talk about us, Kayla. Our

marriage, and our future together. I fucked up . . . I know this. But I

can't stand living without you—the love of my muh-fuckin' life!" He

exhaled as if he was smoking—something he did when he was

drinking— then continued, "Look, I've been living in a fuckin' hotel,

alright. The Marriott has been chewing holes through my fuckin'

pockets, so much so that pretty soon I'm gonna have to start digging into

my savings to cover my stay. I need to be sleeping in *my* bed, in *my*

house, with *my* beautiful wife lying next to me. I'm tired of this

separation bullshit babe. I wanna come back home . . ."

"Isaiah—" I huffed, shaking my head in disbelief and frustration. "You

must really think the world revolves around you, huh? After all the shit

Call It What You Want

you've said and done, you really think I'm so pressed for your attention

that I'd jump back into your arms as if you didn't break my heart and

embarrass the shit out of me? *Pffttt!* I don't fuckin' think so—" I paused

as Blaze stepped out of the front door, his eyes searching for mine to

ensure I wasn't in distress. I held my index finger to my lips as an

indication for him not to speak and walked to the other side of the porch

to wrap up the conversation with Isaiah. "Listen . . ." I began in a

lowered tone, "I really can't get into this right now. Once I am back in

Columbus, we can resume this conversation but on my terms though—"

"On your terms?" he exclaimed, annoyed. "What the fuck is that

supposed mean, eh?" Isaiah snapped like a mad dog.

I could tell by the way the pace of his breathing had increased that he

wanted to cuss at me! He probably wanted to call me all kinds of names

and intimidate me with his aggression, as he had done so many times

before. I wasn't up to take his shit anymore. Before he could utter

another word, I held the power button down on my cellphone until the entire screen went black, slid it into my back pocket, and followed Blaze

back into the house.

*

"Gosh, I swear I wish I did not have to return to Columbus, at least not

as soon as tomorrow." I told Blaze as I prepared my suitcase for our

early flight due the next morning. "You just dunno how much at peace

I've been on during this trip. Thanks again for showing me a great time,

Blaze. I really, really appreciate you!"

"I'm glad to hear you enjoyed hanging with the family and I, because

we have all enjoyed your I'll be coming back in August for our family

reunion; you know that you are more than welcome to join, if you want

too. . ."

"Aww, thanks for the invite, Blaze, but the twins will be home from

their vacation by then, and I want to spend as much time with them as

possible before they go back to school. I'm hoping to close on my condo

in Pickerington before then, so the transition from our old life won't be

as difficult for them as I think it's gonna be.

Call It What You Want

I mean, Isaiah and the boys and I have always been together. Now that things have changed so drastically, I dunno how they are gonna feel, or how they are going to react to things…" I released a tired breath, shrugged, and shook my head. "Things are gonna be a challenging for us, I know. But we'll be alright!" I declared with a confident nod. "I am gonna make sure that those handsome boys of mine are good, no matter what!"

Blaze nodded in agreement and then excused himself as he disconnected his ringing phone from its charger and answered it. I continued to organize my suitcase and think about my children, as he chatted on the phone with one of his relatives. After his phone conversation ended, about 20 minutes later, we enjoyed a *surf 'n' turf* dinner at the restaurant on the first floor of the Sheraton. Then, we took a stroll around the block for sightseeing and for burning off some of the calories we had consumed during the entire trip, then returned to the room, thoroughly exhausted.

Call It What You Want

As soon as we stepped into the room, I kicked my sandals off and flopped down on the queen bed near the window that I had claimed the moment we had arrived in Philly.

Lying back with my head propped up on a few pillows, I powered my phone back up and sent a text message to the twins, letting them know that I loved and missed them and would be flying back to Columbus the next morning. Then, I turned on Pandora radio to listen to some of my favorite old-school jams. As Luther Vandross's "Wait for love..." played through the speakers of my cellphone, my glaze innocently fell on Blaze. He was once again chatting on the phone, while stuffing the pink and purple t-shirts he had purchased for his daughters into his baggage. I was glad that he was completely consumed by his conversation, as it gave me a little time to admire him from afar without any interruptions. Blaze was beautiful—inside and outside.

Everything about him was *dope*—from the way he passionately stared into your eyes when he spoke, grinned, and laughed with his mouth wide open, showing off his perfect white teeth. To the way he listened to

Call It What You Want

others' views with an open mind and made everyone who crossed his path feel appreciated.

From the first day Blaze McFadden strolled into C&O Counselling Center for his initial job interview, he had captured my attention like a bullhorn being blown in a relatively quiet auditorium! I remember him walking into the counselling center with a confident smile, dressed in a gray pinstriped suit, white shirt, and dark dress shoes, which not only made him appear timeless but also prompted all the women to gawk at him as though he was the finest breathing thing to have ever walked the Earth! *And, he smelled so damn good too!*

As if Blaze had read my thoughts during my brief moment of reflection, he turned towards me with a sly grin on his face, which made me blush with embarrassment. He ended his call, hooked the phone back up on the charger, and threw himself onto the bed—next to me. The soothing scent of his cologne wafted into my nose immediately, making me to leap out of the bed as if he had farted! I was too damn vulnerable for him to be so close to me, smelling and looking good enough to be

Call It What You Want

devoured whole. And seeing the fact that being alone with Blaze for those few days made me want him *bad as ever*, I didn't want the distraction of lust to complicate things between us. Once on my feet, I played it cool by digging into my overnight bag for my hairbrush, untying my ponytail, and brushing through my naturally thick and curly mane, as if that was what I had intended to do in the first place.

"Whoa Miss Lady, I didn't realize your hair was that long! What is it, velvet?" He teasingly quoted the movie *Coming to America*, as he watched me brush my elbow length mane from the bed. We both cracked up laughing.

"Uh no, silly!" I giggled. "This hair comes from my Dominican roots. Although my father and baby brother Omar wear their hair short, they've got this same wolf hair that's quite difficult to manage at times."

"Oh yeah?"

"Uh-huh . . ." I nodded.

"Sooo . . . I have a little confession to make," Blaze announced, with his signature grin. "*Hmm*, what's that?" I asked curiously.

Call It What You Want

"I am glad you decided to take this trip with me. You just don't know how long I have wanted to get you alone, just to see who the real Kayla is, outside of work . . ."

I laughed and shot him a silly glance. "Mmm…and your thoughts about me now, if you don't mind me asking?" Blaze chuckled. "All I can say, Miss Lady . . . I ain't tryna *hate* on your husband—he's who he is, as I'm who I am. But, uh . . . he has got to be the most selfish brotha on planet Earth to allow a bright, shiny diamond like you to slip through the cracks of his fingers. You're beautiful, sexy as hell, intelligent, hilarious, and fun to be around. You deserve to be loved *unconditionally* and spoiled and treated like the queen you are, instead of being abused and disregarded. I ain't nothing like ole dude, or even like any of the other brothas from your past. If I were ever given the opportunity to be with you the way I would *love* to be. . . I swear on everyone and everything I love, I would go above and beyond to ensure your happiness. These aren't just words of flattery. This is coming straight from my heart." He said, tapping the left side of his chest with his palm to add emphasis.

Call It What You Want

Chills ran through my body as those words dripped from his lips and oozed into my ears. I stood against the hotel room's chiffonier as stiff as a frozen fish, gawking at Blaze's reflection in the mirror as if a third eye had suddenly appeared on his forehead.

"Oh . . . uh, thank you but, um, yeah so, when did you say your vacation ended?" I asked nervously, attempting to change the topic altogether. Evidently, Blaze had caught on to what I was doing, because he chuckled and nodded his head as I rattled off like Rose Nylund from *The Golden Girls* when she recited one of her humorously peculiar stories of her hometown in St Olaf!

"My vacation starts this Friday, July 1st, and I'll be out of the office until Monday, the 11th. I think I had told you that my baby brother Omar was coming to town to celebrate the 4th of July with our eldest brother, Maxwell. I mean . . . Omar and Maxwell aren't blood related or whatever. Maxwell and I have the same mother while Omar and I share the same father. However, none of that matters . . . we're siblings, and that's that! Anyway, Maxwell normally throws a pool party at his six-

Call It What You Want

bedroom mini-mansion in Grove City, where people come not only to eat and drink until their stomachs are sitting in their laps but also to see how a good 'polygamists' gets down. My mom and I can't stand Maxwell's chosen lifestyle, but we love him along the women who are as in love with him as he is with them, if that makes any sense—"

Blaze chortled and stared at me through dreamy eyes. . .

"What? Why're you looking at me like that, Blaze? Am I talking too much?" I quizzed, with a side-eyed grin.

"Nope! Not at all! I enjoy listening to you talk to me."

"Then what's on your mind, Blaze?" I asked a second time, sneaking a look at my reflection in the mirror to ensure that I didn't have a booger dangling from my nose. "You're just an amazing woman. . . *that's all.*" Blaze smoothly affirmed, as he moved from the bed, took a few steps forward, and stood so close behind me that I felt the warmth of his breath on my nape. I thanked him for the compliment and tried to hide my growing anxiety by moving out of his way. However, he gently placed his hands on my shoulders to hold me in place, brushed his thick

Call It What You Want

lips against my ear, and crooned along with the song streaming from my

cellphone, *"Let me hold you tight, if only for one night. Let me keep you*

near, to ease away your fears. It will be so nice, if only for one night . . .

I won't tell a soul. No one has to know. If you want to beeeeeee, totally

discreet. I'll be by your side, if only for one night . . ." Oh, my goodness,

words cannot explain how his powerful voice, singing one of my

favorite songs by Luther Vandross, sent chills through my body like tiny

ants crawling down my skin! I thought I would faint right then and

there, but somehow, I retained my composure.

My breath quickened, as I felt his hands softly glide down my back,

until they came to rest on my hips. Our bodies swayed back and forth to

the rhythm of his voice and our silent lust.

Once I found the courage to turn around and gaze into Blaze's

hypnotizing eyes, curtained by long flowing eyelashes, I muttered

helplessly, "What are we doing, Blaze?"

He exhaled softly, licked his lips, and then pulled me close enough to

feel that his heart was pounding just as fast as mine. *"Let me take you*

Call It What You Want

home and keep you safe and warm. Till the early dawn, warms up to the sun. It would be so nice, if only for one night . . ." Blaze found my neck and softly sucked on it, cupping my face with his large hands behind my ears. As he caressed my cheeks with his thumbs, his thick soft lips brushed against mine, sending sparks of fire through my body.

"Miss Lady . . ." he whispered, as the tiny space between us became invisible. "Do you want me to stop?" Without a single word or second thought, I kissed Blaze—longingly and passionately. I was completely at his mercy, as his kisses melted like sugar on my tongue. And when he lifted me off of my feet effortlessly, I didn't even fret about my weight or the possibility of him dropping me on the floor. Instead, I wrapped my legs around his waist like a pretzel, continuing to suck on his juicy lips, and enjoyed the short ride to the bathroom.

I hungrily bit down on my bottom lip, as Blaze allowed me to undress him —blessing my sight with the intricate designs blanketing his chocolate chest and back. Ooooh, he was so freaking sexy that I just couldn't keep my hands off of him! That night, Blaze and I made love for the very first time. And by the time he had *smacked it up, flipped it, and licked me down*, I couldn't feel my damn toes!

Chapter 19

*F*rom the first kiss to the final orgasm, the night I spent making love to Blaze was *magical*! I used to be as proud as the queen of Egypt to be able to boast about Isaiah being my first and only lover—a man who seemed enormously more skilled in the art of lovemaking compared to the countless lovers my girlfriends swanked about.

But, after what I had experienced with Mr. Blaze McFadden, my supposition that nobody could love me the way Isaiah did became a big fat red VOID!

Blaze's love was so, so, damn *good*! He had me completely subdued. Every time he looked into my eyes, moaned my name, or kissed my lips, my body lit up like a damn pinball machine— making me want more and more of him! And, in addition, to his *incredible* girth and length, Blaze was as gentle as the moon . . .

Call It What You Want

The following morning, Blaze and I woke up an hour later than we were supposed to and ended up missing our 5-am flight. By the time we made it back to Columbus, it was nearly noon and raining buckets throughout central Ohio!

Seeing no other feasible alternative, we grabbed lunch at one of those ridiculously overpriced airport bistros, chatted it up for a while, and then took a cab to his place. I know this may sound corny, but I was having such a good time with Blaze, that I almost wanted to cry when thoughts of returning to my *"regular life"* seeped into my head. I knew I would have to face my harsh *reality* eventually. But I damn sure wasn't ready for it!

"Miss Lady . . ." Blaze called out to me as I stared out of the cab window, thinking about all the things I needed to do when I got home—particularly the fact that I had agreed to meet up with Isaiah. I could only imagine what kind of tricks that clown had up his sleeves. . .

"Hmm?" I replied, turning my head to face him.

Call It What You Want

"A penny for your thoughts, *beautiful*. But I'll give you 20 dollars if those thoughts are of me and what we shared last night!" We laughed in unison, and then he said, "Slide on over here and talk to me, won't you? Let me hold you for a little while . . ." He smiled and motioned me to move closer. Without a second thought, I slid over to Blaze's side, rested my head on his chest, and concentrated only on following the rhythm of his heart until we reached our destination.

"You know, you don't have to go if you don't want to . . . Blaze suggested softly, after we arrived at his house and he began loading my luggage into the backseat of my car.

"You can just stay the night and go to work from here; if you like. I enjoy having you around. . ." he said.

"Blaze, you are sooo sweet; I swear you are!" I remarked as a blush lit up my grinning face. "But I've got a bunch of stuff I *have* to take care of today. I've gotta check on my parents' house, run by the grocery store, and as I was telling you on the plane, Isaiah finally wants to 'talk'. . . Ugh, only God knows how that entire thing is gonna turn out.

Call It What You Want

Pray for a sistah, wouldja?" Blaze nodded and shot me a serious glance.

"You sure you'll be alright, speaking to him alone and all?" he asked, legitimately concerned for my safety, as I had shared with him several instances of Isaiah's aggressive, and sometimes violent, behavior.

I waved my hands dismissively and smiled.

"Ah, you don't have to worry about me. . . Isaiah's antics can be as unpredictable as his temper, but I am taking all the necessary precautions to ensure my safety *this* time.

I'm gonna see if he'll meet me at a Starbucks or someplace like that— just in case he decides to start up with his typical 'bullying' crap. Regardless of what he says or does though, it changes absolutely NOTHING between him and me. Isaiah and I are over Blaze. I just want to be free . . . free of him and his family. *That's all*. That's not asking for too much, is it?"

"Nah . . . I can't say that it is Miss Lady. But he and I are two different breeds of men, you know what I mean? If you're serious about giving dude his walking papers, I'd. . . uh . . . like to be the man you allow to love you more than that brotha' ever did. I am not trying to rush things between us, but I care a lot about you Miss Lady. *Always have.* I would one day like to be able to call you *my* lady, as opposed to Miss Lady."

I smiled and bowed my head shyly, only for Blaze to gently grab my face and pull my chin up to face him. "I want to discover who are . . . I wanna love you *Kayla,* the way you deserved to be loved." Just like magic, our pheromones were once again enraged! We kissed passionately and stripped each other of our clothes until we reached his bedroom. Blaze buried his face in between my thighs, before the sounds of his headboard *knocking . . . knocking . . . knocking* intertwined with our sensual moans.

About an hour later, Blaze escorted me back into his garage, to my car. As I thanked him for *everything,* and promised I'd give him a call later on that evening, he tilted his head to the side and gazed into my eyes for a few seconds. Then, he smiled and pulled me into a warm, tight embrace, as though we were never going to see each other again.

Call It What You Want

After planting an affectionate kiss on my forehead, he reiterated, "I meant everything I said to you. I can offer you an abundance of truth and loyalty if you allow me to. . ." He softly kissed my lips, then both of my cheeks and smiled. "Do what you have to do with your husband. Remember, *I am only a phone call away*. . ."

Chapter 20

I was less than five minutes away from the house when I felt my phone vibrating in my purse. I quickly dug it out, assuming the call was from one of my homegirls checking to make sure I had safely made it back to Columbus. Much to my dismay, the word "husband" flashed on my screen, making me feel as if I was going to barf—right then and there! Pressing the "ignore" button, I quickly shoved the phone back into my purse and immediately started bawling—my guilt had finally crept in and hit my conscious like a loaded truck.

'You ought to be ashamed of yourself for the low dirty shit you have done, Kayla. You went through all that arguing—bickering, fighting, and whining over Isaiah's affair with Odessa—and now you've turned

around and done the exact same thing. Fucking and sucking the man who you claimed was "just a friend". Just go ahead and admit it, you've been wanting to screw Blaze for what, the last five years or so, eh? All that the man had to do was take you on a cheap trip, treat you a little bit better than your lowlife husband, and BAM—just like that; your legs and mouth were wide open, ready to devour him! You ain't no fuckin' better than your husband! You my dear are a cheater too! Two wrongs don't make a right, sis! Sincerely, your conscience!

Shrugging feebly, I let out a deep sigh and wiped away the tears from my eyes. For 14 years, I had tried to be the "perfect, super wife" that everyone, including Isaiah, believed me to be. But I was now done with all of that! My time away helped me realize that Isaiah had taken way more from my emotional bank than he had ever given me.

After sitting back thinking about all of the horrible things that he had said and done to me, right up to the stunt he and his mother had tried to pull on me in our kitchen, my disgust for Isaiah had multiplied, to the point of no return. . .

Call It What You Want

Turning onto our street, an eerie feeling of déjà vu' crept up my spine, interrupting the confident thoughts that had been floating in my head a few seconds earlier.

Parked in our driveway was Isaiah's F-150, as though he still lived there— just as his momma's minivan had been stationed on the night of our epic "kitchen brawl". Fear sat on me like a pillow covering my mouth and nose, as I blinked my eyes multiple times, hoping for Isaiah's parked truck to be a figment of my imagination.

Once I realized that it wasn't, so many questions began prancing around in my mind that my hands trembled and I felt sick to my stomach!

Oh God, why is he here? How long has he been in the house? Has he moved his things back in? Has he been staying here since I left for Philly? Has he been meddling with my things? Did he simply come by to pick up his mail? Am I safe?

I had not laid eyes on Isaiah since the day I had left him curled up in a fetal position on our kitchen floor, clutching his nuts and groaning like a dying moose. Certainly, he had not forgotten any of that!

~ 294 ~

Call It What You Want

And if I had gauged him right, he had had more than enough time to sit

back and contemplate the many terrible things he would say and do to

pay me back for my unexpected response to him and his sociopathic

mother. I don't think anyone related to Isaiah knew a damn thing about

peace or letting go; it was always about power, intimidation, and more

importantly, revenge . . .

After I parked my car next to Isaiah's, I sent a group text to Symone and

Essence, informing them that I had made it home safely, and that I had

an uninvited *husband* waiting for me inside the house . . . In other

words, HELP ME, because Isaiah could be as unpredictable as Ohio

weather!

With my heart pounding in my ears, the nervousness I felt practically

diluted the dull drumming resonating through my entire being. I slowly

walked around to the passenger side of the car, fixing my eyes on the

front windows to detect any kind of movement inside the house. I

retrieved my bags from the car, and even though it was still pouring

down heavily, I took my sweet time walking to the front door.

Call It What You Want

As I stepped into the foyer, I was greeted by the sounds of *Boney James*, a carpet of beautiful red rose petals along a trail of vanilla-scented candles.

With my mouth hanging wide open from the shock of the matter, I dropped my wet luggage to the floor and followed the candle trail into the living room, where more crushed red roses—with a hint of pink ones added this time—spelled out "I LOVE YOU, KAYLA" across the floor. Any other woman would have been over the moon to be pampered this way, especially by a handsome, dimpled faced man, who could easily trick one into believing that his heart was pure and life was "all about them". It was a nice gesture and the scene was breathtaking, but I was NOT *impressed*!

"Oh, hey babe! How's it going?" Isaiah called out as he sauntered into the living room from the kitchen with one of his "Kiss the cook" aprons tied around his waist. He grinned and hugged me firmly, then said, "Lunch will be ready shortly. Why don't you get out of those wet clothes and meet me at the dining table in about fifteen minutes, okay?"

Call It What You Want

After a hot shower, I applied some of the organic shea butter that I had purchased in Philly to my body, tied my hair into a sloppy bun, and threw on a pair of blue denim cut-off shorts and a tan crop top, along with a pair of matching sneakers. As much as I wanted to slip into a pair of pajamas and sleep for a few hours before running my errands, I did not want Isaiah to get any funny ideas by assuming that he had been invited to please my body—which, as far as I was concerned, would NEVER happen again.

"Ah! There's my beautiful wife!" He beamed when I sauntered into the dining room and took a seat at the head of the table. "I called you earlier to let you know that you don't have to worry about running by the grocery store today; I've already taken care of it."

He beamed proudly at me, as if he was expecting applause, or a standing ovation even. "I bought everything on the list you had stuck on the refrigerator, plus some other little things I know you enjoy snacking on. I even picked up an extra box of Gain, seeing that we were almost out of it . . ."

Call It What You Want

"Oh well, thank you Isaiah. That was very, uh, thoughtful of you," I stated bluntly with a nod.

"How much do I owe you for your trouble?" Although he never replied, I could tell by the way he sighed, clenched his jaw as if he had bitten down on his tongue, and began walking back and forth between the kitchen and dining room, that my honest question had irritated his soul. I sat in silence as I observed him fancy the table up with a large bowl of salad, hot plates of shrimp and chicken Alfredo, warm garlic sticks, and two glasses of red wine, and patiently waited for him to make the next move.

"So, did you have a good trip, babe?" He asked, after taking a seat at the other end of the table and fixing me with a serious stare.

I nodded, nibbling on a small piece of garlic bread. "I *did* . . . thanks for asking . . ."

"Great! I'm glad you enjoyed yourself," He asserted with a nod, flashing his dimpled smile.

Call It What You Want

"But I wish I could've been there with you. I don't like the idea of you traveling all by yourself and shit. There are some real crazy muhfuckas in the world who prey on beautiful women like you. So, the next time you decide to leave the city, whether it's for work or pleasure, I'd appreciate it if you let me know beforehand, so I can come along . . ."

I looked at Isaiah as though he was two kinds of crazy and thought, *Boy, I ain't telling you shit, and you're not going anywhere with me. EVER.*

"So, how much have you missed me?" he quizzed, making me damn near choke on the bread I was about to swallow—so much so that I had to spit it out on a napkin and cough a few times to clear my throat.

"Oh my goodness, that delicious bread must've gone down the wrong way!" I chortled, thumping my chest a few times so as to avoid answering.

Over the next 30 minutes or so, I sat at the dining table with my lips sealed tight, listening to Isaiah blabber on about how much he loved me, how much he regretted being involved in that scandalous affair with the

Call It What You Want

"*garbage-pail kid*", and how desperately he wanted to fix our marriage. I tried to keep my mouth shut for the most part, simply nodding as and when needed, as I would do during an intense counselling session with one of my clients. I didn't want to say anything that would make him think there was any chance of reconciliation. Nor did I want to risk upsetting the fella and receiving the "payback" beating that I was certain he had simmering on the back burner.

"So, did Mama Libby tell you that she and I spoke for about two hours the other day?"

"Huh? What in the world did you speak to my mom about, Isaiah?" I gasped and shot him a glance, clearly annoyed. "Us . . . babe, what do you think, hmm?" Isaiah shrugged innocently. "Us?" I shrieked, grimacing. "What about 'us', huh? I hope you didn't call all the way down south in search of a damn 'pity-party' for the little situation you've got going on with your little redheaded whore! My mom can't handle that type of pressure Isaiah, and I'd rather you NOT invite everyone into our business. This crap is embarrassing enough as it is!"

Call It What You Want

"C'mon now, Kayla . . . don't sit up here and try to play me like I'm a little bitch! I ain't never been the type of dude to be runnin around tryna get mutha-fuckas to feel sorry for me about shit. I'm a grown ass muh-fuckin' man and I deal with my shit in my own fuckin' way, regardless of whether it is satisfactory to you or not! The only reason I called your mom's phone is because I couldn't get in contact with the twins. And when she asked how *we* were doing, I assumed that you had filled her in on the bullshit Odessa's raggedy ass lied about. Especially since you broke your fuckin' neck to tell Symone and Essence's bald-headed ass about it! If I was wrong for that, I'll take that shit on the chin. But let's get one thing straight: I didn't call your momma looking for no muh-fuckin' sympathy—so you can get that thought outta ya mind right now!"

"Symone?" I repeated shaking my head.

"The two of you are really starting to get on my fuckin' nerves! I dunno what kind of slick shit yall have got going on, but it is not a good look!

Call It What You Want

And watch what you say about Essence, Isaiah. Taking childish jabs at my friends doesn't excuse the fucked up shit that you've done, *Isaiah*!

"How the fuck am I being childish?" He barked as he thumped his chest. "What, because I called that bitch *bald-headed*, eh? She is fuckin' bald-headed, Kayla. . . this is a fuckin fact"

He angrily pushed himself up from the table, stomped into the kitchen, and grabbed a beer from the refrigerator. After taking a gulp, he continued. "To keep it real with you and shit, I really don't give a rat's ass about that *hoe*! I've heard a bunch of unflattering shit about Essence's trifling *wannabe* gangster ass, and frankly, I ain't too comfortable with my wife hangin' out with a measly bitch who thinks she's the female version of Don Magic Juan! Ole *bisexual cunt*. . . Keep on hangin with that nasty bitch, I bet she'll be tryna suck on your pussy as I hear she has done many times before to other women."

"Whaat! Now wait a damn minute. Where is all of that coming from?" I asked, essentially waiting for him to confirm my suspicions of Symone running her mouth on Essence's personal business AGAIN!

Call It What You Want

Isaiah took another swig of his beer and dismissed my question with a sweeping hand gesture. "Ahh, the source of my information is neither here nor there, Kayla. Like I said, if I was wrong in telling your mom about something you should've shared with her yourself—way before flapping your lips in front of your nosey-ass friends—I apologize, alright? I been on this earth long enough to know how yall women get down when it comes to gangin up on men for some of the stupid shit we do. I wanted to make sure my side of the story was on the record, before folks stared forming screwed-up opinions and talking shit about me."

"Ah! I see, you don't wanna be talked about as yall have been doing in my face *and* behind my back for years eh?" I lashed back boldly.

"I don't give a hoot about what you say, Isaiah. It was not your place to tell my mother ANYTHING—*period!* I bet you didn't even tell her the whole truth. Probably worked your ass off to minimize as much of your part in all of this embarrassing shit as possible. Huh, Isaiah? Just like you have always done!"

Call It What You Want

"See, there you go—jumping to conclusions again! I WAS completely honest with your mother Kayla . . . you can ask her. After I broke everything down, I even asked her guidance on what exactly I needed to do to make things right and get you back into my life. If your muh-fuckin ass would chill the fuck out and listen to what I'm trying to say, you will see that our conversation had nothing to do with a goddamn pity party."

Isaiah paused, tossed his empty bottle into the trash can, and then sauntered over to the dining table, where I was sitting with my legs crossed. He kneeled next to me and tried to pull my chin so that I would look into his eyes. But I quickly pushed his hand away and turned my head to the opposite direction so that he would get the message—loud and clear: I was not falling for the emotional game he was trying to play with me.

"Look Kayla, I don't wanna fight with you . . . or make shit any worse for us than it already is.

Call It What You Want

All I wanna do is just hash this shit out like a pair of adults, so we can move forward with our marriage. Please . . . please . . . please . . . don't let this one mistake ruin what we have, baby . . ."

"One mistake, eh?" I snapped, glaring at Isaiah as if he had lost his damn mind. "Negro pleeeze! Who the hell do you think you're playing with, huh? Having a full-fledged affair with a freakin' *lunatic* and creating a child in the process is not just a freakin oversight —it was DELIBERATE nasty ass! You knew exactly what you were doing and the risks you were taking each and every time you put your damn lips on that worthless piece of shit or slid your dick into her body unprotected! But you didn't give a damn about who you hurt in the process, now did ya? Of course you didn't! The only person you have ever cared about is yourself! I guess I should be grateful to Odessa for the insight, because had she not showed up at my office that day and aired your dirty laundry, I'd probably still be floating around looking like a goddamn fool, thinking our marriage was solid . . . *Pfftt!*"

Call It What You Want

Isaiah stood up, crossed his arms across his chest, and nodded. "Okay . .

. you're right babe. I've apologized about this shit over and over again.

If it makes you feel better, I'll say it again Kayla, I am fuckin SORRY . .

. what more can I say, hmm?" Isaiah continued, "Getting involved with

that bitch was one of the biggest mistakes I've made in my entire fuckin'

life! *I fucked up*! I gambled our marriage because I was stupid enough to

believe I could use that bitch to get some of the freaky shit I like out of

my system. Things I knew you weren't down for."

"Huh? What the hell is that supposed to mean?"

"It means that I respect you, Kayla. I respect you enough to not force

any of my weird ass sexual fetishes on you. Odessa is a freak with a

helluva lot of experience. I played with it for a while, and after I got all

that I wanted from that skeezer, I bounced—which obviously pissed her

off and prompted her to come see you. Regardless of the bullshit she has

fed you, our relationship was purely sexual. I *never* loved that bitch,

never told her I'd marry her. And I sure as hell NEVER mentioned

anything about her having my baby!

Call It What You Want

That's why I laughed at her dumb ass when she tried to hit me up with that ole 'hood-rat' entrapment bullshit!"

"The what?" I asked for clarity. "Hood-rat entrapment . . . you know how these hood rats pretend to be down for a ninja when they think they're benefitting from some shit. Then, as soon as you let 'em know that the party is over, they very conveniently pop up pregnant. You haven't been away from the hood that long. You know how these worthless bitches are . . ." I groaned, shaking my head in disgust.

"The funny thing about Odessa is that we NEVER had unprotected sex, and she knows this very well. In fact, she'd actually cop an attitude with me when I doubled up on the 'magnums' talking about, "*You treat me like I'm one of those nasty bitches on the streets. . .*" In my mind, I'm like, '*Yeah, that's exactly what you're—a fuckin' nasty bitch! Take this dick, and I'll holla back . . .*' It's bad enough that I wasted more than an hour with a skeezer who is now tryna ruin my goddamn life. But I wasn't gonna risk catching a disease from her ass and bringing that shit home to you. I ain't perfect Kayla, but I've got a little more class than

Call It What You Want

that. Don't you know that, hmm?" I stared at Isaiah for a few seconds with my head cocked to the side, and said, "Interesting . . .Since you brought that up, I do have one question for you."

"Shoot." He nodded, with an *'I will answer anything for you, baby'* look on his face. "So, you claim to have been overly protective about 'our' health—you know, with doubling up on the condoms and all that—what did you use to protect your mouth, sir? I am sure you've sucked on both sets of her funky-ass lips, and God only knows what other parts of her body you've savored . . ." I spat, rolling my eyes.

Embarrassed and completely caught off guard by my question-cum-statement, Isaiah took the insult on the chin and shook his head, mumbling, "Wow! You talk about me being childish, what the fuck do you call that petty shit, Kayla? Here I am—sharing my truth in spite of how awkward all of this is—and all you wanna do is taunt me about some fuckin oral sex? That's petty as fuck, but it's cool. If hittin me below the belt makes you feel better, *have at it*! I still fuckin love you the same. Despite what you might think of me and the shit I have done with this bitch, I'm not the father of her baby, and I put that shit on my life! I ain't tryna put nobody's business on blast but uh—"

"Yeah . . . yeah . . . I already know," I remarked, cutting him off mid-sentence. "She already told me how you forced her to fuck your 'homeboy' yada, yada, yada!"

"Forced her?" Isaiah repeated sharply, shaking his head. "See, this is the stupid shit I'm talkin' bout with this fuckin'skeezer. She's always tryna act like she's been victimized and shit, knowing damn well that she's a thirsty-ass hoe who will do anything for a little bit of attention! Did I pass her on to one of my buddies? *Hell yeah*! But I didn't make her do no shit that she didn't already want to do!"

"So who is this friend, Isaiah?" He paused and looked around the room nervously, then back at me. "Babe, I can't tell you that . . . I ain't the snitching type, you know what I'm saying? That shit is between Odessa and her baby daddy. I ain't got nothing to do with it. . ."

"Huh? Dude, you've got everything to do with it! Because, from what I understand, you're the one who introduced your so-called 'homeboy' to that lunatic in the first place. I just hope whoever this man is, he isn't married, because that'd be real shady of you—pulling another family into your stupid shenanigans!"

"Whatever, woman!" Isaiah snapped dismissively. "I ain't pulled nobody into no muhfuckin' thang. Grown folks do what grown folks do. Period!" By now, I was up on my feet, clearing away our untouched meal from the dining table. With my back to Isaiah, I questioned, "So, what about the other women, Isaiah?"

"Say what?" he asked. "Well yeah . . . while you and your crew were wasting time trashing our house, sir, you dropped your little black phone," I announced, whirling around to face him. "You know the little black phone that housed all your little dirty secrets—text messages, photos, and multiple X-rated videos starring the man who does no wrong!"

Isaiah's face went completely slack; his eyes were as wide as two giant saucers and his body grew so stiff that it was hard to say whether he was still breathing or not!

Call It What You Want

He could not manage a single word out of his pie hole.

All he could do was look at me with pleading eyes before dropping his head shamefully. "How can I fix this, babe? Tell me, please," Isaiah begged, walking up behind me, attempting to circle his arms around my waist. I pushed his hands away and growled, an irritated look on my face, "Boy pleeeze!"

As Isaiah and I continued to go back and forth, I realized that his cellphone had been flashing the entire time we were in the kitchen.

I honestly could not say if he was intentionally ignoring his phone—as I assumed he had done with me when I "thought" we were happy. Or if he had actually been so absorbed in our conversation that he had become oblivious to the back-to-back incoming calls.

Leaning against the sink with my arms folded across my chest as Isaiah continued to plead his case, he must have noticed me eyeing his phone. Abruptly, our conversation came to a halt, as he snatched his phone from his hip and answered it in an exasperated tone.

Call It What You Want

"Wasup Momma? Whatcha need? I'm in the middle of something and don't have much time to talk . . . ." Hearing him say "*Momma*" was all I needed to hear to understand that our conversation was over. I didn't even want to think about Bertha's ugly-musty smelling ass, let alone be compelled to stand around and listen to her manly voice bark on about some inconsequential bullshit.

Isaiah had grabbed the back of my shorts and pulled me so close to him that I could hardly breath. "Yeah, I heard whatcha' said, Momma . . . and like I'm tryna tell you, we're gonna have to discuss that shit another fuckin' time! Right now, I'm with my wife, tryna make shit right . . . you say what? Nah, nah nah . . . c'mon now Momma . . . don't play with me like that, aight? DON'T-FUCKIN-PLAY-WITH-ME! *I swear to God Momma. . .*" I do not know who ended the phone call—Isaiah or Bertha. But whatever she had said made him angry enough to breathe FIRE! His hands were trembling as he embraced me from behind, and his heart was pounding so hard that I could feel it vibrating through my back!

Call It What You Want

The next thing I knew, there was a loud maddening honking outside the house, whose source had to be pretty close by, because both Isaiah and I were equally startled at the same time. All we could hear was a continuous HOOOOOOOOOONK, followed by screeching tires!

"FUCK!" Isaiah yelled, glancing at his phone and shoving it into the pocket of his shorts. "OH-MY-FUCKIN-GOD! This is cannot be happening!"

"What is it Isaiah?" I squawked nervously. "What going on?"

"Look, I'll explain this shit to you later . . . right now, I just want you to stay inside—with the doors locked! Aight? I don't want you involved in anymore of my shit!" He called out over his shoulder, marching through the hallway, towards the foyer. Acting on impulse, I took off behind him in a run. And soon as I stepped foot into the foyer and peered out of our glass door, I closed my eyes and said a quick prayer, because shit had just got real . . .

Call It What You Want

Chapter 21

*F*rom my position behind the glass door, I could see Isaiah standing near the driver's side of the reddish purple Taurus that, I assumed, was responsible for the loud honking that had shaken awake our relatively quiet neighborhood.

With my view slightly hindered because of the distance between the car and me, I was unable to catch a glimpse of who Isaiah was talking to, or make out what was being said. However, the passionate flailing of his arms and the agitated bobbing of his head made it apparent that not only was he pissed off, but some serious shit was about to go down!

Before I allowed myself to get too riled up about the situation happening outside of our house I tried to convince myself that the obvious disagreement was nothing more than another one of Isaiah's meddlesome relatives having an immature temper tantrum because of some kind of bullshit that Bertha's manipulative ass had sowed into their already warped minds. She was known to do messy shit like that—get everyone a little peeved by blabbing their business to others, along with

Call It What You Want

a few amplified lies added to it. Then, she'd sit back and watch as her loved ones or so-called friends went head-to-head with one painful insult followed by another, until the situation became physical and someone ended up getting hurt. . .

Anxiously shifting my weight from one foot to the other, I pondered on whether I should step outside to see what the commotion was all about, or just simply mind my own damn business. I played with the thought of suggesting to Isaiah that he and his "peeps" move their little quarrel over to the next street, or even to a Walmart parking lot—to spare our family the embarrassment of their "ghetto shenanigans".

But, I changed my mind on that thought real quick, because I did not want Isaiah to mistake my suggestion as an indication that I was interested in proceeding with the conversation we were having in the kitchen, before we were rudely interrupted by the blaring horn. *Which I absolutely did not*!

Call It What You Want

Just as I had decided to walk away from the door and leave Isaiah to take care of his own business, the passenger door of the car flung open and out popped Bertha's obnoxious ass.

It felt like someone had instantly punched me in my stomach, as I eyeballed her bald-headed, grisly-looking ass hobble around the car and buck up in Isaiah's face, wagging her funky index finger at him as though he were still a child.

Now, let me make one thing clear: I could not have cared less about what Bertha was saying or doing to her *trifling* son, as he deserved all the bad shit that came his way. The thing that chapped my ass, was that fact that she had shamelessly brushed off my warnings to never show up to or around my home *again* unless she was prepared to suffer some serious consequences!

I swear to God, I *hate* Bertha, and the feeling was probably mutual. If that wicked witch had fallen off the face of the earth at that very moment, I would have been secretly "jumping for joy"!

Call It What You Want

In hindsight, with the tension between she and I being so high, I probably should have simply turned my back on the escalating bullshit in the front of my house, popped in a movie or better, I should have locked myself in my bedroom and read a few inspiring verses from the bible. Instead, I pulled my cellphone from my pocket, texted "3603=911" to Symone and Essence's phones, took off my gold hoop earrings and the matching chain around my neck, and began flying through the house like a bat out of hell, in search of the steel bat I had gotten from Mrs. Maybelle, for *protection*.

As I rushed through the living room towards our attached garage, my attention was drawn to the active scene outside of the bay window. Bertha was screaming obscenities and swinging her fists wildly at Isaiah, aiming for his face.

As I watched him flinch and stagger back in an attempt to block his mother's blows, my eyes unexpectedly fell on the long, pale, freckled face of the driver-ODESSA!

Call It What You Want

In that instant, I lost my train of thought and bolted out of the house at the pace of freaking bullet, ready to *kick someone's ass!*

"What the fuck! Bertha . . . Why did you bring this POOR EXCUSE of a human being to our fuckin' house, huh? What in the hell is wrong with you, lady? Have you lost your goddamn mind?" I yelled, as I stood next to Isaiah, with my fists clenched and my eyes locked on both the uninvited guests.

Bertha flinched at the seriousness in my tone, then flashed a brazen smirk, before taking a few steps backwards to inch closer to the driver's side of the car—next to her newfound friend. Isaiah moved to stand in front of me and tried to pull me into a hug, in order to quell my growing anger at his mother and his side-chick. *I was not having it!* As soon as he started with, "Babe . . . now hold up. . ." I shot him a lethal painful stare, and had it not been for him catching a hold of my tightly clenched fists, I would have tried to knock his soul from his body—just for putting me in such a fucked-up situation!

Call It What You Want

"Get your filthy hands off me!" I growled as anger boiled through my body as hot as lava. "I am so fuckin' sick and tired of you, your mammie, and that dusty, redhead whore's bullshit that I could kill all you demented maniacs and not even bat a damn eyelash!" I yapped while smacking his hands away from my body. Turning my gaze back to Bertha, I said, "Tell me why, Bertha . . . Help me understand why you felt the need to bring HER to our home? The divorce has been filed and I am done dealing with ANYONE linked to your toxic ass. What else do you want from me, eh? If bringing HER over here was one of your attempts to throw some shit in my face, you're wastin' your time Bertha! We all know Odessa is your 'pick',"

I declared with a dramatic sweep of my hands. "And trust me, I am gooood with that! You just dunno know how freakin' ecstatic I'll be when our divorce is final and I'll never, ever, EVER have to be in the company of you worthless pieces of shit! Oh Lord, I cannot wait to be free of all of you EARTH DISTURBERS!" I glanced at Odessa, shook my head, and chuckled sneeringly, "Hmph! And while you're sitting up

Call It What You Want

there grinning like a goddamn fool, I hope you realize what you are about to get yourself into. Regardless of what you have heard about me, that woman right there, standing next to you, is as wicked as they come! Give it a little time, boo, and you will see exactly what I am talking about! *Good fuckin' luck to ya, Odessa!*"

"Kayla, CHILL THE FUCK OUT!" Isaiah squawked hotly, as he yanked on my arm. Pulling me close enough to get a whiff his foul breath. "I told you to let this shit go and take your ass back in the muhfuckin' house. You ain't gotta say anything else to either one of them. Just please . . . please Kayla, go on back inside and let me handle this!"

"Pfftt! As I told you before, get your goddamn hands off of me and move outta my way!"

I snapped boldly while attempting to push Isaiah out of my way, so I could say a few more words to *'Dumb and Dumber'* who were chuckling and whispering with each other. "I specifically told your mom NOT to fuck with me or bring her ass around to MY house and look at

Call It What You Want

what she does! Look at this shit . . ." I yelled, pointing to Odessa, who

seemed pleasantly entertained by all of the drama.

"She brought your BITCH or should I say, your 'baby momma' to our

fuckin' house! Your mother is out of fuckin line *again!"*

As Isaiah desperately tried to calm me down, I noticed Bertha and

Odessa repeatedly glance at each other and snicker at my evident

frustration. This only infuriated me further, making me want to wipe the

smirks off their ugly faces and shove them right up Isaiah's reckless

asshole!

"Oh, so you think this shit is funny, eh?" I snapped at

Bertha. "You're like a sneeze away from your 90th birthday, and

probably should be somewhere knitting a blanket or some fuckin' socks,

but here you are . . . tarnishing relationships and keeping a bunch of shit

going. Why don't you go somewhere else with your bullshit, ya' big

funky bully! And just leave me the fuck alone. . . *Damn!"*

I paused long enough to shake my head at her before continuing,

"Bertha, you are one SHITTY human being. But, you're gonna get what

Call It What You Want

you've got coming real fuckin soon, and I'll be the first one laughing my

fat ass off, as Karma rips your rotten ass to SHREDS!"

Bertha craned her neck backwards dramatically, glancing over her

shoulders animatedly, as though I was speaking to someone other than

her. Turning her head to look back at me, she chuckled lightly and

replied in her everyday ghoulish voice, "Shiid! Gurl, I dunno who the

fuck ya think ya yappin' at, but you betta take ya fat ass on into the

house like Izzy told ya to and stuff ya face with a box of doughnuts or

somethin', foe' I slap your teeth outta ya head! Lemme tell YOU

something, ya big-fat disrespectful cow. I ain't nowhere near 90 years

old, and ya damn well know it! You must have me confused with your

hunchback-of-Notre Dame-lookin' mammie, cause I know for a fact that

I don't look nearly as rough in the face as she does. Hell . . . as a matter

of fact, I look better than your fat funky ass, which is probably one of

the reasons you can't stand me in the first place! Hahaha! And, for the

record, *FATTY* when it comes to my son ISAIAH WARD, I can do

Call It What You Want

whatever the fuck I wanna do, *when* I wanna do it, including coming to

MY SON'S house, whenever the fuck I feel like visiting.

How about that, smart ass?" Bertha leaned against the car and let out a

thunderous belch; then, flapping her crusty hands at me like I was an

annoying flea, she spat, "Now run along, hussy! I'm done talkin' to your

stupid ass. Get the fuck outta my sight!"

"Pahaahaa! Yap, yap . . . that's right Momma B! Go on and let Pigatha

know that her and that little Chihuahua bark ain't scaring no muhfuckin'

body!" Odessa chimed in, as her gigantic sneakered feet hit the

pavement and she pulled herself out of the car. Laughing like a loon, she

stood next to Bertha and crossed her arms over her enlarged breasts—

glaring at me, looking like a pregnant red-haired jolly Green Giant.

Once again, Isaiah was back in my ear, citing reasons as to why I should

ignore his mistress and mother's taunts and not stoop to their level of

pettiness. Everything he was saying at that moment made perfect

sense—this was *his* battle to fight . . . his mom and Odessa *were stupid*

bitches who were merely looking for trouble . . . I was a *better woman* than the either of them could ever be, and I should be the *bigger* person

and walk away. But my anger would not permit any type of peace to

seep into my mind, nor convince me to turn my other cheek. I had to

finish this thing that Bertha had started, even if it included me serving

those bitches up with the beat-down they so deserved. "Oh, blah blah

blah! Enough of all that mushy pussy shit already!" Odessa announced,

causing Isaiah to freeze up on the foiled pep talk he was giving me, and

turn his attention to Odessa. She looked past Isaiah fixated her eyes on

me and jeered, "Unhand my man, bitch! Before you get slammed on that

fat back again, just like you did . . . what was that, like a month ago?

You're sittin' up here, talkin' about how Momma B should be ashamed

of herself. You should be ashamed of how you called yourself bucking

up to the grandmother of your children and ended up gettin' your ass

whooped in your own damn house!

Ugh . . . you are so fuckin' pathetic! Now I see why Isaiah was cheating

on your ass, you big stupid!" "AYE, bitch! Hold the fuck up! Watch

your muhfuckin' mouth when you're speaking to my wife, aight? You can say whatever the fuck you wanna say to me, but degrading my wife ain't happenin'! This is probably one of the reasons your monkey ass is so goddamn lonely—you're a fuckin psycho, Odessa. IN FUCKIN-SANE!"

Odessa had finally awakened Isaiah's inner demon, as he began spitting out hateful words with the ferocity and speed of a firing machine gun. Isaiah's temper was almost like TNT: once the sparks started to crackle, there was very little time to duck and take cover.

The minute I noticed the sudden change in his breathing pattern, I was certain that Odessa's taunts had pushed Isaiah more than was wise, and then some more. Especially when she pulled up her top to expose her big pregnant belly, released a pretentious whine, and began walking towards the back of the car, where we were standing.

"Oh Isaiah, you ain't gotta be gettin' so upset with me, baby. You *know* that you love me, big-daddy, just as much as I love you. I have proven that to you, starting with giving you the beautiful daughter ya weak ass wife was never able to conceive!"

Call It What You Want

Pausing, Odessa curved her lips into a sinister grin and turned towards our neighbors who had gathered on their porches and along the sides of the street with inquisitive eyes and listening ears. "Hey friends! Allow me to introduce myself, since I will soon be your new favorite neighbor. My name is Odessa Starr, and this big fat bitch that yall see in the arms of my man—the father of my unborn daughter—is Isaiah's soon-to-be ex-wife who was never able to produce any more children after birthing those spoiled-ass twin boys! The poor little tink-tink is as barren as death, yall! Ha-ha-ha! Which is one of the many reasons Isaiah has chosen me, over her . . . Ain't that right, Isaiah?"

Before I had any time to react to Odessa's words or even scream at Isaiah for sharing these hurtful bits of MY life with his ridiculous whore, Isaiah pushed me to the side, causing me to lose my balance and fall to the ground. He then grabbed Odessa by her throat and slammed her pregnant body onto the trunk of her car. Rather than expressing signs of fear by kicking, screaming, or even pleading for help, as any normal woman in her right state of mind would have done for her own safety,

this nutcase wrapped her legs around Isaiah's waist and desperately tried
to pull his face down into hers for a kiss, as though she had been turned
on by his aggression!

I was appalled as I watched this crazy woman buck her hips in the air
and reach for Isaiah's dick, seemingly eager for him to fuck her right
there on the trunk of the car, in front of everybody! Two older black
guys ran to Odessa's rescue, prying Isaiah's hands off her neck, yelling,
"Come on, man . . .This is a female, brotha. A pregnant female! You
can't be slamming her around like that. That shit ain't cool, man!"
Releasing the grip, he had on Odessa's neck, Isaiah shoved her away
from him and then jumped into his mother's face, telling her how much
he despised her for what she had done and would never speak with her
again after that day. Bertha had a live audience; so, she began to scream
and holler like a banshee, as if she had done no wrong. . .

Moments later, Essence, Chance, Symone, and Ron came bustling down
the street, their faces wrinkled in worry. Until I actually saw my friends

running towards me, I had forgotten that I had sent out a group SOS text.

"What the hell is going on here? Kayla, you alright, sis?" asked Essence, as her eyes quickly assessed me for injuries. She then glanced over to Odessa, who was pretending to have trouble breathing, as Bertha and a few other people gathered around, pleading for her to calm down and telling her that the police had been summoned.

"Oh, hell no! What the fuck is that bitch doing here?" Essence and Chance screeched simultaneously. "Now, that is one deranged bitch over there!" Chance chimed in as he glanced at Odessa and shook his head in disgust. "I cannot believe that she is still on the same messy bullshit that she was on when she worked at the salon! It's a surprise that she hasn't gotten her ass stomped the fuck out by now, or that someone hasn't buried that troublesome ass troll! Ugh, like when is she gonna grow the fuck up?" I provided my friends with the shortest, quickest version of the story possible, all the while observing Isaiah argue with the two men who had pulled him off of Odessa and were criticizing him for being so reckless and disrespectful to his mother. But as soon as two police cars

and an ambulance turned onto our street, things went from bad to worse!

For starters, when the cops showed up was about the same time I had

looked over at Ron and Symone and realized that they had been so quiet

since their arrival that I had almost forgotten that they were even there!

While Chance and Essence were ready to wring both

Bertha and Odessa's necks for the drama they had brought to my home,

Ron and Symone looked around nervously, as though they wished to be

anywhere other than 3603 Scottwood road. It even looked like Symone

was trying to hide behind her husband's 300+-pound body, which was

extremely weird, because for as long as I had known Symone, she had

never, ever, ever been afraid of a fight of any kind. *Never!* I wondered if

she was acting strange because of Essene's presence and the guilt, she

may have felt due to the mean things she had been saying behind her

back, or if something else was up.

Nonetheless, I had to put that on the back burner and focus on Odessa

who had taken her antics up several notches since the cops had arrived.

Call It What You Want

"Oh officers, I am so glad that you are here!" Odessa exclaimed

dramatically as she waved her arms for the police officers' attention.

With crocodile tears gushing out of her eyes, she began the incident,

obviously making herself sound like a victim when, in reality, she was

the unbalanced *villain*! But, once she laid her eyes on Ron and Symone,

it was as though the world halted and everything changed. Odessa glared

at my friends like she wanted to rip both their heads off and toss them

into the river. Essence, Chance, and I exchanged confused looks with

each other and then glanced at Ron and Symone, who looked nervous

and just as confused as everyone else.

"Well, well, well . . ." Odessa began as her lips curled into a wicked

smile, walking towards us, with the cops following close behind. "It

looks like the whole clan is here; now I can get all of this shit off of my

chest and be done with all of yall stupid mutha fuckers!"

Essence held her palm up, shook her head, and pursed her lips. "Alright

now . . . don't get cute, because the cops are out here, Odessa! Ain't nobody scared of your stupid ass—don't start none, won't be none!" she warned. Odessa threw her head back and laughed.

"Aww . . . Essence. No need to worry your pretty little head, BOSS. This ain't got nothing to do with you, your faggot sidekick Chance, or even your homegirl standing next to you . . . *Pigatha*." She rolled her eyes, returning her attention to my best friend and her husband, who looked pretty close to shitting themselves. Standing within a few feet of Symone and Ron, Odessa looked Ron up and down and began to speak out of twisted lips. "I'd be telling a boldfaced lie if I say it's good to see your worrisome ass again. While you're standing up here with that simple look on your face, I bet you haven't told your wife that you've been harassing the shit out of me, now have you?" Ron attempted to respond, but Odessa yelled at him before he was able to get his words out. " SHUT- THE- FUCK- UP! Don't you say a mutha fuckin word! Imma tell you in front of your wife, so you can leave me the hell alone—*for good*! For the last and final time SIR, you are NOT the father of my unborn child. Okay? You can sit around and let Isaiah play mind games with you, if you want to, but HE is my baby daddy, not you, FAT BOY, with your itty-bitty weenky!"

Everyone's heads whipped around quickly, as we looked at one another in confusion. "What in the hell are you talking about Odessa? How do you know my husband?" demanded Symone. Odessa grimaced and made a harsh sound in her throat before spitting out a yellowish chunk of phlegm on the concrete. "Ugh, unfortunately your slovenly sloppy husband and I became acquainted some months back at the Swinger's club. Isaiah convinced me to let him get his little 'thumb' wet. . .or whatever.

I did that, and just like the other men who got a sample of this juicy pussy, your hubby can't get enough of it, boo! I guess I can understand why you've been cheating on him for years too, *Miss Symone*. That fella's private area almost looks like a fuckin Ken doll!" Symone tried to lunge towards Odessa, but Essence and Chance restrained her, since the cops were standing nearby and she would have been arrested immediately for striking a pregnant woman. Odessa snickered and waved her hand dismissively. "Ah, shit! Ain't nobody worried about you, Symone.

What, you think because your people are out here, it's gonna keep me from busting your fraudulent ass out too? NOPE. WRONG ANSWER, BOO-BOO! I'm pulling everyone's card today. . ." Odessa tilted her head to the side, smiled as she looked into Symone's eyes, and said, "Now see, Miss Holier-than-thou, I was actually gonna be nice and let you slide with your box of secrets, a little while longer.

But since you wanna come at me like you're Billie badass, why don't we discuss the REAL identity of Trinity's father, in front of your best friend and your sweet and loving micro-dick husband, eh? How about that? Matter of fact, . . ." She paused and placed her hand above her eyes, as though she was shielding her eyes from bright light, and looking for someone. With a sigh and a slight chuckle Odessa continued. "Well I'll be damned. It looks like Isaiah's scaredy-cat ass has already gone ghost on us, ladies and gents. The sneaky ninja must have jumped in his truck and pulled off while my back was turned. Tsk, tsk, tsk. . . I guess you can never expect a coward to face their own shit, huh?"

With a callous shrug and a wicked smile etched on her face, Odessa turned to Ron and me and said, "I was gonna call Isaiah over so he could further explain what he and this bible-thumping whore has been doing right under y'all's noses. But he's probably somewhere hiding and the party must go on!" Odessa taunted, as she peered into Symone's eyes. "My unborn baby girl and I aren't Isaiah's only secrets. Now ain't that right, Symone?"

Chapter 22

"Whoa, whoa, whoa! Hold it right there, BITCH!" I interjected, pointing my finger at Odessa's face. "What you're NOT gonna' do is attack my friends with your filthy lies. It's not *our* fault that you decided to get involved with a married man, who used your stupid ass and tossed you into the garbage can—where trash belongs! You're a big girl. Deal with the shit that you've gotten yourself into on your own miserable time and leave us the fuck alone!"

Call It What You Want

I was so fed up with Odessa's constant bullshit that I would have much rather punched her right in the face and dealt with the consequences of striking a pregnant woman, than to continue to listen to her grating voice antagonize me and my friends. Clouting Odessa would only have added fuel to the fire-this I know. But it sure as hell would have felt *damn good* to knock that big goofy bitch on her back like a cockroach, and laugh in her face as she begged for mercy.

"First of all, Pigatha, contrary to what yall *uppity bitches* might think about me, Isaiah IS head over heels in love with me. It's *allllllllll* a part of God's perfect plan, Boo-boo, and there ain't a damn thing any of you can do about it!" Odessa declared, snaking her neck in the same way she had the first time we met.

"Like I told you before, God has confirmed that me and Isaiah were made for each other. And as soon as he gets his shit together, we're gonna' get married and have a house full of beautiful little babies— rather yall like it or not. However, what I *do* have a problem with is being called a goddamn liar. Now *Pigatha*. . . I can understand that you might be a little, uh heartbroken or whatever after being rejected by an

entire family who despises your fat and bougie ass.

But let's not get it twisted, sugah-face, okay? I ain't gotta lie about a

mutha-fuckin' thing! My word stands steady. And my truth is THEE

fuckin truth!" Odessa stopped her tirade for a few seconds, rolled her

eyes, and whipped her head around to shoot Symone a nasty glare.

Shaking her head as though she was thoroughly disgusted by Symone's

presence, she continued, "Now, as I was saying, Miss Holier-than-thou,

since yall wanna sit up here and pretend like you mutha-fuckas are

squeaky clean of any scandal whatsoever, why don't we discuss the true

identity of your 17-year-old daughter Trinity's father. Hell, while we're

on the subject, we might as well include your youngest daughter too—

what's her name, umm Luna, right? Cause from what I hear, those little

girls share the saaaaaame crooked ass papa. And uhh, '*biggie smalls*'

you already know it ain't you, sooo. . .?" Odessa taunted, glancing at

Ron, as her lips curved into a cruel sneer. Everything that had come out

of Odessa's mucky mouth since the day we had met in my office was outrageous, perplexing, and even mind-boggling. But as I listened to the

way she questioned Symone on the paternity of two of her four

daughters-with some type of self-proclaimed authority, All I remember

thinking is, *this is not going to end well. . .*

"Bitch, I swear to God—" spat Symone, as she lunged towards Odessa,

swinging her fists wildly which almost successfully connected with

Odessa's jaw. Essence and Chance had restrained Symone right in time-

reminding her of the cops' presence, and how she'd be escorted to the

county jail in handcuffs, if she so much as PINCHED the bitch!

Odessa chuckled waving her hand dismissively. "Ah Symone, you swear

to God what? Pfftt! Simmer the fuck down, cause you ain't gonna do a

goddamn thing but stand your sheisty ass right there with your friends

and *listen* as I read your funky ass like a book!"

Odessa jeered, before throwing a glance over her shoulder to Bertha,

who stood between the two police officers, puffing on her white-tipped

cigar. I saw Bertha flash Odessa a smile of approval, giving her the

green light to make her next move. And I promise, if I had had a frozen can of pop in my hand at that moment, I would have flung it at Bertha, hoping to have knocked her damn lights out! *I hated that woman and everything she stood for!* "You know, the two of you are *something else*—Ron and Symone Butcher," Odessa began, as she leaned back on her double-jointed legs, rubbing her belly and glaring at my friends. "Here you are, the son of a respected pastor, gulping liquor like its water, snorting cocaine, parlayin' at Swinger's clubs with random women, and harassin' me over a goddamn paternity test of a child that you THINK belongs to you.

 Meanwhile, little Miss Super-Cali-Biblicous over here is runnin' around town—fucking, sucking, and breeding babies with the husband of her beloved best friend!" She shook her head and continued, "Tsk, I hate to burst yall's bubble, but uhh . . . don't neither one of you fraudsters have the room or the right to say a goddamn thing about anyone and their flaws. Yall are THEEE biggest, most scandalous hypocrites I've ever known in my whole life! Especially your funky yellow ass, *Symone* . . .

Call It What You Want

"For the longest time, I wondered about what was going on between you and Isaiah. Every time we were together, kickin' it and tryna' enjoy each other's company, here'd come your needy ass blowing up his cellphone and sending text messages with questions of his whereabouts, as if you were the fuckin' wife! And to make matters worse, his punk ass would stop whatever WE were doing to answer his phone, and listen to you babble about how anxious you were to leave your " micro-dick" husband to be with HIM- the husband of your *supposed* best friend! Actually, Kayla—" Odessa paused as she turned away from Symone to look at me. "I *hate* to be the bearer of bad news, but your bestie here must have really, really, REALLY had Isaiah wrapped up tight around her little finger, girlfriend. Because uh, he'd take her phone calls in a heartbeat, while your calls went straight to voicemail each and every time you called."

Turning her attention back to Symone, Odessa nodded and continued, "*Mmm-hmmm.* And that right there was enough to shoot my antennas up real quick and force me to put my investigative skills to use. After about

Call It What You Want

a week or so, I had yall janky mutha-fuckas all figured out. I found and *copied* the text messages and emails that you had sent Isaiah— requesting more money, outside of the thousand dollars he'd been paying you faithfully each month to keep yall's dirty little secrets on the *hush*. Oh, and when your trifling ass wasn't beggin' for money. . ." Odessa jerked her head to face Ron and I, and pointed over her shoulder at Symone. "This tramp was beggin for Isaiah to come by the house so she could either" *look at him*" or so that he could play her lil' stankin pissy-pussy while the *family* was away from the house! Yall can say whatever the fuck you wanna say about me, but I swear to God, Symone is one low down and dirty bitch!"

Trying to remember how to breathe, feeling tongue-tied and completely flabbergasted by the words that fired out of Odessa's mouth like pellets, I somehow managed to look over at Symone. She was still being held back by Essence and Chance, but she was no longer flailing about like she had been only a few minutes earlier. Instead, she looked sapped, wounded, and completely defeated.

Call It What You Want

Her skin had turned grey, her mouth hung open, with her lips slightly parted, and her eyes were filled with tears. As much as I would have loved nothing more than to believe—without a shadow of a doubt—that each and every allegation made against my best friend were barefaced lies. The guilty energy wafting from

Symone's soul—the woman who had been my best friend since junior high school—spoke volumes.

"Symone! Tell me she's fuckin' lying," I lashed out like an enraged panther and moved towards my friend with my fists clenched. " Tell Odessa that you would never do no shit like that to me, or Ron. . . Tell her right fuckin now, Symone! *Now*."

"Oh, no, no, no, no, no... wait Kayla, that is only half of what this sneaky bitch has been doing behind your back, sis." Odessa squawked, forcing me stop in my tracks and direct my full attention to her. Pointing over her shoulder again at Symone with her thumb, Odessa continued, "Symone is a perfect example of why you cannot trust those goddamn bible-thumpers. They can read and recite the bible through and through, yet they are the most malicious mutha-fuckas walkin' on this earth.

Thankfully I have a solid relationship with GOD—so all of that bible

babbling shit means a nothing to me. I am blessed and highly favored!

Amen, amen, amen!"

Beaming with sick pleasure, Odessa carried on with her unwarranted

yakking—her voice loaded with sarcasm. She shot Symone a glare that

appeared to have sucked something out of her. Symone was visibly

wilted, as Odessa continued with the godawful revelation.

"*Ahhht, ahhht, ahhht*! Don't you dare start up with all of that cryin

bullshit now! Those fake tears don't mean shit to me! Especially when

you call yourself trying to interfere with my fuckin life! Suck those punk

ass tears right on up, and tell your bestie and husband how you are *still*

fuckin around with Isaiah to this very day. . .

Yeah, go on and tell em' how you've visited your "DAUGHTER's

father" at least five or six times since he's been staying at the Marriott—

for the past month or whatever. I mean, it could have very well been

more visits than that, but the five or six times were when Momma B and

Call It What You Want

I caught your lanky ass sashaying in and out of his hotel room, like you were supposed to be there. Call it whatever the fuck you want BITCH, because your ass is sooo fuckin busted!" Odessa laughed, wickedly. "There were several times where, you stayed in the suite with Isaiah for hours, then come strolling out, looking all fresh and clean—and fulfilled, like I used to feel after making love to *my man*. While other times you were in and out within 30 minutes— which were probably the times where you stopped by to give him some of that sloppy-toppy, since according to your text messages, you are the best '*Monica Lewinsky*' in the state of Ohio. . ."

With a meaningful smirk, Odessa turned to Ron, who looked as if his entire world had fallen apart, and gave him a quick once over. "Tsk tsk tsk. . . Aww, you poor fella. A part of me *actually* feels sorry for you Ron, cause you're probably a good man who unfortunately fell for a two-bit self-absorbed whore who doesn't think about anyone but herself. But at the same time, *baaaybeee* you should've known that your thimble of a dick wouldn't be good enough to keep *any* woman satisfied, sugah.

~ 343 ~

Call It What You Want

Let's be honest here, you've got less meat in your pants than there is in a vegetarian restaurant! Ya' catch my drift, lil' man?

Can't nobody get "jiggy' with that itty-bitty shit!" Symone finally turned towards me, and the moment our eyes locked, I felt as though my head had been suddenly thrust under water. Everything around me became slow and muddled up. Her expression reminded me of one of those pop-eyed toys from the claw machines that are normally placed in supermarkets, restaurants, and movie theaters—*perfectly stiff and funny!* I rolled my eyes at her and focused on Ron, who had begun to pace back and forth like a caged lion. It was almost as if he had tuned out Odessa's taunts about his " short comings" and was concentrating solely on the dirty deeds of his beloved wife. Ron's eyes displayed deadness—a stillness that made me shudder. The man who laughed so often—the person whom everyone considered to be a generous and doting friend—had become as stiff as a rock. He looked as though he wanted to cry, but his anger forced back the tears. . .

Call It What You Want

"So, you mean to tell me that you have been foolin' around with Isaiah, all of these years, Symone? Huh?" Ron asked his wife angrily, continuing to pace about. Symone looked down at her feet before she glanced back up to catch my fuming eyes. Ignoring her husband, she said, "Kayla, can we please go inside the house and discuss this? We need to pray about this, like now. . ."

"Huh?" I shrieked. "Oh hell no! We're not going in my house to discuss a damn thing, Symone! I'm with your husband on this—have you been fuckin' my husband right under our noses? And is *he* the father of your daughters, huh?"

"But. . . Kayla. . ." Symone mumbled and whined nervously, with tears falling from her eyes. "Please *Bestie-Boo* . . . let's just—"

"Answer ME, goddamnit!" Ron roared, catching us all off guard—including the two cops, whose hands immediately went to their sides and gripped their guns.

Call It What You Want

"So, Isaiah *is* the mutha-fucka' you nicknamed '*Fresh*' eh? The sorry mutha-fucka who you claimed to have fucked ya' brains out at a little house party back in the day, and left you all high and dry, huh? Is he?"

"Baby . . ." Symone cried, breaking her arms free from Essence and Chance's grip and rushing over to her husband.

"Ron. . . please calm down. You're scaring me. We can talk about his in private. I promise I'll tell you everything. But not here baby. Not in front of everyone. . ." Shoving her hands away, Ron shook his head.

"Nah . . . Don't even try to act like a warm and loving wife now, *bitch*! Answer the goddamn question, Symone . . . Is Isaiah Trinity and Luna's father or not? You don't have to write a fuckin essay about it. It's simple question that requires a simple yes, or a simple no. Which one is it, Symone?"

"Oh Jesus, Ron . . . will you please stop yelling at me? I'm scared baby! Please let's go home and pray. I will tell you everything. *Please let's just go!*"

Call It What You Want

"YES OR FUCKIN' NO, BITCH!" Ron roared; sweat pouring down his face and pooling around his chunky neck. Bawling her eyes out, Symone finally nodded her head and yelled, "YES! YES! YES! Isaiah *is* Trinity's biological father. We were young and foolish back then—it was a freakin accident! But baby, I have documented proof that you *are* Luna's daddy. I had a DNA test done after she was born and you are 100 percent proven to be her father.

Plus, she looks just like you and your mother—" Before Symone was able to sum up the large list of lame excuses she'd compiled to explain the foul shit she had done behind our backs, Ron balled up his fist and rained blows into Symone's face as if he meant to smash her into the earth! It took two Tasers and a few whacks with the officer's baton, before Ron was pulled off of Symone, handcuffed and tossed into the back of the police cruiser.

I stood as if I were paralyzed from the neck up, gibbering nonsense unable to fully comprehend all that had just occurred. I watched as the paramedics had lifted Symone's bloody and unconscious body into the

Call It What You Want

ambulance—originally called for Odessa's malicious ass, and shoot off of our street at an aggressive speed. A part of me wanted to be seated in the ambulance with her, holding her hand while reassuring her that everything was going to be okay. While the other part of me was as done with the friendship I shared with her, as I was done with my marriage. *Screaming sobs*, caused me to look over at the police car, where Ron was positioned in the backseat. Once I made eye contact with him, he shook his head sorrowfully and sobbed, " Oh my God Kayla, I'm so sorry for what I have done—you have gotta believe me! I love Symone and my kids. . . I *just*—Please pray for me. Tell my babies I love them very much. I am sorry for what I did to their mother. God knows I never meant to hurt her like that. I never meant to hurt *anyone*. I'm still a good guy. . .you know me Kayla!" As the police cruiser began slowly pulling off of my street, from the backseat came the most hysterical cry that I had ever heard from a grown man. My false-hearted, *best friend's* husband, Ronald Butcher cried as if his brain was being shredded from the inside. . .

Call It What You Want

Epilogue

Odessa speaks . . .

You just don't know how much I would have loved to be a fly on the wall after Symone's stankin' ass was rushed in an ambulance to Riverside hospital. Ron and his big ole bear paw knocked the *shit* out of that sneaky bitch after I exposed her for the reckless creep that she is! All I can say is, behind all those scriptures. . . Symone wasn't nothing but a goddamn HOE. A crooked one at that! I can only imagine how fuckin pathetic Pigatha, Essence, Chance's faggot-ass along with

Call It What You Want

Symone's weeping relatives looked—sitting slumped over in the hospital's waiting area, boohooing and drumming up all kinds of weak-ass hymns and prayers for the biggest bible-babbling bitch in the entire fuckin' state of Ohio.

I say FUCK THE BITCH! Okay? I don't care what anyone says! Symone Butcher got exactly what she deserved! I know I may sound a little bitter, but this is the thing. . .

I had known all about this lil' "Love Jones" bullshit that Symone shared with Isaiah for quite some time. I could've exposed their shady asses a long time ago. But, being the kind-hearted woman that I am— naturally, I had decided not to utter a word of the scandal to anyone besides "Momma B" until after the birth of my daughter . . . *well that was the initial plan.* After my special delivery, I was gonna bless the shiesty bitch with the same gallant visit that I blessed her best friend with at the damn C & O counselling center. I was gonna lay out my demands—for her to STAY THE HELL AWAY FROM MY MAN, then we'd all live

Call It What You Want

happily, ever after. But, *nooooo*! This dumb cunt fucked

evvvvvverything up the moment she started pokin' around in my mutha-

fuckin business and talkin' shit about me . . .

Momma B had rung me earlier that morning, before our lil' visit to the

Ward's residence, to fill me in on a juicy conversation she had

overheard the day before. "Now listen here, Odessa," Momma B had

said. "You know I ain't one to gossip, but uhhh . . . you ain't gonna

believe the crazy shit that Imma bout' to tell ya! I hope you are sitting

down, cause this SERIOUS!" Momma B cleared her throat, and

continued. "Yeah, so Izzy came by the house the last night around 7

o'clock or so. I dunno if he was drunk or what, but he parked in my

driveway and was yakking his goddamn head off on the phone for a

good 20 minutes.

You know Izzy talks loudly when he is on the phone . . . and chile, I was

all ears! From what I gathered, he was chattin' with that high-yella girl

who's been stickin to my Izzy and his wife for years. Oh shit, what is her goddamn name, again? You know, Kayla's friend, the one married

to that fat Albert lookalike, the pastor's son?"

"Ugh! You must be talking about Symone..." I answered, instantly

irritated. "Symone! Uhn-hunn . . . yep that's her!" Momma B affirmed

strongly. "I dunno why I couldn't remember that cow's name . . .

probably cause' I can't stand her snooty-boot ass either. But anyway, so

I'm standing near the kitchen window adding a few spices to pot of

chitterlings I had simmering on the stove, and all I hear is my son and

that girl talkin' bout you like you're a filthy stankin' mutt. I ain't tryna

hurt cha feelins or nothin' like that—but uhh I don't think Izzy is as

fond of you as you think he is, baby . . ." Momma B paused for a

second. I heard the flick of her lighter and instantly pictured a dark

skinned heavy-set woman in her mid-60's sitting at her dining room

table with a tall glass of Wild Irish Rose, drawing puffs from one of her

prized Black and Mild cigars. With a loud exhalation, she continued,

"Guuuurl, Izzy told that ole ratchet wench that you are as crazy as bat

shit, and that he hates ya fuckin' guts! He even went as far as makin'

Call It What You Want

jokes about invitin' you on one of those fancy cruise ships, just so he could get cha drunk and push ya off into the ocean with the goddamn sharks—like those rich white men do when they wanna get rid of their pesky wives. Laaaawd Jesus! I could not believe my damn ears when I heard MY BOY talkin' about cha like that. Don't gemme wrong now; Isaiah ain't no saint—he's got that mean streak in him like his daddy. But I have never known him to be that damn hateful!

"Umph, umph, umph. . . listen, I ain't tryna make up any excuses for Izzy's behavior. But his head is all jacked up these days Odessa, and his momma is worried sick about him. I may be wrong, but ever since that snooty wife of his filed for divorce, Izzy has been trippin', like he's losing his mind or something. One minute he's actin' like he is oh sooo happy that their marriage is ending— braggin' about all the 'hoes' he's gonna have on his team to play with whenever he feels like it. Then in the same damn sentence, the fool speaks of renewing his vows with that funky bitch in Italy or Hawaii. . .

Call It What You Want

I hope he ain't still *sniffin'* on that shit you told me about. But if he is,
we need to get him some damn help! I just dunno what's going on with
Izzy anymore, but I am most definitely worried about him . . ."

I was almost certain Isaiah was still using cocaine, especially if he was
still hanging out in the swinger's club. But that was neither here nor
there. I was more concerned with the fact that Isaiah had the nerve to
talk shit about me to a bitch who didn't know me from a can of paint,
than his use of street drugs.

My blood pressure literally shot through the fuckin roof when Momma
B told me that before Isaiah ended his conversation, she heard Symone's
stankin' ass tryna' persuade him to file harassment charges against me!
According to the funky bitch, who had been fucking around with her
best friend's husband for damn near 20 years- I am *craaaazy*,
deraaanged and *unpredictable*, like one of those "lifetime movie"
bitches who stalk and harass people for the heck of it . . . yeah,
whatever!

Call It What You Want

I was so fuckin pissed off when I heard that foolishness that I could've beat the shit outta both of them, *on sight*. Instead, I laughed my ass off at Symone's corny attempt to make me look like the villain. The poor lil' tink-tink was just tryna get me out of the picture for good so she could keep Isaiah for herself—or at least continue to secretly share his dick with Pigatha. *Shiid*! Symone had me all fucked up. Pigatha wasn't strong enough to push me away from the man that God had created specifically for me. So that dumb bitch should've have known that she didn't stand a mutha-fuckin chance against me! After the little altercation I had with Pigatha and dealing with the embarrassment of Isaiah tryna show off for his wifey-boo and the neighbors by slinging my big, pregnant ass around like a ragdoll and talkin' shit as if he never loved me, locking eyes with Symone was the last thing I expected to happen.

Granted, the presence of my old boss, Essence and her *fairy* friend Chance was a shock on its on- as I had no idea that they were friends of Pigatha's. But when I caught a glimpse of Ron and Symone galloping

Call It What You Want

through the crowd to Pigatha's rescue and eyeballing me with their

noses turned up as if I was out of line . . . it did something to me.

Something bad! With God as my witness, I swear, had it not been for the

precious princess baking in my belly, I probably would have knocked

that fraudulent bitch's head clean off her shoulders, and kicked Ron in

his big ass stomach!

But I decided to hit those mutha-fuckas where it was REALLY gonna

hurt. . . Airing out their nasty lil' secrets in front of their peeps—

unapologetically! I blasted Symone in front of the entire neighborhood

on the affair she'd carried on with Isaiah for decades, right along with

the secret kids she had with him. If I had more time on my hands, I

would've probably have whipped out the pictures I had of her funky ass

creeping in and out of Isaiah's hotel room. Or the pictures I had snapped

of them meeting up at Panera Bread on East Broad Street every third

Wednesday of the month, where he would slide one of those bank

envelopes into her purse, after grabbing her by the waist and slobbin'

her down right in the goddamn parking lot as if she were his girlfriend!
Well, in a bizarre type of way, I guess she was.

Apparently, my truth was enough to eke emotions from everybody who
had decided to poke their nose into our business. Because while Pigatha
and the bougie crew stood before me with the dumbest expressions I've
ever seen on a group of people who considered themselves holier than
the Lord. I witnessed Ron's love for his precious wife swiftly evaporate
from his eyes. All it took was for Symone to admit to her husband that
what I had said about she and Isaiah's love affair was God's honest
truth—before Ron huffed and puffed, cocked his arm back, balled up his
large bear paw, and socked that bitch in the face with so much force that
her head spun around like the girl in the exorcist!" Considering the way,
Symone was sprawled on the ground, with blood squirting from her nose
and ears, I thought that Ron had killed her. *Unfortunately, there is no*
such thing as luck. Later on that evening, I reached out to a couple of my
associates employed at Riverside hospital, who gave me the scoop on
Symone's condition—and promised to sneak me a few pics of her once

Call It What You Want

her family and friends had left. Ole sneaky-thongs survived the beating.

But from what I was told, she was pretty damn fucked up!

Symone suffered a stroke or whatever, that left one side of her body

temporarily paralyzed. Oh, and that beautiful face of hers, which she

apparently thought was "*all of that*," was a thing of the past! According

to my reliable sources, her eyes now drooped and her lips were twisted

to the side like Popeye's— causing that bitch to look more like a

monstrosity than a damn beauty queen. Tsk, tsk, tsk! This are the types

of things that happen when people call themselves messing with the

daughter of the King! Gotta be careful of the ditches you did for others.

Cause' guess what? Your dumb ass just might be the one to tumble in to

it first!

At exactly 2:53 am the following Thursday, I was startled awake by

loud, enraged banging on the front door. I knew it couldn't be anyone

but Isaiah's ignorant ass. I didn't really deal with too many people like

that, and the ones that I did deal with on a regular basis had enough decency to ring my phone before banging on my door in the middle of the fuckin' night.

As I stood with my hand on the doorknob and a watercolor Kimono robe wrapped tightly around my body, I begged Isaiah to stop banging on the door, go away, and call me when he was sober. I didn't have to peer into his face to know that he was as drunk as a skunk; his slurred words gave him away. Instantly. "Odessa . . . open this mutha-fuckin door, bitch . . . I ain't gonna do shit to you . . . if that's what you're worried about . . . I just wanna holla' at you . . . for a minute . . . lemme in this muh-fucka . . . before I kick the goddamn door down!"

I could only imagine how he swayed back and forth on my stoop, trying to maintain his balance and talk shit at the same time. And I won't lie— the mere sound of his voice had my emotions all over the place, slurred speech and all!

A part of me wanted to pull him inside, so we could debate about who was right and who was wrong, call each other all kinds of foul names, then fuck and make up like we had done so many times in the past. But

Call It What You Want

my rational side, on the other hand, was screaming, *Girl, you'd be a*

fuckin fool to open the door . . . he's gonna beat your ass!

You would think that after this man had unashamedly ignored my calls

and pleas for months, I would have had enough sense to understand

exactly why he was at my doorstep at that moment. But love . . .true

love sometimes made people *think* and *do* some of the craziest shit!

When the banging on the door stopped, I thought Isaiah had taken my

advice and simply walked away. That was until he tapped on the door

lightly, speaking in that smooth sexy voice that always made my pussy

purr like a kitten, "Odessa . . . listen to me baby . . .I know that you're

mad at me . . .for dodgin' your calls . . . and not being around for you

and the baby . . .and all that shit.

I'm sorry, alright? I've got a lot of shit going on in my life right now . . .

tryna' sort shit out . . .ya know what I'm sayin'? Please . . .open the door

. . .I could really use a friend right now . . ."

Against my better judgement, I unlocked the door and eased it open,

hoping to fall right into Isaiah's strong arms. But, before I had the

Call It What You Want

chance to even get a good look at him, I had fallen to the floor from the force of an unexpected punch to my face.

As I scrambled around on the floor trying to comprehend what had just happened and get back up on my feet up, Isaiah locked the door that I had just let him through, snatched out his thick leather belt from his denim shorts, and began whooping my ass, as if I was one of his children!

The searing pain and the ripping sensation felt like the kind I'd only seen characterized in historical dramas like Alex Haley's *Roots* or *Amistad* where slaves were thrashed and humiliated for merely blinking! I howled as loud as a wolf in search of fits pack as he beat me, which was pointless. The gay couple I shared a stoop with was away on vacation— therefore no one could hear my cries.

Once Isaiah had stopped whopping me, he dragged me to my bedroom by my hair, forced me on all fours, and for what seemed like an eternity, butt-fucked me as hard and rough as you can imagine. . .

Call It What You Want

With each agonizing thrust of his dick in and out of my ass, the love I had for him turned into sheer hatred—and there is no hatred stronger than the one born of violence.

"Now, you see what the fuck your dumb ass made me do, bitch!" Isaiah barked from behind me once he was finished with his business. "I told your monkey ass to move the fuck on and leave me and my family alone, but you're fuckin hardheaded Odessa! You don't listen, do you? Shit, I guess you thought you were just gonna punk me into being in a relationship with your trifling ass, eh? Even after you've sucked and fucked damn near every muhfuckin' ninja in the city of Columbus? *Traaaaaamp* be FOREAL . . . Don't nobody want that ole stank ass COMMUNITY PUSSY!"

I cannot recall much of what Isaiah said after that; I had gotten distracted by the cramps in my belly. I still had six weeks before my due date, and a premature delivery was the last thing I wanted for my beautiful baby girl.

Call It What You Want

So, I turned a deaf ear to Isaiah's tirade of traumatizing taunts and focused solely on my breathing and the baby kicking frantically in my belly. Eventually Isaiah left my apartment, and as soon as I was sure he was gone, I checked myself into the hospital.

I was in a whole lot of pain, but thankfully the baby was okay. The hospital staff along with a set of aggravating detectives bombarded me with questions about the purplish welts and bruises covering my entire backside, but I didn't tell them shit!

I could've easily pointed the finger at Isaiah and had his sorry ass arrested for what he had done to me. But I deliberately *lied*, telling them that I had been mugged and robbed by some scruffy looking white guy during a late-night stroll through my neighborhood.

Call it what you want, but vengeance was MINE! I was gonna make sure Isaiah paid the piper for the fucked-up shit he had done to me and my unborn baby, without the presence of witnesses or authorities.

On the night of the 4th of July, I parked my car across the street from 3603 Scottwood residence and waited for Isaiah or that bitch Pigatha to arrive home. I waited for those stupid mutha-fuckas for so long that I ended up falling asleep, only to be awakened moments later by the distinctive sound of a slamming car door.

I slowly raised my head over the steering wheel for a quick peek, hoping to steal a glance of my man one last time. Although I didn't get a chance to physically see Isaiah or Pigatha enter the house, the shiny pickup truck I had been waiting for was now parked in the driveway. Pulling a Newport cigarette from my glove box, I drew the smoke deep into my lungs, remembering all of the warnings but not giving a flying fuck! Once the cigarette was short enough to burn my fingers, I flicked it into the peaceful early morning summer air. With my pregnant body wrapped in a dark burqa and a matching niqab covering my face, I pressed the trunk release button, marched to the back of my car to put on the plastic gloves I had purchased from the hair store. I pulled out the large can of gasoline I had purchased the day before, and tiptoed across the street like a thief in the night. I crept around the perimeter of the house, dousing it with the flammable contents of my can. Then,

Call It What You Want

crawling on my hands and knees, I slid into the slightly ajar garage door, where I rummaged around until I found an additional can of gas positioned behind a beat-up Honda and a bunch of white, unmarked, stacked boxes. I dumped as much of the gas in the garage as I could—including inside the parked car.

After I unlocked and tiptoed through the side door of the garage, my stomach tightened up again, causing me to double over in pain. To avoid alerting anyone with my agonizing cries, I covered my mouth and prayed for those damn Braxton hicks to chill.

Thankfully, the contractions subsided long enough for me to make it out of the garage, and into the middle of their driveway. As I glanced at the matchbox in my hands, I thought about the love I had for Isaiah. I had sacrificed so much for that man and would have done just about anything for him. But he hurt me bad . . . to the very core of my being. There was no fuckin reason for him to have done me the way he did. *I was good to him*! Playin with Odessa's emotions was a big "No-no".

Call It What You Want

Isaiah had to pay, just like the other mutha-fuckas who thought they could cross me and get away with it!

The first strike of the match was a complete failure, but with the second stick, I held it firmly between my thumb and first finger near the gunpowder end. Then, with violent ferocity, I struck it against the sandpaper strip and watched as the match flared up in the darkness. Without an ounce of remorse, I tossed the burning match into the garage. Within seconds, it seemed as if the fire had spread everywhere! I watched as the flames began rising up from the house in colors I had never imagined. The burning smell dominated every breath I took, and the flames were louder than I had ever expected—roaring as they consumed what had once been once a fine house owned by a selfish man. As I entered the freeway speeding towards my apartment, those damn Braxton hicks returned with pain that took over my entire body. The agonizing pain would pass for a minute or two, only to return with more intensity than anything I had ever experienced in my life. Nothing could have been more brutal—not chains, whips, or harsh words from the man who had once claimed to love me forever.

Once I felt a huge gush of fluid escape from in between my thighs, it became clear that my first child, Legacy Ann Marie Ward was on her way into this cruel world.

As far as I was concerned, she would never get the opportunity to meet her father- in the *flesh*. But, she'd have way more in common with him than genes, or any of his other children. Isaiah's tragic death and Legacy's birthday would be one and the same . . .

Call It What You Want

Call It What You Want

About the Author:

Qiana Moss is a wife, mother of three and graduate of Kaplan University with a bachelor's degree in Behavior and Social Science. She has been reading and writing short stories for over 20 years now and has authored the book "*Call It What You Want*" along with several upcoming novels.

Connect with Qiana on Social Media

@AuthorQianaMoss

P.O. Box 1583 Columbus Ohio, 43216

ThreeMindzPublishing@gmail.com